A Dead Man's Honor

Frankie Y. Bailey

An Imprint of The Overmountain Press
JOHNSON CITY, TENNESSEE

This book is a work of fiction. All names, characters, places, and events are either the product of the author's imagination or are used fictitiously. Any resemblance to actual events or persons, living or dead, is entirely coincidental and beyond the intent of either the author or the publisher.

Hardcover ISBN 1-57072-170-X
Trade Paper ISBN 1-57072-171-8

Printed in the United States of America

1 2 3 4 5 6 7 8 9 0

Acknowledgments

I would like to acknowledge the help, assistance, and support of a number of people who have played important roles in helping me to complete this book and in my evolving development as a mystery writer.

First, my thanks once again to the members of The Wolf Road Irregulars—Joanne Barker, Caroline Petrequin, Christopher Myers, Audrey Friend, Emer O'Keeffe, and Ellen Higgins—who have been there both as writing group and friends, nurturing me through the second book as they did the first.

To Joycelyn Pollock, who has been my friend longer than almost anyone else I know, and who can be counted on always to provide candor, good advice, and a quick read.

To Alice Green, another longtime friend, who came through for me once again with a recipe from the Orleans Café and a great cover photograph. Take two bows, Alice.

To the police officers in my two favorite Virginia cities, who kindly answered my questions. And to Officer Christopher Myers, for technical assistance, and University Police Chief J. Frank Wiley, who took the time not only to tell me about being a university police chief but to brainstorm a plot twist. However, I should state here that any errors regarding the work or practices of police officers in this book are completely my own.

To Charity Harris, who greeted me with all the enthusiasm any author could ask of a reader during my visit to Creatures 'n Crooks in Richmond. And to all the bookstore owners and readers who have given me much-needed confidence with your response to my first book.

To the family and staff at Silver Dagger, who work amazingly hard not only to support their authors but to accommodate their needs. And to Stacey Amos for another wonderful cover.

Finally, my gratitude to my family. This book is dedicated to my mother, Bessie Fitzgerald Bailey (1917-2001).

Author's Note

For the benefit of readers who might be somewhat confused by the use of the word *lynching* to describe the event that occurs in this book, I should explain that although we often think first of a hanging when we hear the word *lynching*, a lynching occurred whenever a mob or a group of individuals took the law into their own hands and carried out the punishment of an alleged offender. The victim of a lynching might be hanged, burned, shot, and/or drowned. He—more rarely she—might also be tortured and mutilated.

Historically, in the United States, the origin of the practice of "lynch law" is generally traced to the activities of citizen-vigilantes during the Revolutionary War. During this era, the term referred to the whipping or other nonlethal punishment of offenders such as horse thieves and Tories. It was in the 19th century that lynching as a practice evolved into the killing of alleged offenders by vigilantes, whether mobs or posses. Many readers will associate lynching with the Western frontier and the punishment of outlaws. Images of such lynchings are captured in two classic American novels (later films) about frontier law: *The Ox-Bow Incident* and *The Virginian*.

However, the majority of lynchings occurred in the South and border states in the late 19th and early 20th centuries. The campaign against lynching was spearheaded by the National Association for the Advancement of Colored People (NAACP) and by individuals such as courageous journalist Ida B. Wells-Barnett. These reformers were eventually joined—in their efforts to end lynching—by white female reformers in the South such as Jesse Daniel Ames and by others, such as congressmen and outspoken newspaper editors, both black and white.

The wave of lynchings in the United States occurred at the same time that race riots in the United States were becoming more frequent in both the North and the South. The year 1919 was known as "The Red Summer" because of the approximately twenty-six race riots which occurred across the country. And in the spring of 1921, a major race riot occurred in Tulsa, Oklahoma.

Although the effort to pass federal antilynching legislation was never successful, a number of factors—including media coverage, international reaction, fear of federal intervention, and the social, political, and economic changes brought about by the Depression and two world wars—contributed to the eventual decline of lynching events.

Chapter 1

TUESDAY, OCTOBER 31

If dead grandmothers were supposed to be sweet, comforting presences, Hester Rose, my grandmother, had not been paying attention when that particular celestial lesson was taught. Since my arrival in Gallagher, she had been raging—like a five-foot-two fury—nightly through my dreams. But I had done something she had told me plainly not to do, and being disobeyed never did sit well with Hester Rose, even when she was alive.

It took me a while that morning to shake off our most recent nocturnal encounter, but by a little after ten, I was out and about.

I found the used book store, which Joyce Fielding had told me about, on a side street, tucked between an engraving shop and a real estate agent's office. As I entered, the proprietor peered at me over the top of his chunky black glasses and then went back to the chess game on his computer monitor. The only customer in sight was a large pink-cheeked woman with a trace of a mustache. She was occupying an armchair near the door. She darted a glance at me and began to snatch up the books she had piled on the floor beside her. A few minutes later, as I started down the first aisle of bookshelves, I heard the jangling bell over the door signal her departure.

I hadn't meant to run her away. But there was nothing I could do about it if I fell into that category of people she found scary. Or maybe she had wanted the place to herself. I could understand that. I felt kind of possessive myself as I contemplated the empty aisles and the shelves crammed with books.

But my browsing was being done with the clock ticking. I allowed myself one hour, and then down to business. I was working my way through the history section when a volume on a bottom shelf caught my eye: *A History of Gallagher, Virginia, 1785-1939* by Harry Glover. I gave an unladylike whoop and dropped the other books I had collected onto the top of the bookcase. With reckless disregard for my last pair of panty hose, I got down on my knees and eased the volume from the shelf. The public library's copy of Glover's history was in Richmond being rebound. Until now I had been stymied in my efforts to get my hands on this book.

The pages were yellowed, the print small. But in the middle section were the photographs that documented events and personages in the history of the city. A July 4th picnic in 1898 with girls in summer frocks and two small boys in sailor suits in front of the town bandstand. A 1905 photograph of Captain William Calhoun, the gallant young Civil War hero who had served as mayor of the city from 1872 until he died in 1919. After his death, a statue had been erected in his honor on the courthouse steps.

The next photograph was a formal portrait of the directors of the Mercantile Cotton Mill seated around their conference table. That was followed by the 1915 graduating class of Piedmont Military Institute. I studied the painfully young faces of the cadets. How many of them had died in World War I? Glory turned to dust.

I turned the page and found myself staring down at a grainy, black-and-white photograph of a man, perhaps in his late twenties, his face somber above his stiff uniform collar. Not a soldier's uniform. A police officer's. According to the caption, the man in the photograph was Officer Thomas Kincaid of the Gallagher Police Department.

"Find something?" a squeaky male voice said above my head.

I jumped and almost dropped Glover's history as I grabbed for the edge of the bookcase to steady myself.

The proprietor of the bookstore had left his perch behind the front counter. He backed up a step as I got to my feet. "Sorry about that," he said. "I didn't mean to startle you." Sunlight seeped through the dusty window behind him, sparkling on the gold hinges of his glasses. He pushed them up on his nose, hunched his shoulders, and gave me a lopsided grin.

"My fault," I said. "I was wool-gathering. And, yes, I have found something. A book I've been looking for."

He took the book I was holding out and nodded. "You're lucky you found this before someone else did. Glover's really popular around here. I have a hard time keeping a copy in stock."

"Is Glover accurate?"

"Accurate? Well, you know what Mark Twain said about that. He said, 'Get your facts first, and then you can distort them as much as you please.'" Another lopsided grin. "Glover's about as accurate as most city historians. Little details here and there that longtime residents like to debate. But for the most part, he seems to have gotten it right."

"Would you ring me up now, please," I said. "I really need to get out of here."

"Sure. I didn't mean to hold you up." He hunched his shoulders again as he spoke.

"Wait . . . I didn't mean to sound— I'm a little. . . ." I searched for a word. "Unsettled."

His bespectacled gaze went from my face to the book in his hand. "Is it something in this?"

"Yes." I plucked up the other books I had put down on top of the bookcase. "I'll take these, too, please."

"Let's go up front," he said. "I'll give you your grand total."

I followed him to the front of the store. The chess game on the computer monitor had been replaced by a screen saver featuring the cast from "Star Trek: Voyager." A light was blinking on and off in one corner. "I've got mail," he said.

He glanced from my books to me. "Casey Jones, huh? You have a child?"

"I was a child," I said. "My grandfather worked for the railroad."

"What about this one about duels?"

"I'm interested in honor," I said. "And the Army survival manual is in case I ever find myself stranded in the desert without water and dying of a rattlesnake bite."

I was doing my best to hold onto my patience. But he must have sensed that he was not making me happy with his slow, methodical process of opening each book, pushing up his glasses, licking the end of his pencil, and then writing the price of the book down on the pad in front of him.

"Hope you don't mind," he said. "I never use the cash register unless it's a big purchase. I like to add things up in my head. Keep it simple when I can."

"Oh," I said.

"That'll be forty-four seventy-five. Sorry, the Glover was twenty-five. You're at the university, aren't you?"

"Yes," I said, handing him three twenty-dollar bills.

"I thought so. You look like the professor type. What department?"

"Criminal justice," I said and reached for the bag containing my books.

"Cool! Serial killers and all that, huh?"

"No, I do crime history. Excuse me, I really do have to go. My change?"

"Oh, sure. Hey, if you need help finding anything else, just come on back by or e-mail me—the address is on the bookmark—and I'll try to track it down for you."

"Thank you," I said. "I'll keep that in mind."

"Have a good day," he said over the jangle of the bell as I opened the door.

A good day? That hardly seemed likely. It was All Hallows' Eve, and I had just found something wicked in my bag of treats.

There was a telephone booth on the corner. As I waited for John Quinn to come on the line, I stared at the four-letter word someone had scratched into the metal wall. Too bad I could never bring myself to use it. It certainly fit the present situation.

"Chief Quinn speaking."

"Quinn—" I began.

"Lizzie? It is you. When Sergeant Burke said Professor Lizzie Stuart was on the line, I thought he must have gotten the name wrong."

"What . . . why would you think that?"

"Because, Lizabeth," he said, "this is the first time in the almost fifteen months of our acquaintance that you've ever called me."

I never knew how to respond to teasing. Light quips never came to me. I stared at the scratched metal wall of the booth and fumbled for a response. "You . . . before I arrived in Gallagher, you called me twice," I said. "The first time was when you got here, to give me your new address and contact information. The second time was when I was about to leave Drucilla. You called then to remind me to check my spare tire for air and to watch out for speed traps. Other than that, Quinn, you always e-mailed."

"Yes, but in the two and a half months since you've been in Gallagher," he said, "I have been calling more often. You, on the other hand, have never called me. Until today."

I shoved at the telephone booth door with the toe of my pump, creating an opening wide enough for a stream of hot air to enter the smoke-stale space. "All right," I said. "I haven't called. I didn't know you wanted me to call. I'm calling now because I—"

"Thanks, Mike. Is the September report here too?"

"What?" I said.

"Sorry. Sergeant Burke just handed me a printout."

"Quinn, I need to talk to you about—"

"Lizzie, you don't know how much I hate to ask this when you've called me—but may I call you back? I have to do a press briefing at noon about that brawl in the student center."

"What brawl?"

"Last night. The aftermath of a billiard game. Stitches required and arrests made. Three of our students and a couple of local—"

"Quinn, I saw a dead man."

"You what?"

"I saw a man who is supposed to be dead."

"Happy Halloween," he said. "Are you in your office? I should be done in an hour or so, and then I'll—"

"Quinn, I am not joking. I'm holding a book in my hand." I unclenched the fingers of that hand. "A history of Gallagher. I found it in a used bookstore a few minutes ago."

"What does this book have to do with—"

"It has a photograph of Thomas Kincaid. The police officer I told you about. The one Mose Davenport shot."

"And he's the dead man you saw? Was he sitting up or lying down?"

"Quinn, this is not a joke," I repeated. "I'm looking at Kincaid's photograph, and the caption beneath says, 'Killed by a Negro felon in 1921.'"

"The Negro felon would be Mose Davenport. And if he shot Kincaid in 1921—"

"I know that," I said. "But about two weeks ago I saw a man who looked like Officer Thomas Kincaid. Who looked enough like him to be his double."

"All right. Where were you at the time? What was this man doing?"

"I had driven onto campus," I said, remembering that morning. "I was trying to get to my office before the rain started. You know how much I hate storms, and the sky was so dark I thought— Anyway, just as I turned onto College Avenue, it began to rain. To pour. And there was this man standing on the corner at Alumni House waiting to cross the street."

"Thomas Kincaid's double?"

"Yes, but I didn't know that at the time. All I knew was that he was getting soaked. So I stopped to let him cross. As he passed in front of my car, he turned his head and looked at me. He looked right at me," I said. "And he smiled and waved. The rain was pouring, and he was smiling."

"Definitely a sign that he was up to no good," Quinn said.

"Quinn, will you please—"

"Okay. You saw this man. And now you've found Kincaid's photograph, and there's a resemblance. And you think what?"

"I think I want to know what's going on. You're the university police chief."

"Believe it or not, Lizabeth, I'm not clairvoyant."

"I'm not asking you to be clairvoyant. I just want you to help me think this through. Do you think he was a relative? A descendant of Kincaid's?"

"Unless you believe in ghosts, that's the most likely explanation."

I rubbed at the dust on the cracked book cover my hand was resting on. "Today is Hester Rose's birthday. She always said she'd die on Halloween too."

"But she didn't," Quinn said. "Your grandmother died in summer. Well over a year ago."

"I know that. And I know I sound half-hysterical, going on about seeing a dead man. I know how I sound. But last night I had a dream about Hester Rose—"

"What kind of dream?"

"An unpleasant one," I said, remembering the dream of the hissing baby snake curled up on Hester Rose's dressing table beside her hat and gloves. Of Hester Rose appearing in the doorway with snakes coiling around her head and Medusa fury in her eyes. Definitely a very Freudian dream. "An unpleasant dream," I said again to Quinn. "And now, today, on her birthday, I find this photograph of Thomas Kincaid—the man she saw shot to death when she was twelve years old."

"And you think the two things are connected?"

"She told me never to come to Gallagher."

"But you are here."

"Yes, I'm here," I said. "But maybe I shouldn't be."

"Why?" Quinn asked. "Because you think you've stirred up the restless spirit of a dead man?"

"No, because the tiny hairs are standing up on the nape of my neck, and I feel sick to my stomach. And I don't think I really want to know what happened in 1921."

"Then maybe you should stop digging into it."

"I came here to do research," I said.

"Lizzie, I need to get moving."

"Sorry," I said. "Your press briefing. And I'm meeting someone for lunch."

"Who?" he said.

"Richard Colby."

"Colby? I thought you said he had an attitude problem."

"I— When did I tell you that?"

"It must have been during one of those rare conversations," Quinn said, "when you actually talked to me."

Stifling inside the telephone booth, I shoved the door wide and spoke above the roar of a bad muffler on a passing car. "When I actually talked to you . . . what does that—"

"Why are you having lunch with Richard Colby?"

"Because he invited me. What did you mean about—"

"He's married. His wife is a professor in the psychology department."

"I know that. We've having lunch, not meeting for a rendezvous at a cheap motel."

"Good," Quinn said. "You can pick up all kinds of things in cheap motels. About this Thomas Kincaid-double thing—we'll try to figure it out later, okay?"

"Don't worry about it," I said. "I'm all right now. What did you mean about my not talking to you, Quinn? We've talked about all kinds of things."

"Yes, we have, haven't we?" he said. "We've run the conversational gamut. Our jobs. Events in the news. Health and fitness. Movies, books, politics. All kinds of things. Nothing too personal, though."

"If you've been finding our conversations so superficial. . . ," I said, feeling a hollowness in the pit of my stomach. "You were the one who initiated this whole 'let's be friends—'"

"Is that what we are?"

"I don't know what you—"

"I know you don't," Quinn said. "And I don't have time right at this moment to discuss it. I've got to go do the damn—"

"Press briefing," I said. "Happy Halloween."

"Lizzie, whoever your mystery man was, he wasn't a ghost."

"Of course not," I said. "I don't believe in ghosts."

Chapter 2

AUGUST 11, 1921, GALLAGHER, VIRGINIA

From her hiding place in the bushes, Hester Rose watched a man in baggy overalls come sneaking around the corner of the house. He crouched his lanky body down low as he edged past Ophelia's bedroom window. Then he straightened to his full height and glanced back toward the front of the house and over his shoulder toward the woods.

Hester ducked down. She swallowed and almost choked on the trickle of spit that ran down her dry throat.

When she dared peep again, he had a box of kitchen matches. He struck one and held it to the rag-swabbed stick in his hand. He took two steps backwards and tossed the torch up to the tarpaper-and-shingle roof. Then he turned and ran back the way he had come, bending low as he scurried past the window.

The flames on the roof caught and began to spread. Hester watched for a moment. Then she started to push back the bushes and rise. She had to tell Ophelia and Mose. They were still inside.

But someone in the crowd had seen what was happening. A woman's voice, shrill and excited, cried out, "Look there! Fire! The house is on fire!"

A cheer went up. Hester sunk back down.

She shivered in the clammy dress that was plastered to her with her sweat. Blood still trickled down her arm from the nail scrape that she had gotten when Ophelia shoved her out through a back window. The other two policemen had been busy dragging away the one that Mose had shot, and Ophelia had wanted Hester to get away. But Hester had gone no farther than the wild tangle of shrubbery at the edge of the narrow yard.

Acrid smoke blew toward her now, and she rubbed at her eyes. Tears ran down her cheeks, tears from the smoke. She was not crying. She would not cry.

She swatted at the fly buzzing around her face. Moving to the left, she craned her neck until she could see the fringes of the crowd that had gathered out in front of the house. She couldn't make out their faces, but she knew that if she could, she would find people among them that she knew. All sorts of white folks had come to watch. They had dropped whatever they were doing and come running to see what would happen. A colored man had shot a policeman.

The policeman in charge had roared up on a motorcycle with a side-car. He had jumped off and yelled at his men to keep the crowd back to the other side of the street. But that had been right at the beginning, when Mose had still been shooting. Now there was no sign of life inside Ophelia's house. Only the fire eating away at the roof and the wooden frame.

Out in front, a man—probably the one in charge—yelled, "Miller, get the damn fire department!"

But it was too late for that. The house was going. The nearest side of the roof crashed down in flames and smoke. Hester buried her head in her arms.

Someone in the crowd yelled, "Here he comes! He's coming out!"

Hester scrambled up on her knees, trying to see. A branch snapped behind her. She twisted around.

The white man grinning down at her had a wad of tobacco in his cheek. He turned his head to the side and spit out a dark stream of juice. "Well," he said. His voice was slurred with the whiskey she could smell on him. "What we got here?"

Behind her, Hester heard yells and the crackle of gunfire. The man took another step toward her. She scrambled backward, her fingers searching for a rock. . . .

Years later, she had reason to speak of that day again. She spoke of it to a man who would not listen when she told him to go away and leave her be. His name was Walter Stuart, and he was a big, slow-talking man. A man with a smile in his eyes. He worked for the rail-road, and he had seen her working there at the hotel. He had seen her one day when they'd had her out in front, scrubbing the porch steps. He started coming by after that, seeking her out. He kept coming, even when she told him not to. He said he was courting her. So—to make herself plain to him—she had told him about that day in Gal-lagher. She'd told him about that day and about how it was that night when she left.

"The moon had blood on it," Hester told him. "Four people was dead in Gallagher that day. And the moon that night was bright as it could be and red as blood."

It was that strange moon that had lit their way as Hester and her friend Henry crept down to the railroad tracks. They had found an empty freight car, and Henry had helped Hester to climb up into it. Then he'd jumped down to the ground. "Bye," the boy said as he backed away. "Bye, Hester."

When the train started to move, Hester Rose crawled into one of the dark corners of the freight car. She was twelve years old, and she was leaving the only home she had ever known.

Chapter 3

TUESDAY, OCTOBER 31

I closed the door of my car and dropped the bag containing the books I had purchased on the seat beside me. I reached for my briefcase. I was supposed to be meeting Richard Colby, one of my new colleagues, for lunch in less than fifteen minutes, but I had to do this first.

I pulled out the folder containing the newspaper stories I had copied from microfilm.

The *Gazette*, Gallagher's only newspaper, had carried a number of articles about Officer Thomas Kincaid's death and its aftermath. I paused over the one about the memorial service:

The Gallagher Gazette, August 16, 1921

City Mourns Lost

Yesterday at noon over five hundred citizens of Gallagher gathered at the steps of City Hall. There, Mayor Otis paid tribute to the memory of Patrolman Thomas Kincaid. As this newspaper has reported, Officer Kincaid was slain on Thursday afternoon as he and a party of two other officers attempted to arrest Mose Davenport, the negro wanted for the brutal murder of Dr. Daniel Stevens.

The negro, who was known to have operated gambling dens and who was suspected of selling cocaine to local colored people, came to this city less than a year ago. On Thursday afternoon, shortly after Dr. Stevens's body was discovered, Officer Kincaid, accompanied by Officers Finch and Benedict, went to look for Davenport.

They found him at the house of Ophelia Hewitt, the deaf-mute woman who had been Dr. Stevens's housekeeper. Davenport met them on the front porch carrying a shotgun. He was asked to surrender. Instead, he fired the shotgun blast which ended Officer Kincaid's life.

The negro himself was killed when other officers rushed to the scene and citizens of Gallagher surrounded the house, forcing him from inside.

Having served with honor and distinction in the recent world conflict, Thomas Kincaid had returned to Gallagher in 1919 to resume his position as a police officer. Married and the father of an unborn child, Officer Kincaid was considered by all who knew him to be an exemplary young man with a bright future ahead of him. . . .

I flipped through the folder until I came to the editorial that had appeared in Richmond's black newspaper:

The Richmond Voice, August 18, 1921

Lynching in Gallagher

Mose Davenport, a ne'er-do-well, a gambler, and a roustabout, who even colored people will admit was not as good as he might have been, met his death at the hands of a lynch mob last Thursday. Driven from his refuge in a house on Bigelow Street that had been set ablaze, Davenport was shot to death by armed citizens.

Whether or not Davenport was guilty of the crime of which he was first accused—the murder of city physician Dr. Daniel Stevens—remains unknown. When Davenport shot one of the police officers who came to arrest him, he signed his own death warrant. It was for this crime that he paid with his life.

Colored citizens in Gallagher tell us that they expect no more violence. Calm has returned to the city. But the actions of the mob that intervened in police business and lynched Mose Davenport remind all of us of the colored race that lynch law still prevails during moments of high emotion. . . .

I closed the folder and put it back in my briefcase.

There was a logical explanation, of course. I had not seen Thomas Kincaid walking about on campus. Thomas Kincaid was long since dead, and I did not believe in ghosts.

Not even on Halloween.

No matter what Hester Rose would have said about this, I did not believe in ghosts.

Chapter 4

AS I DROVE ACROSS THE DOWNTOWN BRIDGE toward my lunch date with Richard Colby, my mind drifted back to a year and a half ago in Hester Rose's hospital room. I had walked into my grandmother's room and found her staring down at her withered right hand, glaring at it as if it belonged to someone else and had been grafted onto her wrist.

"Hello," I said and hugged her.

Her rigid body resisted my embrace.

"Have you seen the news?" I said and clicked on the television. "They have flooding in Gallagher."

During that first week in May, a storm had swept out of the Atlantic. It had torn through North Carolina, then swooped into Virginia, bringing torrential rains. In Gallagher, the Dan River had crested at over seven feet above its banks. The floodwaters were providing spectacular aerial footage for CNN's report on the aftermath of the storm.

In Kentucky, Hester Rose and I watched the news report on the television in her hospital room. As the CNN reporter announced that he was standing in the middle of the one-hundred-two-year-old Mt. Zion Baptist Church, my grandmother said, "My daddy was one of them that started that church."

The reporter pointed out the destruction around him and noted with irony that the flooded church was located in a section of the city known as "Lucktown." The residents of Lucktown had not been lucky this time, he said.

And Hester Rose said, "Ain't nobody never been lucky there."

The CNN coverage ended. I clicked off the television.

"Grandma," I said, "we need to talk about something."

"What's ailing you, girl? Speak up."

Her body might be frail, but Hester Rose's tongue had lost none of its bite. At any other time, that would have amused me.

"I saw the hospital's patient-care coordinator this morning," I said. "She says we need to move you to a nursing care facility—"

"No! I ain't going to one of them places. You take me home."

"Grandma, I can't yet. They're still concerned about your blood pressure and your kidneys. You need special care, more than I or a home-health-care person could provide. But as soon as everything is under control—"

Her hooded eyes looked at and dismissed me. "I took care of you from the moment you came into this world," she said.

"Grandma, please. . . ." I touched her hand. "I promise I'll take you home as soon as—"

"If you put me in one of them nursing homes," she said, "I'll die there."

"You won't die there," I said. "The nurses will be there to give you round-the-clock care."

"Go on, girl. Go on back to your work." She turned her head away on the pillow and closed her eyes.

I kissed her on her sunken cheek and went back to my work.

In my campus mailbox, with the rest of the morning mail, was the latest criminal justice newsletter announcing positions open. Piedmont State University in Gallagher, Virginia, had a position open for a visiting scholar, women and persons of color encouraged to apply. I stared at it for a long moment and then tossed the newsletter into my overflowing "in box."

It was still there four months later in September when I was cleaning out my "in box" in preparation for fall semester. By then I had buried Hester Rose, who had died during the summer. By then I was back from my less-than-relaxing vacation in Cornwall, England.

I had always respected Hester Rose's feelings when she was alive. I had stayed away from Gallagher in spite of my curiosity about the place where she'd been born and about the lynching that had made her leave. But Hester Rose was dead now. And that day as I sat at my desk watching students stream into the building for the next round of classes, I felt the restlessness that had been plaguing me since I returned from Cornwall.

I was finally tenured. My academic life had settled into a comfortable pattern. But, if nothing else, Cornwall had shown me that sometimes patterns needed to be shaken up. That afternoon I drove to the post office and sent my letter of application out by express mail.

And that was how I came to be in Gallagher, Virginia, on an unusually warm—make that hot—day in October a little more than a year after mailing that application. Hester Rose had once said to me—long ago, when I was a child—*"I came into this world on the witches' sabbath, and I guess I'll go away from here on that same night."* She had been wrong. But the fact that today was her birthday—and the nightmare I'd had about her last night—was enough to fill my head with thoughts of her. Not that being in Gallagher wasn't already having that effect.

Gallagher was not what I had expected. Contrary to the impression I had gotten from the CNN footage, the city was not flat. It rose in hills and slopes from the banks of the Dan River. The river ran through the middle of the city, cutting it in half. Two bridges, one downtown, one uptown, linked the two halves together. The business district was on the south side of the river where Alexander Gallagher had established a trading post in 1743. On lower Main Street, the venerable gray granite courthouse was flanked by an ultramodern, black glass municipal building. Up the hill, a new public library had been done in clear glass and red brick. This was a major change from the library's former facility, a Victorian mansion.

According to local legend, both a group of Confederate officers and later the Union officers who'd vanquished them had been received at that mansion and been entertained with equal grace by the lady of the manor. Of course, legend also had it that the lady had considered poisoning the Yankee officers' stew. Only the fact that they had furnished the meat from which the stew was made, and thereby bound her to the rules of civility, had stayed her from doing away with her dinner guests.

That mansion, now the city's Civil War museum, was located on upper Main Street in the area that natives of Gallagher used to call "Millionaire's Row." Those four blocks of Victorian houses were listed in the historic registry. The Row had been used for location shooting when a film crew came to town last spring—before the flood—to make a movie about Amanda Norris, the Gallagher native who, in the 1900s, became an "heiress bride" to a titled relative of the British royal family. But it was the adventurous and somewhat scandalous life she had led after her first husband had broken his neck while riding to the hounds that had prompted a filmmaker to think a movie about her life would attract an audience. According to *The Gallagher Gazette*, the residents of Gallagher had greeted the news of the movie and the arrival of the film crew with both enthusiasm and concern about how the image of the dashing Amanda would fare in the hands of Hollywood.

The movie was due out early next year, and Amanda Norris and Millionaire's Row would bring attention and—the city council hoped—tourist dollars to Gallagher. But Amanda was not the only legendary resident of Gallagher. Among others, there were the Todd brothers, James and Bertrand. In the post-Civil War era, the powerful Todd brothers had built their cotton mill in an unincorporated township that they had called Mill Village. The houses they had built there had been for their white workers. The village was now a part of the city of Gallagher, and the mill was still the city's largest employer. It lay east of Millionaire's Row, past the city's park and recreation center complex and a bit beyond the hospital (medical center).

Down the hill from the Mercantile Cotton Mill was the Swan Street bridge. If you crossed that bridge, turned left, and drove about five miles, you would be at the main entrance of the university campus. The land the campus was located on had been donated by a city father to establish Piedmont Military Institute, but the military school had been forced to close its doors in 1927 because it was unable to compete with Virginia Military Institute (the renowned VMI). Recognizing a bargain, the state had stepped in and purchased the land for use as a university campus. That university had grown significantly in the last ten years. Piedmont State University now had a population of over 26,000 full- and part-time students. The presence of the university and all those students and faculty and staff had rather a significant social and economic impact on the city.

But the reminders of Gallagher's history were everywhere. On the same side of the river as the bustling campus, along Riverside Drive, you could still find the tobacco warehouse district that had been there since before the Civil War. During the war, the warehouses had been used as temporary barracks for captured Union prisoners. Of course, that bit of history had been blurred to the naked eye by the fact that the refurbished tobacco warehouses had been joined on Riverside Drive by auto dealerships, gas stations, mini malls, fast-food restaurants, dance clubs, and a veterinary hospital. And about five years ago, a splendid shopping mall-hotel complex had been built on one of the hills overlooking Riverside Drive.

From that hillside there was an excellent view of the river. While Hester Rose and I had been watching the flooding of the Dan River on television, people here in Gallagher had probably been up on that hillside getting a much better view of the river than they really wanted. But on this Tuesday noon, the Dan River slumbered in the sunshine, and the residents of Gallagher were going about their business.

The traffic light changed, and I turned onto Spring Street in downtown Gallagher. I was on my way to the Orleans Café. Yesterday Richard Colby had invited me to have lunch with him there. I had accepted because I was curious about why he had invited me; aside from one snide remark, he had ignored my existence for the past two months.

Joyce Fielding, one of the other faculty members in the school, had introduced us. We were in the faculty lounge. Richard had glanced up from *The Wall Street Journal* spread out on the table in front of him and said, "A pleasure to meet you, Professor Stuart. And for future reference, we don't cater to jocks here."

"Pardon me?" I said.

"I said, we don't cater to jocks. We don't adjust our academic requirements for the guys on the football team or the basketball team. Track stars don't receive special treatment either."

"I'm sorry, I don't understand why you're telling me this," I said.

“I’m telling you because I know universities like the one you’re coming from,” he said. “All the jocks at your university either major or minor in criminal justice. Or, at least, take two or three easy courses. And they get a walk-through in the program because of their athletic prowess. It doesn’t work that way here.”

“Thank you for explaining that to me,” I said.

When we were out in the hall, Joyce nodded toward the closed door of the lounge. “Ignore him,” she said. “Sometimes Richard can be irritating enough to make a pacifist contemplate violence. If he weren’t so damn brilliant, the rest of the faculty would hire a hit man.”

In light of our exchange in the faculty lounge and his complete silence toward me thereafter, I had been caught off guard yesterday when my office telephone rang and it was Richard Colby calling to ask if I was free for lunch today. I had managed to stammer “yes.”

Now I wanted an explanation. Why was he suddenly interested in fraternizing with a visiting professor from one of those second-rate universities where all the jocks majored in criminal justice? And, just as a matter of curiosity, why did he have Noah Webster, an ex-jock, as his graduate assistant?

Noah, I was told, had been a star running back on his college football team. So why had Richard taken Noah on as his assistant? Maybe Richard was willing to tolerate ex-jocks who arrived in graduate school with the kind of undergrad academic record I’d heard Noah had and who then managed to live up to it.

Whatever the explanation, this was another one of those occasions when curiosity triumphed over my other emotions. I wanted to know why Richard wanted to have lunch with me. If I didn’t like his reason, I could always get up and walk out.

Or I could have, if Hester Rose hadn’t spent the formative years of my childhood and adolescence filling my head not only with her endless supply of superstition and folklore but with frequent lectures on good manners. Although she had never come right out and said so, my grandmother had made it quite clear that good manners were essential when you were the illegitimate (father unknown) daughter of a headstrong teenage mother who had left town five days after you were born. Moreover, good manners were essential because I was not going to embarrass her and my grandfather by acting like a child with “no home training.” Undoubtedly, good manners were one of the reasons I hadn’t turned Richard down when he invited me to lunch. I was too polite to tell him to go to hell.

As I closed my car door, I glanced across the street and saw Richard waiting for me outside the café. Why hadn’t he gone inside? Good manners on his part? Somehow I doubted that.

My glance was drawn from Richard to the two-story red brick

building on the corner. Yesterday, at the university library, I had seen an old newspaper photograph of that building. Now I looked at it with fresh interest.

Lounging on the steps of the porticoed entrance was a man who looked unkempt even from a distance. In this weather, he had a bright red scarf wrapped aviator-style around his neck. He tipped his head back and took a long swallow from the bottle inside his brown paper bag. If it had been 1921, Andrew Clark would have come charging out of the doorway of his store in that building with a broom handle in his hand. Clark had been famous for his broom handle. He was a staunch prohibitionist, a "dry man." To his annoyance—and that of the other members of the Law and Order League—even after national Prohibition was declared, drinkers in Gallagher had still found ways to quench their thirst.

But in spite of his limited success as a reformer, Andrew Clark had been known as a savvy businessmen. After getting his start selling produce at the Saturday curb market, Clark had gone on to open his own general store in that red brick building. In the full-page newspaper ad announcing the grand opening, he had boasted, "We are the most up-to-date establishment in the city. We stock the finest merchandise to be found anywhere."

The windows of that establishment were boarded up now. But according to one local historian, Clark's store had been at the hub of the bustling commerce on Union Street. On any Saturday afternoon, country folks mingled with mill workers and society matrons. Motorcars darted around farm wagons and pedestrians. Children frolicked, and dogs barked.

Today Union Street drowsed. The crowd-drawing stores were gone, replaced by a municipal parking lot and a few small businesses. First State Bank on one corner. The downtown liquor store on the other. A barber shop and a used furniture store. But the Orleans Café was still there on Union Street. The Orleans had served its first meal in 1912.

When I had mentioned to Joyce Fielding that I had been meaning to stop by the café and talk to Miss Alice, the owner, Joyce laughed and said that I'd better wait until our October heat wave was over. Some days they used air-conditioning at the Orleans Café. Some days they didn't. So I had decided to wait.

In truth, that wasn't the only reason I had decided to wait. I had told myself that it wasn't that urgent that I talk to Miss Alice yet anyway. She might have known my grandmother. But that was all the more reason to make sure that I had done my research before I introduced myself to her. Then I would know what I wanted to ask her.

But yesterday Richard Colby had thrown a monkey wrench into my game plan. He had invited me to lunch at the Orleans Café. So here we were.

And he was still waiting for me by the door.

I started across the street. Nothing was coming. I jaywalked.

It was hot. I was sweating. Not Richard. His short-sleeved white cotton shirt was open at the collar, but it looked laundry fresh. His khaki slacks still had their crease. And the precise cut of his hair would have passed muster with any barber—make that "stylist." Hands in his pockets, dark glasses shielding his eyes, Richard looked "cool" in both senses of the word. Cool as that proverbial breeze. Cool as an urban sophisticate. What puzzled me was why he had come back to Gallagher. I knew he had been born here. But why would he and his wife Diane have left Berkeley, California, to move back? Individually and as a couple, they were definitely more Berkeley than Gallagher.

"Sorry I'm late," I said as I walked up to Richard. "I made the mistake of stopping at a used bookstore on the way and completely lost track of the time."

Richard took off his dark glasses and slid them into his shirt pocket. His clear eyes, amber brown under arched brows, studied my face. He said, "And I was standing out here wondering if you'd changed your mind and stood me up."

His amused tone threw me again. "Changed my mind? Why would I do that?"

"Women sometimes do change their minds," he said. "Wait until you taste Miss Alice's gumbo. I promise you it's worth the trip downtown." He opened the iron-grilled door and ushered me inside.

Ceiling fans circulated lazily. Jazz played in the background. Pungent odors of meat and spices and simmering greens provided a counterpoint to the laughter and conversation of the customers. They were a diverse group. Interracial. Some white-collar types in ties or dresses. Other more casual diners in blue jeans or shorts. All sitting on hard wooden chairs around tables covered with red-and-white checked oilcloth.

Only two tables in the long room were unoccupied. Other businesses on Union Street might have died or fled, but the Orleans Café still flourished.

Chapter 5

RICHARD GUIDED ME toward one of the empty tables. "Hey, Clo," he called to the woman behind the counter. "You saving this one for me?"

The smile that had started to spread across the woman's brown velvet face wavered when she saw Richard was not alone. She put her hands on her hips. "Didn't you call and tell me to save you that table, Rabbit?"

Richard flashed me a glance and made a comic grimace. "Clovis, how many times I got to tell you not to call me that in front of people?" He pulled out a chair for me.

Clovis came out from behind the counter and picked up a menu. She was a big woman. Big, not fat. She was wearing a white United States Navy uniform, complete with bell-bottom trousers. Her Halloween costume, I assumed. A jack-o'-lantern sat on the counter, and cardboard witches and goblins were scattered about on the yellow walls. The centerpiece on our table was a black candle inside a skull-shaped holder. Obviously, Clovis got into Halloween.

She moved toward us in time to the jazz in the background, a hip-swaying walk that made her beaded braids swing. She looked to be in her late forties. Richard's age. Someone who had known him when he was a boy nicknamed "Rabbit." Someone who was still allowed to tease him with that nickname.

"Hi," she said as she handed me the menu. "I'm Clovis. Miss Alice's granddaughter."

"Hello. I'm Lizzie Stuart." I glanced at Richard. "Richard and I are colleagues."

Clovis's limp fingers closed around the hand I was holding out to her. Then what I had said registered. She grinned, revealing the gap between her two upper teeth. It was a magnificent grin. "Oh, you're the one Rabbit told us about. The new professor from Kentucky."

Richard said, "Clovis, I'll pay you two dollars right now to call me by the name my mama gave me."

"You still know how to talk your way out of a fox's mouth?" she asked him.

He smiled. "When I have to."

"Then you're still 'Brer Rabbit' to me." She tilted her head as she looked at me. "The rice and beans are good. But they're kind of heavy on a hot day. You might want to try the wings and some potato salad."

Richard said, "I been bragging to Lizzie about your grandma's gumbo."

"It's too hot for gumbo," she said.

He glanced around the room. "Half the people in this place are eating the gumbo."

"They're as crazy as you are, Rabbit," Clovis said. "You want the wings and potato salad?" she asked me.

"All right," I said. "If that's what you recommend."

"Your colleague here has sense," she told Richard. "I'll bring you the gumbo."

"You do that, Clo."

He watched her hip-sway away. "I love that woman," he said. "I've loved her since the day she beat me up on the playground for calling her gap-toothed."

I must have looked stunned by that announcement, because he laughed and shook his head. "Hot, young blood, Lizzie. If my mama hadn't sent me away to keep me out of other kinds of trouble, Clo and I would probably have gotten married before we were out of high school."

I managed to get out, "Better not let your wife hear you say that."

Richard brushed a finger across his upper lip. "I'm not sure that she would care. Diane and I are having our problems."

Had he invited me to lunch to tell me about his domestic troubles? "Most couples do now and then," I said. "What are those photographs on the wall over there?"

"Those are the great jazzmen. Clovis's father fancied himself a musician. Used to treat the crowd to trumpet solos every Saturday night. Miss Alice would only let him play once a week."

"Is Miss Alice here now?" I asked, seizing on the opening. "I'd like to meet her."

Richard called out to Clovis, "Hey, Clo, where's your grandma today?"

"At home," Clovis said. "Cousin Jean's here visiting."

Richard pointed at the empty table by the kitchen door. "When Miss Alice is here, she sits over there."

"I'd like to talk to her about the old days here in Gallagher," I said. "Do you think she would?"

"You don't know Miss Alice. Big Daddy Sam used to say the woman would talk to the Devil if she could get him to sit still long enough."

"Big Daddy Sam?"

"Her husband. He died years ago. Before I left town."

I leaned my elbows on the table and gave in to curiosity. "You mean when your mother sent you away to keep you out of trouble? Where did she send you?"

"To live with her sister in Texas. My aunt and her husband had a ranch they were trying to make a go of, so they were happy to get another hand. And my mama was happy to get me away from the stuff I was getting into."

"Kid stuff?"

"On the way to being big-time. I was hanging around with the town's bad boys."

"Did you like ranching?"

"There were some days when it wasn't as bad as others," he said. "The good part was that I learned self-discipline—how to get out of bed before sunrise and put in a full day's work. I also realized I didn't want to spend the rest of my life breaking my back. So I finished high school and applied to some colleges. I ended up at Emory University."

"I've heard it's a good school," I said.

"I stopped there last week on my way back from a conference in Savannah."

"For old time's sake?"

"To see one of my buddies," Richard said. "Ted James. We were undergrads together. The guy was a crazy man. Gave the professors nothing but grief. Now he's on the faculty."

"He must have mended his ways."

"Not hardly. Ted's still a crazy man. We spent Saturday evening in the hospital emergency room with his sprained ankle because he wanted to play a pickup game with some kids we saw out on a basketball court." Richard leaned back in his chair, smiling. "But, crazy or not, the guy's a political scientist now, and he's back at Emory. Been there nine years. Living the good life in *Gone with the Wind* country."

"If you don't mind my asking, how did you end up back here in Gallagher? You and Diane were at Berkeley, right?"

Richard's smile froze in place.

"Here you go." Clovis set a bowl of pretzels on the table in front of us. "Help yourself, Rabbit."

She walked away, signaling to the young man who was helping her wait tables. He was tall and skinny, blond hair caught back in a ponytail, azure blue earring dangling from one earlobe.

"I'm sorry," I said to Richard. "I didn't mean to pry."

He scooped up a handful of pretzels and popped one into his mouth. He chewed and said, "Diane and I came back here because I was going through what's popularly known as a midlife crisis."

"Oh," I said.

"Oh?" he said. "Don't you want to know the details?"

"It sounds personal."

"But that's what makes a story interesting. All the personal details." Richard sat back in his chair. "Diane is my second wife. My first wife was Delores. I make it a practice to marry women whose names begin with *D*."

"Obviously."

"Delores and I were married right after I got my first teaching job in Indiana. We stayed married for fourteen years. Twelve of them were good years."

"Twelve good years is probably better than average these days," I said. "Did you have children?"

"A son," Richard said. "He died four years ago."

"Oh, I'm sorry."

"Me too. I had a hard time dealing with it. Kevin was eighteen years old when he died of a drug overdose. He—" Richard shook his head. "Sorry. As I was saying, Diane— You've met my lovely spouse? You know she's a psychologist?"

"Yes, I know that," I said.

"When my son died, Diane did her best to comfort me. But when I took a good look at my life, I wasn't particularly pleased with what I saw. I went into a depression. My midlife crisis."

"And that was when the two of you decided to come back here to Gallagher?"

"It happened that my crisis coincided with Amos Baylor's efforts to recruit a new faculty member. Amos and I had met before, and he called and asked if I would consider applying. He was impressed by the fact that I came complete with Ph.D., M.B.A., and a national reputation. As for Diane—she thought getting back to my roots would cure what ailed the two of us. So she applied to the psych department. When they offered her a full-time position for the next year, that cinched the deal."

"So it all worked out," I said—and then realized what I had said. His son was dead. That part hadn't worked out.

Richard shrugged. "I stopped moping around the house in my bathrobe. Diane thought that was real progress." His gaze focused on my face. "But enough about me. How do you like Piedmont State? Or more specifically, the School of Criminal Justice?"

"I like both the university and the school."

"Really?"

"Yes, really. I like the CJ faculty. I think the students are great."

"Some of them," Richard said. "As you'll learn, our students range from dull-mediocre to brilliant."

That word again. Joyce had used *brilliant* to describe Richard. Not that I hadn't heard it applied to him before I arrived at Piedmont State. He had a reputation as one of the outstanding theorists in the area of white-collar and corporate crime. He was a celebrity of sorts among African-American criminologists. There weren't that many of us around, and he had achieved both name recognition and status among our white colleagues. But Richard and I had never met because he didn't attend the two national criminal justice/criminology conferences that most people in our field attended each year. Probably because he didn't need to.

The truth was, I had hoped to have the opportunity to get to know Richard during my year at Piedmont State. But his first response to my arrival had been so discouraging that I had kept my distance.

I picked up on his last remark about the quality of the students in the criminal justice program. "So, who would you include in the brilliant category? I've heard good things about Noah Webster, your grad assistant."

Richard nodded. "Noah has the brains to match all that brawn. And we have a few others who show more than occasional signs of intellectual activity. Drew Phillips, for example."

"I haven't met him. Or is it her?"

"Him. He's not around a lot. He's working for the state while he finishes up his dissertation."

"What about the women students? Any of them brilliant?"

"One or two. Megan Reed is going to whiz right through the program. She came in with an M.B.A."

"Aah," I said. "So she started out with a gold star in your book."

"Definitely. Although, every time I see her with Eric Walsh, our resident prankster. . . ."

"Maybe Eric will turn out like your crazy friend Ted. Besides, being brilliant has nothing to do with who one falls in love with, does it?"

"Very true. As I can testify."

I laughed. "Richard, low self-esteem is not one of your problems."

"Only on dark winter days and rainy Mondays."

"Both depressing," I said.

"So we've established that you like it here. Now, tell me about this research you're doing."

"Are you confessing that you didn't read the research agenda I included with my application?"

"I read it. But it was somewhat vague. Crime and justice in Gallagher in the post-World War I period? What does that mean exactly?"

I hesitated as I remembered Officer Thomas Kincaid's photograph, then said, "Actually, what I'm really interested in is the lynching that happened here in 1921."

"1921? You mean Mose . . . what was his name? Mose Daniels?"

"Davenport."

"Mose Davenport. So the book you intend to write will be about that lynching?"

I nodded and launched automatically into my twenty-five-words-or-less summary. "And the general climate of criminal justice and race relations in the South during that period. I want to understand why he was lynched."

"You know why he was lynched," Richard said. "He was a black man, and he shot a white cop. What about the other accusation against him? Who was it that they said he killed? A doctor?"

"Dr. Daniel Stevens. The city physician." I paused and then said, "But my grandmother didn't believe he did it."

"Your grandmother?"

"Her name was Hester Rose. She came from Gallagher. She was there in Ophelia Hewitt's house when the police came to arrest Mose Davenport."

Richard looked surprised. "Your grandmother was in that house?"

"She was only twelve years old at the time," I said. "Ophelia made her run and hide. Then that night she—my grandmother—left town."

"And your grandmother said Davenport was innocent?"

"That was what she believed," I said.

"What she believed. But from what I remember of the story, Mose Davenport wasn't exactly squeaky clean."

"I know. My grandmother said he was a gambler. The articles in *The Gallagher Gazette* alleged he was a drug dealer too."

"And a doctor would have drugs in his office, wouldn't he?"

"Yes, but Ophelia, Mose's girlfriend, was Dr. Stevens's housekeeper. My grandmother said Ophelia was very fond of Dr. Stevens."

"So what you're saying is that Davenport wouldn't have tried to rip off his girlfriend's boss because she was fond of the guy?"

"What I'm saying is, my grandmother didn't think Mose Davenport was a killer."

"He shot a cop."

"That was an accident. My grandmother saw what happened. Mose panicked."

"Suppose the doctor walked in when Davenport was ripping off his office and Davenport panicked then too?"

"That's possible," I said. "But the police apparently never even looked for another suspect. After Mose shot Officer Thomas Kincaid, there was a presumption that he had also killed Daniel Stevens."

Richard said, "There would be, wouldn't there? So that's why you're here. To solve an eighty-year-old murder mystery. To identify the culprit and—"

I shook my head. "That particular trail is pretty cold by now. I think I'd better settle for describing the lynching—the environment in which citizens could take the law into their own hands and—"

"We know that stuff already," he said.

"I know there's a significant body of research on lynching, including other case studies, but I think—"

"But you think you're going to find something different with this one?"

"Not necessarily. But I do think that it's important to do comparative research in which we examine the dynamics—"

"Examine the dynamics? Save that crap for your students, Professor Stuart." He leaned toward me. "Come on, Lizzie! How about looking for the truth? Why don't you figure out who killed Daniel Stevens and tell that story."

"And just how am I supposed to do that?" I said. "I'm a crime historian, not a detective. For all I know, Mose Davenport did do it. And even if I wanted to investigate, the police records aren't there. They were destroyed in 1927 when the police station burned down."

"Excuses, Lizzie, excuses. Do you think the police records would have had anything useful in them, anyway? And I thought crime historians prided themselves on their detecting abilities. Isn't that the definition of any good historian?"

"I think, Richard, that depends on how one practices history."

"And you practice history by evasion?"

"Did you invite me to lunch to insult me?"

He smiled, a slow, almost sweet smile. "If you really want to know, I invited you to lunch because I've been wondering what goes on behind your unruffled brow."

"And you decided to ruffle it?"

"Okay, so I have noticed a slight ruffle now and then." He gave me a sly look with arched brows. "And maybe I was pushing you a little just now. But I do find you interesting."

"Why, thank you so much," I said. "I find you interesting too."

"Now that we've established rapport, would you care to tell me all about yourself? Your deepest, darkest secrets."

"I don't have any," I said.

"Not even one?"

"None. Do you?"

"A few." His smile flickered, then returned. "What about something about Lizzie Stuart that I could look up anyway? Like what the *T* stands for."

"The what?"

"Your middle initial."

"Oh, that," I said.

"That bad, huh?"

"If you must know, it stands for Theodora."

"Your parents were into Byzantine rulers?" Richard said.

I gave him several points for looking completely innocent when he asked the question. My mother, Rebecca, had gifted me with the name of a woman who had begun life as the daughter of a circus bear trainer. Although that woman, Theodora, had become the strong and capable wife of an emperor, her detractors took pleasure in claiming that before her marriage to her emperor, Theodora had been not only an actress but a prostitute. That little zinger—the likelihood that Theodora had been a prostitute—undoubtedly had been what smart and rebellious Rebecca had been thinking of when she proposed my middle name.

My grandmother—pleased to have something good to tell a child about her absent mother—told me that Rebecca had named me after a queen. Later, when I was old enough to read about Theodora, I could almost imagine the wicked laughter in my young mother's eyes when she made her little joke. A joke that had gone right over her own mother's puritanical but uneducated head and ended up on my birth certificate.

"My grandmother chose my first name," I said, daring him with my look to make further comment. "My mother countered with my middle name."

Richard said, "My mother named me after an uncle of hers. He was a drunk, but damn good at making money and generous to his relatives."

"Not the worst namesake you could have," I said. "So, tell me about why you have both an M.B.A. and a Ph.D."

"Oh, that. I wanted a fall-back position."

I laughed.

"Careful, now," a drawling voice said. Pete Murphy was standing there at our table, grinning down at us. "Watch out for this guy, Lizzie."

Richard and I had been so involved in our conversation that we had missed Pete's arrival. He was hard to miss. He was built like a gladiator, and he had a bushy blond beard, circa 1860. Pete participated in Civil War reenactments.

"Hi, Pete," I said.

"Peter," Richard said, relaxing back in his chair.

"What kind of snake oil is this guy trying to sell you?" Pete asked, giving me a wink.

"I was telling Professor Stuart that she should really try to find out why some white cops found it convenient to make a black man the fall guy for a murder."

Pete, who had been a cop, frowned. "What?" he said.

I intervened. "Pete, Richard was encouraging me to try to find the solution to a murder that happened in 1921. Remember last week—when I did the brown-bag lunch about my research on Gallagher—I mentioned the Mose Davenport lynching?"

"Davenport?" Pete said. "You said he shot a cop."

"But you see, Peter," Richard said, "even though Mose Davenport shot the police officer, Professor Stuart doesn't believe he murdered the city physician."

"I didn't say that, Richard."

Pete tugged at the side of his beard. "If he didn't do it, who did?"

"I don't know," I said. "For all I know, he did do it."

Richard smiled. "Cop out, Professor Stuart. Forgive the pun, Pete."

I frowned at Richard and turned back to Pete. "Pete, please sit down and join us."

"Thanks, Lizzie, I'm just here to pick up takeout. I'll see you both later."

"Sure thing," Richard said.

"See you back at school, Pete," I said.

He raised a hand in farewell and walked off toward the counter.

I turned to Richard. "Why did you do that?"

"Do what?" he asked.

"You know what. You were deliberately rude."

"Me? I'm always sweet as honey."

"Tell her another one, Rabbit," Clovis said as she arrived with our lunches. She set a bowl of steaming gumbo in front of Richard. It looked good.

So did my chicken wings and potato salad. I swallowed my irritation with Richard and told her so.

She grinned. "I'll be back later to see if you want to try the peach cobbler."

When we were alone again, Richard said, "So, tell me about life in Kentucky?"

"Tell you what about it?" I said.

"All right then, I'll talk about me."

And he did. By the time he had gotten halfway through a story about his first year in graduate school, I was nodding my head. For the next hour, Richard and I traded stories—some funny, some sad, some enough to make us both mad—about our respective adventures in higher education.

We ordered the peach cobbler, topped with vanilla ice cream. And then Richard asked if I'd gone to the last Kentucky Derby. He groaned when I admitted I'd watched it on television. One of his dreams, he said, since he had discovered horses on his aunt's ranch in Texas, was to own a thoroughbred race horse. I said that was on my fantasy list too.

Richard insisted on paying for lunch because he had invited me. And after the hard time he had given me about Mose Davenport—not to mention the incident with Pete—I let him pay.

As we were leaving, I asked Clovis to mention me to her grandmother. Please tell Miss Alice that I would call one day soon. Tell her that she might have known my grandmother when they were both children.

Clovis said she would do that.

Out in the parking lot, Richard escorted me to my car. "Thank you for the pleasure of your company at lunch, Professor Stuart."

"I enjoyed it too," I said.

"We'll have to do it again soon," he said. He waved his hand and walked away toward his shiny black BMW.

I got into my beige Focus—not as snazzy, but it did what I needed done—and reached for the "to do" list I had left on top of my briefcase.

First the Hall of Records. Then back to campus to take care of—

Richard tooted his horn as he passed me still sitting there.

I started my ignition. I had at least five things I needed to get done before the murder mystery party tonight.

Chapter 6

I SPENT THE NEXT COUPLE OF HOURS going through string-tied boxes in a back room at the Hall of Records. I was looking for any criminal cases in which Mose Davenport had been a defendant. *The Gallagher Gazette* had reported at least two occasions on which he had been hauled into Police Court. The first time, he had been fined fifty dollars for disorderly conduct. The second time, he and several other suspected gambling-den operators had appeared at their hearings represented by a lawyer named Jonathan Caulder. The police court justice had dismissed the cases for lack of evidence.

The records I was looking through now were of cases which had gone up to Corporation Court. The trouble was, it required opening and reading each case packet because the index to the files was only partial.

I paused over an arrest warrant that had been issued for Fay Lincoln, accused of operating a house of ill fame. She was one of the alleged gambling-den operators who had been arrested with Mose Davenport. I jotted her name down on an index card. That was something I needed to get started on. I needed to identify Mose Davenport's criminal associates.

When I walked out of the municipal building into the late afternoon heat, sweat popped out in my armpits. The air-conditioning inside had been turned up full throttle.

In the parking lot, a woman in a honey-colored silk suit was getting out of a pale green Mercedes. Her license plate said MSLAW.

I should have gone to law school. Lawyers never got dust all over their clothes. I closed my car door and swatted at my black skirt.

The paper bag containing the books I had bought that morning was still there on the passenger seat. I hadn't mentioned Thomas Kincaid to Richard during lunch because I saw no reason to have him think I was crazy. I might as well stick with someone who already thought that I was. That would be University Police Chief John Mackenzie Quinn.

I started the car and headed back toward campus. With any luck, Quinn would be in his office when I got there.

As he had said, we had met almost fifteen months ago. We were both on vacation in Cornwall at the time. When we met, Quinn was a Philadelphia homicide detective with a job offer he was considering. I found out later that the offer was from an old Army buddy who wanted Quinn to take over as head of the Toronto, Canada, office of his security consulting firm. Quinn was giving the matter serious consideration. However, he passed on Toronto because he suddenly decided that he wanted to be a university police chief in Gallagher, Virginia. He had found out about the job vacancy because I had mentioned the university to him in an E-mail.

Not that I had ever expected to find myself exchanging E-mails with John Quinn. We had said good-bye in Cornwall. I had gone back to Drucilla, Kentucky, and he had gone back to Philadelphia. And so much for that kiss in a hospital waiting room that shouldn't have happened and that was much better forgotten. He had agreed with me when I told him that. When he called the next day, I pointed out to him—before he could fumble his way through a speech intended to let me down easy—that it would be ridiculous to take that kiss seriously. We had been brought together by a dramatic situation, the kind of situation that novels and movies programmed us to think should be romantic. But this wasn't a movie, and we were two people with nothing at all in common, and we lived hundreds of miles apart. So we would be much better off simply saying "Nice meeting you, good luck, and good-bye."

My succinct analysis of the situation during our telephone conversation did not include mention of the nightmare straight out of *Rosemary's Baby* that had awakened me in the wee hours of the morning. But that was irrelevant. I had dreams all the time.

And it wasn't as if Quinn had shown any inclination to argue with what I'd said. What he said was, "You're probably right. Why complicate our lives when we don't have to? It was nice meeting you, Lizzie Stuart. Good luck in your future endeavors." And then he'd hung up the telephone.

In between worrying about all the other things I had to worry about that day, I spent a fair amount of time wondering if I could have handled the situation with Quinn better. Maybe I had been too abrupt, had hurt his feelings—or his ego. But I didn't have a whole lot of experience in dealing with situations like that. And at any rate, it was over.

Or at least I had thought it was over. Then a few months later, just before Christmas, Quinn e-mailed me at the university. His three-line message read: "I spoke to Janowitz last night. He asked how you and Tess were doing. I said I'd find out."

Janowitz was his friend and ex-partner, now retired to Cornwall with his Scottish wife. Quinn had been visiting them when we met. Tess Alvarez was my best friend and roommate from college. She was a travel writer, and I had been there to spend a week with her.

I stared at those three lines on my computer screen for a long time and finally decided that it would be rude not to respond to a simple inquiry about my health and well-being. I typed back that I was fine and that Tess was a lot more pregnant than she had been in Cornwall, but she was all right too.

And that was how our E-mail exchanges had begun. Without mention of that kiss. As if it had never happened. We had moved our exchanges from our office computers to home and fallen into the habit of chatting several times a week.

But I hadn't anticipated the result of our friendly little chats. I hadn't anticipated that John Quinn and I would both end up here in Gallagher, Virginia. That certainly had not occurred to me when I mentioned that I had been offered a visiting faculty position at Piedmont State. From what I had seen of him, John Quinn was level-headed, rational, and in control, not at all the type to do impulsive things. Why would I have imagined that he would go to the Piedmont State Web page, see the position announcement for a new university police chief, and decide to apply?

Even when he told me about it in a "guess what" E-mail, I had thought nothing would come of it. I'd gone back to the Web page to find out what qualifications the new chief was expected to have, and I had been pretty sure the university administration would not think Quinn met the criteria. After all, even though he had been promoted to lieutenant when he returned from his vacation in Cornwall, he was still a big-city homicide cop. An odd match for a university campus. I was sure the recruiting committee at Piedmont State would dismiss his application as the whim it probably was.

When he e-mailed a few weeks later to say that he had been invited to Gallagher for an interview, I was surprised. I was even more surprised when three days after the interview they offered him the job. It wasn't until several months later, when I read an on-line story at the university Web site titled "New Chief Will Bring Unique Qualifications," that I began to understand why he had beat out the other candidates. It seemed that not only had Quinn attended West Point (something I had known), but he had been a major when he was in the Army, the executive officer in a military police battalion. Airborne, no less. The military police part I had known; the major and Airborne, I hadn't. I also didn't know about the "several courses" he had taken at the FBI Academy. And it seemed John Quinn also more than met the education requirement specified in the position announcement. He had not only an M.A. in criminal justice, but another M.A. in public administration. That was news to me too.

And it was just a little annoying that at forty-six (according to the article), Quinn had been successful at two different careers and was now raring to go on to a third. Or maybe it just meant he had difficulty sticking to things. At thirty-nine, that was one problem I did not have. Rut was my second middle name. Or, at least, it had been, until my big move to Gallagher—my big move that had the unexpected consequence of putting me in the same city with John Quinn.

So here we both were in Gallagher. And whatever doubts I might have about his decision, Quinn seemed to have settled readily enough into his role of top cop on a university campus. From what I'd read in faculty and student publications, both groups were pleased so far with his "evenhanded" and "innovative" approach to campus policing.

So maybe I'd been wrong. Or maybe Quinn was just enjoying a honeymoon period.

I guided my car into the last vacant spot in the small parking lot reserved for visitors to the university police department. Located across the street from the garage for the university shuttle buses, the police department was housed in the Public Safety building. One set of doors was marked PARKING MANAGEMENT; double doors of the adjoining wing bore the notice POLICE. When I entered, the young officer in the glass-fronted reception cubicle looked up from the paperwork on the counter in front of him. He had taffy brown hair, happy brown eyes, and freckles across the bridge of his nose. He looked about nineteen. But there was an efficient tilt to his head as I approached. "Yes, ma'am," he said. "May I help you?"

I shifted my briefcase containing Glover's history of Gallagher to my other hand. "Yes. I'm Professor Stuart from criminal justice. I don't have an appointment, but I need to speak to Chief Quinn, please."

The officer's face had relaxed into a grin halfway through my spiel. "Professor Stuart. Yes, ma'am, I recognize you from your picture."

That confused me. "What picture?"

"The one in *The Tattler.* With that piece they did about how you're here for the year as a visiting scholar, and you're doing research on crime in Gallagher in the 1920s."

The Tattler was the campus newspaper.

"You have a good memory," I said.

L. Thorpe—according to his name tag—grinned. "I try to work at remembering things."

"Me, too," I said. "But sometimes I forget what I wanted to try to remember."

Thorpe laughed at my little joke. "I'll see if the chief is available," he said.

He picked up his telephone receiver. I turned to look around me. When I'd first arrived back in August, Quinn had invited me to come over and have a look around. In fact, he had made it a point to stop by my office on my second day on campus with a welcome-to-campus gift, a bag of miniature chocolate bars for me, the confessed chocolate addict. But his visit was the reason I had never come to his office. I had felt much too awkward when he had shown up at mine. How should a brand new visiting faculty member explain why the university police chief was sitting in her office? When Joyce Fielding had asked later why he'd been there, I'd mumbled something about having met him before—and had been very glad that I wasn't a fair-skinned blonde so she couldn't tell that I was blushing. Blushing because I had picked that precise moment to remember that kiss in the hospital waiting room.

That had been Quinn's first and last office drop-in. Maybe he had found it awkward too.

But now here I was on his turf, in his police station. I glanced around the reception area, where framed scenes of campus life and sports posters decorated white walls. Blue tube chairs were provided for visitors. One of those chairs was occupied by a drooping young woman in grubby jeans. She was twisting a lock of brown hair, that could have used a washing, around her fingers. I assumed she was not with the campus All-American sitting three chairs away. Clean-featured and clear-skinned, he looked as if he should be doing milk commercials, white teeth flashing as he lowered the carton and wiped his mouth with the back of his hand.

Officer Thorpe put down his telephone receiver. "I'm sorry, Professor. I'm afraid the chief's not here."

"Oh—will he be back later today?"

"If he does stop back in, it won't be until sometime this evening. Sergeant Macklin says the chief went to Roanoke for a training seminar. I'm sorry, I just came on duty so I didn't know."

"I guess they didn't expect anyone to come looking for him."

"It was more a case of I didn't ask and nobody thought to tell me," Thorpe said. "Sometimes the chief will be back there with his door closed trying to get some work done."

So they had already adjusted to their new chief's work habits, had they? Well, he had been here since June. He'd beaten me to Gallagher by a good two months.

I brushed my hand over my damp forehead. It was the weather. It was too warm for the last day of October.

"Is it something that someone else could help you with, Professor Stuart?"

"No," I said. "But I would like to leave a message for Chief Quinn."

Thorpe reached for a pen and a pink message pad. "Go ahead, ma'am."

"Would you tell him, please, that I stopped by and that I would like to speak with him at his earliest convenience." I paused. "But I won't be at home tonight because I have to attend a Halloween party at the Performing Arts Center. Tomorrow I'll be at home in the morning, and in the office by early afternoon."

I gave Thorpe my home and office telephone numbers. Not that Quinn didn't already have those numbers. As he'd said, since I'd been in Gallagher he had supplemented his E-mails with occasional telephone calls.

He had also shown up a couple of times at the house I was renting to give me a hand with weekend chores that I was trying to get done. Both times, he had pitched in with the work, then I had served him lunch and he'd gone on his way. Actually, I hadn't found that nearly as unsettling as having him drop by my office. Except, of course, for Mrs. Cavendish, my neighbor across the street who had appeared with a plate of gingerbread the first time Quinn came over. He had introduced himself, telling her more than I would have, while she looked him up and down and reached her own conclusions. I was quite sure she had her eye trained to her window every time she saw his black Bronco pull up. And he seemed to be pulling up more often lately. He had been back twice since those two Saturdays when he had dropped by to help with chores. Once with some Chinese takeout and a video we had both wanted to see. Once with a housewarming gift, a small painting full of desert light and shadow from his sister's art gallery in Sante Fe—the sister he hadn't mentioned having until he handed me the painting.

But then, I hadn't told him a lot about my family either. Definitely not about my parents. Exchanging confidences wasn't something that I found that easy to do . . . and what it came down to was that I didn't know how to deal with Quinn. How to act. We had eliminated romance from the agenda, and we seemed to be edging slowly toward being "buddies." Except I had never had a buddy like John Quinn.

"Ma'am? Professor Stuart?" Thorpe said, snapping me out of my reverie. "Ma'am, I was saying that I'll put your message on the chief's desk. Is there anything else I can do for you?"

"No, that's— Yes, one more thing, please. Something else for my message. Would you also tell Chief Quinn that the answer to his question is *They Drive by Night.*"

Thorpe stared at me. "Pardon me, Professor?"

"The answer to a question he asked me," I said. "Tell him the answer is—"

"They Drive by Night," Thorpe said as he wrote it down.

"It's a movie title," I said.

"Yes, ma'am. As long as the chief understands the message."

"He will. Thank you, Officer Thorpe."

The movie trivia game Quinn and I were in the midst of had started with a throwaway remark on my part about a film noir festival on a movie channel. He had responded with a quote from a movie and challenged me to identify it. Since then, we had been shooting challenges back and forth each week. Each of us had been stumped twice. Third time the loser. Prize as yet undetermined. I had suggested three of the winner's favorite movies on video. He had said we ought to be able to come up with something better than that.

Not that I was particularly concerned about how much paying up was likely to cost the loser. When it came to movie trivia, Quinn was good; but if his last attempt to stump me was anything to go by, I was better. The line he had quoted with such certainty that I would never get it was "The doors made me do it!" It was what deranged widow Ida Lupino had said in *They Drive by Night* about why she'd killed her husband. It had taken me the length of a cup of peppermint tea and a bowl of oatmeal with almonds and honey to remember. I had flipped through a video guide as I was thinking, but that was acceptable. The only rule was that we could not resort to Internet Web sites in search of the quote. Now all I had to do was come up with a surefire zinger of a movie quote that would be Quinn's downfall.

Assuming, of course, the game was still on after our conversation this morning.

I slammed my car door and put my briefcase down on the seat beside me. I hadn't come to see Quinn about movie trivia. I had wanted to follow up our earlier discussion about Thomas Kincaid. If Kincaid's look-alike had been crossing the street in front of Alumni House, it was quite possible he had been there. It should be simple enough for Quinn, as university police chief, to make an inquiry of the staff at Alumni House. I could even provide a photograph—Thomas Kincaid's.

But for now, there was nothing else I could do until I could talk to Quinn.

I hated waiting.

Chapter 7

THE ELEVATOR CREAKED to a stop on the fifth floor. I sidestepped around a group of grad students and Pete Murphy, who were in the middle of a football debate. Pete waved his hand as I passed, and I returned the greeting. He went back to what he was saying about Sunday's game.

The School of Criminal Justice had more than its share of sports fans, and Pete was one of them. Oddly enough, Richard, of the no-slack-for-jocks mandate, was included in that number. In fact, Joyce had told me a story about one occasion when Richard and Pete had been in complete agreement. Last spring, Joe Larsen had hosted a Sunday afternoon buffet at his house to celebrate an award he had won for a book he had written on 21st-century criminal justice technology. He had gone all out with prime rib, shrimp, and assorted delicacies prepared and served by his housekeeper. (Joe was a widower.) But when they learned Joe's television was broken, Richard and Pete had gulped down their food and then led an exodus to the nearest sports bar to catch the big game.

Joyce had been a little shamefaced when she admitted she had gone along with the rest of the bunch. Joe had said he understood, had apologized for not thinking to get the set repaired, and had urged them to go. He had joked about all the bets they had down. They had taken him at his word. It wasn't until later that Joyce had felt bad about it. Richard, Pete, and the other male members of the faculty had never expressed any remorse.

The other two female faculty members, Carol Yeager and Vicki Davis, hadn't been there. And it had probably been hard for Joyce, as the only woman present, to force the men to behave well. But I did wish she hadn't told me that story, because every time I saw Joe, I thought about it.

While I was thinking about Joe, I shuffled through the criminal justice magazines and newsletters on the coffee table in the reception area outside Amos Baylor's office. His door was closed, but Greta, his secretary, had held up her hand for me to wait. She was listening to someone on the other end of her phone line. "Yes, we understand that. However, let me say again, Dean Baylor does expect you to have the tables set up for the party no later than 6 P.M." She listened again. "I understand your difficulty. That is unfortunate. However, we do need those tables by 6 P.M. Thank you so much for doing that for us. You take care now."

She hung up the phone and shook her tightly curled gray head. "Caterers for the murder mystery party tonight. Trouble with their staff. And I'm not surprised, given all that work they expect them to do and the little bit of money they pay them. Now, what can I do for you, Lizzie?"

"Amos left a message on my phone that he wanted to see me."

"Well, he's out right now. Let me think what that might have been about." Greta closed her eyes behind her steel-rimmed glasses and rested her forehead on her hand.

"If you want me to come back later, Greta—"

"No, no, I know what it was, let me just think a minute. . . . Oh, wait, I've got it now. It was about Black History Month."

"What about it?" I said.

"We always get a request from the president's office to have someone serve on the university planning committee. We usually don't have a representative, because Richard refuses to serve. He says he is not our token black faculty member. Not that we think of him like that, of course. But you know Richard doesn't hesitate to speak his mind. And he has this thing about not being people's black whatever. So since you're here this year, Amos thought he'd ask you if you'd like to serve. Unless, of course, you object on general principle too."

"Let me think about it," I said, trying not to laugh.

"No problem. Just get back to Amos when you've made up your mind. He needs to know by next Friday, so he can let the folks in the president's office know."

"Will do," I said. I liked Greta. And actually, neither Richard nor anyone else around this place seemed to have a problem speaking his or her mind when it suited him or her.

Out in the hall, I almost missed the latest addition to the student bulletin board: HEADLESS BODY IN TOPLESS BAR. Someone had photocopied the old tabloid story and tacked it up between an internship announcement and a reminder about the topic and speaker at next week's brown-bag lunch. In the photograph which accompanied the story, a homicide detective pointed at the corpse. Two other men knelt beside the body which was covered with a sheet.

There had been no photograph of Officer Thomas Kincaid's body. That kind of newspaper photograph was much less common in 1921. And even if an enterprising photographer had been at the scene, Mose Davenport's shotgun blast at close range must have—

I shook my head to get rid of that thought. I needed to check my mail. That was what I needed to do.

I was opposite the door of Richard Colby's office when it was flung open. The kid who ran out with tears in his eyes and a curse on his lips charged into me, sending me spinning sideways. He didn't stop. I didn't try to stop him. Instead, I rubbed the shoulder he had almost dislocated and bent down to pick up my briefcase and the plastic bag containing the videos I needed to return.

When I straightened, I saw that Richard's door was standing open. The sound of softly playing classical music drifted out into the hallway. I went over to the door and looked in. Richard was standing by the window, looking out.

"Are you all right?" I asked. "That kid seemed pretty upset."

Richard turned. He smiled. "That kid was pretty upset. I do know how to upset people when I put my mind to it."

"You're lucky he knocked me sideways with his exit instead of punching you in the nose. What did you do to him? Give him an F?"

Richard walked over to the high-tech black metal bookcase next to his teak desk. He picked up a plain blue coffee mug. "I told him the truth. People don't like hearing the truth."

"Not usually," I said. My eye had been caught by an object on top of the bookcase. "What is that?" I asked, pointing to a perforated slab of wood attached to a long slanted handle which was holding down a collection of assorted newspapers.

"A molasses skimmer," Richard said.

"A what?"

He gestured for me to back out of his doorway. "A tool used in making homemade molasses," he said as he closed the door and joined me in the hallway.

"Why do you have it in your office?" I asked.

"It belonged to that drunken uncle I told you about at lunch. My namesake. But the man did make some mighty fine molasses. He sold jars of the stuff at a roadside stand."

Richard had turned toward the faculty lounge at the end of the hall. I assumed he was on his way to get some coffee. The mail room was in the same direction.

"Was that how your uncle made his money?" I asked.

"One of the ways," he said. "The man was a first-class example of black entrepreneurship."

"And so the skimmer's a memento," I said.

"Of sorts," Richard said.

I veered toward the door we were passing. "Be sure to duck the next time you tell a student the truth."

Richard went on toward the faculty lounge as I stepped into the doorway of the school mail room. The space was slightly larger than a walk-in closet, but it held a table stacked with wooden cubbyholes into which faculty and graduate student mail was sorted. Since mail was delivered twice a day, it was also a place where people ran into each other and stopped for conversation.

Ray Abruzzo, who specialized in corrections, was in conversation with two students. Actually two of the students Richard had mentioned during our lunch. Megan Reed, whom Richard deemed brilliant, and her boyfriend, Eric Walsh, who was likable even if he was prone to silly jokes and juvenile pranks.

"Hi, everyone," I said.

Ray, who was about 5'9" and about thirty pounds overweight, waved me into the crowded space. "Squeeze on in here, Lizzie."

"Hi, Professor Stuart," Eric said as I edged around him. His brown hair was still damp from what he had told me was his daily afternoon swim at the university rec center. He brushed a dark strand back behind his ear as he went on with what he was saying to Ray: "So we checked the library for Van Buren's book."

"But it's out," Megan said. "Hi, Professor Stuart," she said as she stepped aside so that I could reach into my mailbox. Megan's blonde ponytail swayed as she spoke. Obviously being inseparable did not include joining Eric in his aquatic exercise. Or maybe she had spent a few minutes with a hair dryer.

"I did a recall at the library," Eric said. "But if we have to wait for whoever has the book to bring it back, it'll be too late to use it for Professor Yeager's paper. So we were wondering—"

"If you could borrow my copy," Ray finished for him. "All right, but I want it back in the condition you're receiving it in. I've had that book since I was a grad student, and all the flashes of incredible insight I had as I was reading it are scribbled in the margins."

Eric grinned. "Hey, great! That takes care of my paper."

"He's only kidding, Professor Abruzzo," Megan said. "We promise to have your book back to you first thing Friday morning."

Half-listening, I was sifting through the mail in my hand. Flyers, memos, an academic press catalogue. And a plain white letter-size envelope with no name or address. I put my other mail down on the table to open the envelope and make sure it was intended for me. My gasp stopped the conversation behind me.

"What's wrong?" Ray asked.

I held up the single sheet of paper so that they could see it.

"Someone's Halloween joke?" I asked, looking at Eric.

"Not mine," he said. "Honest, Professor Stuart."

Ray took the sheet of paper from my hand. He and Megan and Eric studied the cartoon of a grave and tombstone. The tombstone had my name on it. The caption read REST IN PEACE.

"The vulture on the tombstone is a nice touch," Eric said. "But I swear I didn't do it, Professor Stuart. I can't even draw."

"I'm sure it's someone's idea of a joke, Lizzie," Ray said. "Joyce was telling me she had a rubber scorpion in a gift box in her mail this morning. And when Carol came back from lunch, she found a paper skeleton with a dagger through its heart shoved under her door."

Megan frowned. "Is it only the female faculty this person is doing it to?"

Ray shook his crewcut head. "No, not just the women. I haven't gotten anything, but Pete Murphy had something in his voice mail. The theme music from that slasher movie—the one with Jamie what's-her-name."

"Jamie Lee Curtis," Megan said.

Eric said, "Somebody's just getting into the spirit of the holiday. Having a little fun with you guys."

"And you're sure it's not you?" Ray asked him.

Eric held up his hand in a three-finger salute. "Word of an Eagle Scout."

Ray wadded the cartoon coffin into a ball and leaned sideways, angling toward the trash can.

"Wait, Ray," I said. "If Eric didn't send that, I think I should keep it."

"Why?" Megan asked.

"Because. . . ." I didn't know why. "Because I just think I should keep it." I held out my hand for the crumpled piece of paper, and Ray gave it to me.

"Excuse me," Joe Larsen said from the doorway. He looked worried and a little uncertain.

"Just a minute, Joe," Ray said. "We'll move out so you can get in."

"No, not that," Joe said. "I was wondering if anyone knows what's going on with Richard and Joyce."

Ray said, "Going on with them?"

"In the lounge," Joe said. "They seem to be having a disagreement. A loud disagreement."

Joe stepped back to let us out of the mail room.

The fifth floor of Brewster Hall was identical to the other four floors. Two corridors of offices ran parallel to each. The dean's suite was in the foyer facing the elevator. At the other end of the hall, at the base of the corridors, the faculty lounge was adjacent to a seminar room.

Carol Yeager was in the doorway of the copying room with a sheaf of papers in her hand. It was obvious her ears were trained to catch what was being said in the faculty lounge.

"What's going on?" Ray asked.

Carol said, "Joyce is in a major rant over something. Something about a student."

The door to the lounge opened, and Richard strolled out with his coffee mug in his hand. A look of annoyance crossed his face when he saw us.

I couldn't blame him.

"I'm not finished, Richard." Joyce was hard on his heels. Her face was flushed, and her mane of streaked blonde hair was flying outward.

"Joyce," Richard said. "We seem to have attracted an audience."

"I don't care what we've attracted. I want you to listen to me."

"I've been listening to you for the past five minutes. I have already stated my position—"

"Your position! You treated that kid like dirt."

"You shouldn't have sent him to see me," Richard said.

"I thought if you saw him and spoke to him in person as I did—"

"We've been through this, Joyce. You're a member of the admissions committee, not an advocate for rejected applicants."

"That kid deserves a chance," she said. "You, of all people, ought to understand—"

Richard turned and fixed his gaze on her. "I didn't get here by way of affirmative action, Joyce."

She glared back at him. "Good for you! Let's have a round of applause for your ability to zip right on through that obstacle course. But some kids—"

"Some kids goof off and then expect to be handed opportunities they haven't earned."

Joyce looked from Richard to Pete, who had joined our hallway gathering. She said, "I don't understand why the two of you won't even consider—"

"We did consider," Pete said. "We voted no."

Richard said, "But Joyce seems to be having an extraordinarily difficult time accepting that."

"No, I don't accept it," Joyce said. "I want to give a kid with promise a chance to prove himself. We could admit Michael for spring semester and give him a chance to—"

"To fail?" Richard said. "Because that's what he would do if we let him into this program. Now, if you'll excuse me—unless there is another confidential matter that you'd like to discuss out here in the corridor."

"What is it with you, Richard?" Joyce said. "You tell Lizzie she ought to try to uncover the truth about a racial episode that happened before any of us were born. But you don't give a damn about a young black man whose life you're going to ruin."

"If not getting into this school is going to ruin his life, then it wasn't much of a life to begin with." Richard glanced over at me. "Now, I wonder where Joyce heard about the conversation you and I had over lunch, Professor Stuart." He was looking at Pete as he finished speaking.

Pete tugged at his beard. "Hey, I didn't know it was a state secret.

I just mentioned it to Joyce when she said you didn't care about your own people."

"My own people?" Richard said.

"Hey, you know what I mean, Richard."

"Sure I do, Peter," Richard said. He walked around us and down the hall to his office. He went inside and closed his door.

There was a moment of silence. Then Eric said, "That's all I need. I'm supposed to meet with him in half an hour to talk about my prospectus."

Megan touched his arm. "Then you'd better go over it again so that you'll be ready to answer his questions."

"Oh, come on, Megan, if he's in a mood—" Eric broke off. "What I mean—"

Ray said, "We know what you mean, Eric. For the past few months, Professor Colby has been somewhat temperamental. If he were a woman, I'd think he had a permanent case of PMS."

"Ray," Joan and Carol said together.

I opened my mouth. But it was Megan who spoke. "Perhaps Professor Colby has been dealing with some personal issues, Professor Abruzzo. But as far as I can tell—and I'm sure most of the students in his two classes would agree—it has not affected his teaching or his ability to provide effective mentoring."

Bravo, Megan.

"And when we had lunch today," I said, not as eloquently, "I didn't notice that Professor Colby was at all temperamental. Excuse me too, please."

"Lizzie." Joyce caught up with me as I rounded the bend into the opposite corridor where my office was next to Carol's. "Lizzie, wait a minute."

"What?" I said.

"Lizzie, I like Richard. We all like Richard. But the truth is, he has been a royal pain in the butt lately."

"Whatever Richard has been lately, I don't think Ray's remark was appropriate in front of students. In fact, it was just plain inappropriate."

"I know," Joyce said. "And it was hardly professional of me to yell at Richard in the corridor. I've got a big mouth, and Ray can be a sexist pig. But we aren't bigots. Okay?"

Joyce had invited me to dinner a few days after I arrived. She'd treated me to a feast of grilled salmon, fancy green salad, and almond chocolate torte. She'd even closed up her two pampered Siamese cats, Ming and Ling, in her bedroom when she thought I was finding their demands for attention annoying.

"Okay," I said. "You aren't a bigot. A bleeding-heart liberal, yes. But not a bigot."

"Ah!" Carol roared around the corner, still carrying her sheaf of papers, but now waving what looked like a letter. "I'm going to murder him!"

"Who?" Joyce and I said at the same time.

"That moron I was married to. We finally have a decent offer for the cottage, and he refuses to sell." She went into her office and slammed the door.

Joyce sighed. "It's the full moon. We'll all be fine tomorrow."

"Let's hope so. But we still have that party to get through tonight."

Joyce raised her eyes heavenward. "Claire Baylor. May God bless her."

Claire Baylor was the chairperson of the theater department. She was also Amos Baylor's wife. Which explained how the murder mystery evening she had dreamed up had become a joint project of the theater department and the School of Criminal Justice.

It also explained how I—Amos's newest faculty member, too new at the time to know how to say no—had found myself working with Claire on the script for her "interactive mystery." It might have been fun if Claire hadn't made General Patton look like a gentle taskmaster.

"Yes, God bless her," I said.

Joyce laughed, a full-bodied, earthy laugh that went with her buxom figure. "Well, at least you'll be done tonight. And it could be that a party is just what we all need."

"It could be." I fished in my shoulder bag for the key to my office. "Let's hope so."

"See you later," Joyce said. "I've got errands to run, including picking up my costume. Wait until you see it."

"Can't wait," I said.

But what I was looking forward to was the end of this day. I'd had about enough of Halloween.

Chapter 8

I HAD FALLEN ASLEEP when I'd only intended to rest for a few minutes. I rolled over and watched the digital reading on my clock radio change from 6:39 to 6:40. The murder mystery evening was scheduled to begin at eight.

Right about now, Claire would be snapping out orders to her troops as she supervised the transformation of the atrium of the Performing Arts Center into the Hollywood mansion of Thaddeus Fairfax. One hand waving as she issued a command, the other would be feeling for the watch she wore on a chain around her neck.

"All right, Amos, where is she?" Claire would ask her husband.

And Amos Baylor, white brows furrowed, would say, "I have no idea, my dear."

Lizabeth Stuart, his visiting faculty member, was late. One demerit for tardiness. Another for distressing his spouse. Professor Stuart really had better shape up if she wished to be considered for a continuing appointment to the faculty. If that was what Professor Stuart wished. Maybe she just wanted to go back to her boring job in Kentucky.

I sat up and wrapped my arms around my knees. "Get moving, Lizabeth."

It was biological—or at least some of it was. That time of the month was approaching, and I'd been eating too much sugar and way too much salt. That was why I felt out of sorts. That—and then, of course, there was the matter of my earlier encounter with the photographic likeness of Officer Thomas Kincaid.

Thomas Kincaid, who had died on a fly-buzzing August afternoon, when he had led two other Gallagher police officers up the overgrown path to the steps of Ophelia Hewitt's little house.

And according to Hester Rose, Mose Davenport, who had seen them from the window, had grabbed up his shotgun and strode out onto the rickety porch with the shotgun held at his side.

"A fine good day to you, officers," he greeted them. "You be looking for Ole Mose?"

"Good day to you, Moses." This from Thomas Kincaid. "Why you carrying your gun?"

And Hester Rose, my grandmother, huddled with her friend Ophelia there inside the house, heard Mose Davenport laugh. Heard through the open window that deep rumble of pleasure that always accompanied Mose Davenport's nonsense. Heard the fear that was in the laughter this time.

"I's carrying it because I might be needing it, Mr. Officer, sir. And I begs your pardon, but my name be Mose."

"Mose, then," said Thomas Kincaid. "Mose, you know why we're here? You know there's been some trouble over at Dr. Stevens's place? We're here to talk to you about that, to ask you some questions."

That brought a grumble from one of the other officers. "Questions? We don't need to ask this nigger no damn questions, Kincaid." This was the one called Finch. Whose belly lolled over his belt. Whose reputation was bad among the colored people.

Thomas Kincaid said over his shoulder, "Finch, keep your mouth shut for a minute." Then to Mose Davenport: "Like I was saying, Mose, we've got some trouble, and we need to talk—"

"Talk, hell," Finch said. "We come to get you, you murdering black son of a bitch!"

"Dammit, Finch, don't—"

Hester Rose, huddled by the window with Ophelia, saw the glint of Finch's revolver.

Saw Mose Davenport's arm come up from his side.

Heard the heart-stopping blast of the shotgun.

And the crash of the door as Mose Davenport hurled himself back inside the house.

"Lord God, that tore it." Mose fumbled the bolt across the shattered door. "That tore it."

Outside, Thomas Kincaid was being dragged to safety by Finch and the other officer. But he was already dying. Or dead. He had grabbed for Finch's gun and been hit by the shotgun blast Mose Davenport had intended for the man he thought was about to shoot him. . . .

Standing under the shower, I shivered as the warm water struck my body. I reached for my new bar of lavender-scented soap and scrubbed my arms and shoulders with the mitt.

Thomas Kincaid had been dead for these eighty years. The man I had seen during that cloudburst on campus was a flesh-and-blood man. No ghost. No trick or treat.

If, by tomorrow afternoon, Quinn had not gotten back to me, I would call him. Tonight, I would put the matter out of my mind.

Chapter 9

"SMILE," NOAH WEBSTER SAID, pointing his camera at me. He was at the top of the stairs that led up from the lobby to the second-floor atrium.

"Noah, I hate having my—"

He snapped the picture and lowered his camera on its neck strap. He grinned down at me, brown eyes crinkling in his chocolate brown face. Noah was 6'4" and at least 220 lbs. He was a former college football star who had suffered a neck injury and ended up working as a parole officer. Now he was back in school, working on his Ph.D. And according to Richard, his brains more than matched his brawn. "Where's your costume, Professor Stuart?" he asked.

"Here in this bag. I thought someone might try to hire me if I wore it out in the street."

Noah laughed. "You're probably right."

I blinked as Megan Reed danced over. "Doesn't the place look great, Professor?"

Girl-next-door Megan of that afternoon, Megan, the serious student, had been replaced by a pale blonde vision. The vision was clad in a gossamer, blue silk gown with puffed sleeves, her hair caught up over one ear with a silver hair clip.

I nodded in response to her comment about our attempt to create a Hollywood mansion in the atrium. "The place bears a striking resemblance to an old William Powell movie set," I said.

Megan giggled. "Enter the Thin Man," she said and then opened her blue eyes wide. "Tell me again, Professor Stuart—why am I one of the suspects?"

I took my cue. "Because, Megan, Thaddeus Fairfax, the award-winning, wealthy, and lecherous Hollywood director, was trying to blackmail you into marriage."

She lowered her lashes. "And wholesome young thing that I am—in spite of those spicy lingerie photos I posed for—I would rather see him dead than be at his mercy."

"Exactly."

Megan brushed back the blonde hair that curled around her throat. "But how can you imagine I could do such a thing, Detective?"

Noah groaned. "Ever heard of being over-rehearsed?"

Megan made a face at him. She pointed at the shoulder holster complete with real-looking gun that Noah had strapped over his white shirt and natty stripped suspenders. "Ever heard of being over-costumed?"

"Over-costumed? I'm playing the director's bodyguard, woman. I have to go armed."

She giggled. "This is going to be fun. If only graduate school were always like this."

"One long costume party?" Noah said. "We could even dress up as prisoners being tortured for our comp exams."

"Ah, good, here you are, Lizzie." Amos Baylor's distinctive voice came from behind the cardboard box he was carrying up the stairs.

I looked down at his legs. He was wearing fringed white buckskin pants and tooled white leather boots.

"Need some help with that, Dean?" Noah asked.

"Thank you, Noah." Amos passed the box over. Revealing his fringed shirt. "Lizzie, Claire's looking for you. In fact, she's about to send out a search party."

"On my way," I said.

Everyone was in high spirits. The room looked great. The buffet tables were in place. Too bad they hadn't already brought out the food. The tuna sandwich I had gulped somewhere between the shower and my car had left something to be desired.

At a few minutes before eight, I slipped into one of the dressing rooms to do a final check of my costume. I was patting the lace collar of my maid's uniform into place when I saw Eric Walsh's reflection in the mirror.

"Eric? Did you want to use this?"

"Thanks, Professor." He stepped up to the mirror. He twisted his tie askew and tilted his felt hat to the back of his head. Getting into character. He was the tough-guy police detective called in to investigate the murder of the Hollywood director.

"See you at the murder," I said and started out the door.

"Professor? I was wondering about something." Boyish, earnest, he was more Jimmy Stewart than Dana Andrews.

"What were you wondering about, Eric?"

"I know you helped write this. But isn't it kind of a stereotype for you to play the maid?"

"You could say that. But in Hollywood in 1939, if I had gotten into this fancy bash, I would have been here as. . . ."

"The maid?"

"Or as an actress who played one."

I glanced at myself in the mirror and gave another small tug to my crisp white apron, courtesy of Claire's costume wardrobe.

Eric said, "But you might have been somebody like Lena Horne."

"Not likely. I can't sing a note. And I don't particularly like being in the spotlight."

"So why did you became a professor?"

"Singing isn't required. And being in the spotlight in front of a class balances out against job security. And respectability. And the time to do research and write."

"So if you had it to do over again—"

"I'd probably do the same thing."

"If I ever manage to get my dissertation finished, I want to give it a try."

I almost asked how his meeting with Richard had gone. Instead I settled for vague reassurance. "It takes time, but I'm sure you'll—"

Claire Baylor stuck her head in the doorway, her feathered hat set at a rakish angle and her gossip columnist's glasses perched on her nose. "And what's going on in here? Something my readers should know about?"

The three of us laughed.

"Let's get cracking," Claire said. "We're on."

Chapter 10

FROM MY VANTAGE POINT beside one of the potted palms, I watched the party guests.

Amos Baylor, dignified, Canadian-born Dean of the School of Criminal Justice, had come to this costume party as an American cowboy hero. He was chatting with Eugene Irving, vice president of Academic Affairs, who was dressed as a desert sheik.

Not all of the criminal justice faculty were present. Several faculty members were out of town. Some were otherwise occupied. Ray Abruzzo—looking a bit sheepish—had caught me as I was leaving the office to say he had to go to a dinner party his in-laws were giving. Britt and Vicki Davis were at home with their new baby.

But apparently Carol Yeager had recovered from her upset over her annoying ex-husband and decided having a good time was the best revenge. The tall man in the Elizabethan costume, whom she was laughing with, seemed to appreciate her vintage Joan Crawford black gown.

In his black tux and cummerbund, Joe Larsen looked a bit like Peter Lorre.

And Joyce Fielding had come as Mae West. No doubt about that.

Richard Colby, her antagonist of the afternoon, was here as—who? Tweed jacket with elbow patches, pipe in hand. A Hollywood writer? A black Hollywood writer in the 1930s? Scarce as hen's teeth. But maybe Richard was a tawny Raymond Chandler. Or a fictional character—William Holden's down-and-out writer, first seen floating facedown in Gloria Swanson's swimming pool. Or it could be Richard had said to heck with it and dressed for comfort.

"Is that stuff edible or just a stage prop?"

"Edible," I said, holding out my tray.

Scott Novak helped himself to a cheese puff. Scott was the director of the university's Early Childhood Development Center. I had first encountered him when he spoke to my cohort of new faculty about the day-care facilities for children of faculty and staff.

Since I had no offspring, I had only half-listened.

It was Scott's face that had held my attention. He had a wayward-angel kind of face. Big brown eyes and long lashes. A cupid's-bow mouth. But a jutting chin and crooked nose saved Scott's face from being pretty, and the awareness in his eyes denied any notion of innocence.

An interesting face. But not one that I was comfortable around.

"Have you figured out whodunit?" I said.

Scott reached for another canape. "Too early in the game."

Half an hour ago, the theater major who was playing the Hollywood director had clutched his throat and died after a series of dramatic coughs, groans, and convulsions. Now the party guests (faculty, staff, students, and townspeople) were supposed to question each other, try to separate truth from red herrings, and come up with the solution.

"What about the butler?" I said. "He's over there. Have you talked to him yet?"

Pete Murphy, by day burly policing professor, was tonight the dignified butler. He was surrounded by five or six guests. They were questioning him about how strychnine had gotten into his employer's champagne glass. That was why the script had called for the butler, not the maid, to serve that glass of champagne.

"Trying to get rid—" Scott broke off in mid-sentence. "Hello, Inez."

The woman he was speaking to turned, the bracelets on her arms jangling. She was clad in the flowing, semi-bare costume of a sideshow fortune-teller. The costume had the unfortunate effect of emphasizing her bony face and skinny body. She smiled. "Well, hello, Scott Novak."

"Who are you on the prowl for tonight, Ms. Buchanan?" Scott said.

"What a thing to say to a lady, Mr. Novak." Her blue gaze then fell on me. "I've seen you somewhere before. You're new on campus, aren't you? I work in the vice president's office, so I see just about everyone eventually. But I can't remember your name."

"Lizzie Stuart," I said. "I'm a visiting professor in criminal justice."

She nodded. "I'm Inez Buchanan. So you know Pete Murphy, then?"

"So, he's the target," Scott said.

"I don't know what you mean," Inez said with what she must have intended to be a coquettish smile.

"Happy hunting," Scott said. "If you ladies will excuse me, I see someone I need to speak to."

"Speaking of hunting. . . ," Inez said, watching Scott's progress across the atrium.

He was headed toward the blonde woman in a black tuxedo who was turning heads with her arrival. Richard Colby's wife. Diane Price Colby. With a cigarette holder between her fingers and a top hat on her head.

"Marlene Dietrich," I said.

"And our Scott does fancy Marlene," Inez said. "The question is how far he's gotten."

“She’s married,” I said. “And just because they— Scott runs the Early Childhood Development Center. Diane specializes in child psychology. They must work together occasionally.”

“Yeah,” Inez said. “Maybe play together too.”

Across the room, Scott, feet splayed at an angle in the floppy shoes that went with his patched Hollywood-funnyman pants, was greeting Richard’s wife. She was listening to what he was saying, with a Dietrich smile on her face.

“It’s gone pretty far, I’d wager,” Inez said. “Not that I give two hoots.” She fingered the gold coin belt at her waist and looked in Pete’s direction. “I think I’ll go offer to read Pete’s palm and see myself in his future. Now that the redheaded bimbo from his Civil War reenactors group has taken herself out of town, I might just have a chance.”

“Pete is busy right now,” I said. “He’s supposed to be giving the guests information about the murdered Hollywood director.”

“So I’ll ask for information.” She jangled away, making a beeline for Pete.

I looked around for Richard and found him standing beside Joyce Fielding. The same Joyce Fielding with whom he had exchanged public insults a few hours earlier. Both Richard and Joyce were watching Scott laughing with Diane.

“This place is absolutely fascinating,” I said to the air. “Tune in tomorrow for the next installment.”

A voice, rough-textured and amused, inquired, “Do you always carry on conversations with yourself, Professor?”

I whirled around and found myself staring up into John Quinn’s silver-gray eyes.

And with a mind of their own, my hands decided to let go of the tray I was holding. Since I was standing on the uncarpeted edge of the brick floor, the tray fell with a resounding crash. Every head in the room swung in our direction.

Chapter 11

CLAIRE, STANDING BESIDE one of the university chaplains, struggled to hold her smile in place.

Dropped tray at 9:15 was not in our script.

"Sorry, ladies and gentlemen," I said. "It was an accident."

But no one was listening. They were all noting the dropped tray on their clue cards.

Wonderful. I turned the tray over and began to gather up the battered cheese puffs.

Quinn hunkered down beside me to help.

I could smell the faint scent of his aftershave. What on earth was wrong with me? It wasn't as if this was the first time I had ever seen the man.

He held out a handful of canapes.

"Thank you," I said. "I'll get a broom for the crumbs."

We both straightened and stood facing each other.

Quinn was wearing a gray suit, discreetly patterned gray tie, and white shirt. Obviously he had not come for the costume party. "You wanted to see me," he said.

"I— Yes, but I didn't expect you to come here."

His mouth tightened. "Lizzie, it's been a long day. Since I am here, why don't you tell me what you wanted."

"Nothing, if you're going to take that tone of voice. I'm sorry everyone was staring at us. But I wouldn't have dropped the tray if you hadn't startled me."

"Startled you? I startled you? Why is it—" He stopped, took an audible breath, and shoved his fingers through his hair, making the silver strands in the dark auburn more visible. "All right," he said. "Let's just— No, let's not. I've had about enough. Would you please explain to me why you're always as jumpy around me as . . . as a virgin at a satyr convention?"

He said that last part like a man snatching a simile out of thin air, and I choked back the giggle that almost erupted from my throat. I was too old to giggle. And it wasn't actually funny.

Quinn turned his head and glared at someone. I turned too. Several of the party guests had moved closer, apparently assuming our conversation was laden with clues to the mystery they were trying to solve.

"Excuse us," Quinn said. "This is a private conversation."

"This has nothing to do with the mystery," I said, trying to smile at them. "Dropping the tray was really just an accident."

"Are you supposed to tell us that to throw us off?" The question came from a man who was dressed as a pirate, complete with cutlass.

"No, really and truly. It was an accident." I edged toward the ante-rooms behind me. "Excuse me, I need to find a broom for the crumbs."

But John Quinn was not done yet. He was right on my heels as I stepped into one of the empty rooms. He pushed the door closed behind us. "Lizzie—"

"I'm sorry you find our relationship awkward," I said. "But—"

"Why can't you ever relax around me?" he asked. "Do I look like I make a habit of throwing women to the floor and having my wicked way with them?"

"If I thought that. . . ." I swallowed past the tightness in my throat. "If I thought that, I would avoid being alone with you. We have been alone together on several occasions. I'm alone with you right now, and I'm not screaming for help."

"No, you're not screaming. But dammit, Lizzie, you never seem at ease around me either. Why is that? Because I'm white? Because I'm a cop and you don't trust cops? What?"

He sounded annoyed. He sounded exasperated.

I opened my mouth and closed it. How could the man not know why he made me nervous? I was not known for my poker face.

"I come from Drucilla, Kentucky, Quinn. I was born and raised there, and except for college and grad school, I've lived there all of my life."

"What does that have to do with what we're talking about?"

"There aren't a lot of men like you in Drucilla. In fact, I find you a completely unique experience."

He folded his arms, obviously not pleased. "Unique in what respect?"

Good grief, the man was obtuse. What did he want me to say? You set my heart all aflutter? Not that it made any difference what effect he had on any part of my anatomy. "If you don't mind," I said, "I would rather not continue this conversation."

"But I do mind. Your choice. We can have this conversation now or have it later."

"Based on the assumption that I have to talk to you about something that I don't want to talk to you about? Has no one ever told you, Quinn, that some things are better left alone?"

"I have heard that on occasion, Lizabeth. But if you were one of those people who believed that without question, you wouldn't be here in Gallagher when your grandmother told you to stay away."

"That isn't the same thing—that's different. I'm doing research."

"Research on something that scares you."

"My research does not frighten me. I was just unnerved today when I called you—"

"And you're unnerved when I'm around you. So maybe if you tried applying the same principle—"

"You mean think of you as research?"

"That might not be a bad idea." He was smiling slightly now. "In fact, that might actually get us somewhere."

I didn't ask where it was we wanted to get. What I needed was a rejoinder that would effectively close the subject. But nothing came to mind.

I slid around him and headed for the door. "I need to get back out there. Claire will wonder what happened to me."

"Wait a minute," Quinn said. "We need to—"

But I had the door open and was halfway through it. And whatever he was about to say was preempted by the shout that rang out from the other side of the atrium.

"Eric!"

Chapter 12

"ERIC!" The shrill summons echoed around the room.

Conversations sputtered to a halt. We were in the middle of a murder mystery party. Amateur sleuths shared questioning glances, surprised but still ready to be entertained.

"Eric! Come on out, Eric."

The crowd parted obligingly, leaving the group containing Eric (the tough-guy detective) and Megan (the ingenue) center stage.

My grip tightened on the tray of damaged cheese puffs that I had forgotten to leave in the anteroom. A young woman was making her way toward Eric. She wore blue jeans and a blue parka, open over a red sweater. I recognized her. She was the girl from the campus police station. But now the fingers that had been twisting her hair were clutching a gun.

"There you are, Eric. You know what, Eric? I'm going to kill you and your slut."

His slut? Megan?

Eric Walsh stepped forward, hands outstretched toward the girl.

"Trace, come on. Let's go outside and talk."

"Talk?" she said. "We've already talked. You told me you didn't want me anymore."

I had forgotten about Quinn until his hands clamped down on my shoulders. His mouth brushed against my ear. "Is this part of the entertainment?" he said.

"No," I said, shaking my head. "No."

He mumbled a curse that blistered my ears, and stepped away from me.

"Tracy," Eric said. "Baby, you're drunk. Come on, let's go get some coffee and—"

"Stay away," Tracy said.

A woman in an Egyptian costume said, "I think this is for real. I think this—"

"Don't run," Quinn told the woman in a low voice. "Get down on the floor. Slowly." He motioned to the rest of us on that side of the room to do the same. "Get down and keep still."

That said, he turned away from us and gave his attention to the matter at hand. "Tracy," he called out to the girl. "Tracy."

Tracy and the gun swung in his direction.

"Tracy, I'm Chief John Quinn of the University Police Department," he said, displaying his badge so that she could see it. He held up the badge with his left hand. His right hand was slightly behind him, holding the gun that he had drawn from the holster that angled over his back pant pocket. The holster that his suit jacket had concealed. He had taken a slow step toward Tracy as he spoke.

On the other side of the room, several people were edging toward the stairs.

"Police," Tracy repeated, slurring the word. "I went to the police station today. But I left."

"That's okay. We can talk now," Quinn said. He took another step toward her. "Put down the gun, and let's talk. Just put it down there on the floor in front of you."

Tracy shook her head. "Can't," she said.

So much for that. She was on the other side of the room. Now what?

"Tracy, I can see you're upset," he said. "But you don't want to do this. This is a really bad idea."

"He lied to me," Tracy said. "He lied!"

Eric said, "Tracy, you misunderstood."

Tracy and the gun swayed back toward Eric. "You lied to get me into bed. Then you told me you didn't love me."

Eric held out his hand again. "Tracy—"

"Eric, stay where you are," Quinn said to him. "Tracy, listen to me. This isn't what you want to do. I know you're hurting, but this isn't going to solve anything."

A movement caught my eye. Richard Colby, who was much closer than Quinn, was edging forward, obviously intending to try to come up on Tracy from behind.

Eric saw what Richard was trying to do, and he started to talk, his voice shaking slightly. "Trace, please. Baby, I'm sorry. You know how much I like you. We're friends."

"Friends? Do you sleep with all your friends?"

"Trace, it wasn't like that. I told you, we— The two of us couldn't be—"

"How could you do that, Eric? If you didn't love me, how could you take everything from me? I was a virgin, damn you!"

Was she? Virgins all over the place tonight. But Eric didn't really look like one of Quinn's satyrs. He just looked scared. Well, he was the one she was pointing the gun at. Except she probably had enough bullets for a few more of us.

Of course, Quinn did have his gun. I could almost feel the tension radiating from him as he watched Tracy and Eric and Richard. He was a lot closer now than he had been, but still too far away to get to her.

"Tracy," he called out again. "Tracy, look at me."

The girl swung toward him.

"Put the gun down, Tracy. You need to do that right now."

"No, he—"

"It doesn't matter what he did. You have to put it down now before someone gets hurt. Please, Tracy. Then we'll try to sort this all out."

"No." She shook her head. "I came here to—"

Eric sprang forward, grabbing for the gun, and Tracy staggered back.

A gasp went around the room as Richard caught her from behind and knocked the gun to the carpeted floor.

Quinn slid his gun back into his holster. He walked across the room and held his hand out for the gun Richard had picked up. He said something to Richard and then to Eric. Both nodded. Carrying the weapon as casually as if it were a book instead of something lethal, Quinn retraced his steps past people who were picking themselves up from the floor.

"Sit down somewhere," he said as he saw me getting stiffly to my feet. "I've got to call for backup."

I turned and watched his gray-suited back disappear into one of the anterooms. He was the one who looked as if he needed to sit down. He looked as if someone had just sucker-punched him in the stomach and he was trying hard not to throw up.

I made a half move to follow him. But before I could decide if I should, Eugene Irving, the vice president for Academic Affairs, brushed past me with a frown on his face. He was headed for the anteroom where Quinn had gone.

I turned and glanced around me. Motion had begun again in the atrium. Conversations broke out in staccato sounds of relief and amazement.

"Girl with gun terrorizes university murder mystery party," Joyce said as she joined me.

I tried to muster a smile. "Details at eleven on your local news."

On the other side of the room, Tracy was sobbing. Harsh, throat-tearing sounds. Eric put his arm around her and guided her toward a chair.

"I wonder if that was why Richard played hero," Joyce said. "To get his name on the news."

"When I saw the two of you standing within ten feet of each other, I thought you'd made it up," I said.

"Made what up?" Joyce said. "Our spat this afternoon?"

"Yes, that," I replied.

"But that was only the tip of our iceberg," Joyce said. She was looking across the room as she spoke. "And there's the tip of another one."

Diane Price Colby was standing in front of her husband. Her face had lost its glamour. It looked taut. She said something to Richard, then she walked away from him toward the stairs.

Richard made no move to follow her. But Scott Novak did. He hurried after Diane. He said something and slid a hand under her elbow. Diane glanced back at her husband. Richard smiled and shrugged. Diane turned away and let Scott guide her down the stairs.

I looked at Joyce. "Things don't seem to be going very well between Richard and his wife," I said. But Richard had said as much over lunch, hadn't he? He just hadn't mentioned the Scott Novak factor.

"That's an understatement," Joyce said in response to my comment about the state of the Colbys' marriage.

I wanted to ask questions, but I didn't. If I wanted to know about his business, I should ask Richard.

Quinn walked back out past us. He flicked a glance in my direction. His color was better than it had been a few moments earlier. What had he done with the VP of Academic Affairs? Irving was probably on the telephone working on damage control. Undergrad with gun at campus Halloween party was not something that parents would find comforting.

Two university cops—one male, one female—were coming up the stairs. Quinn motioned to them, and the three of them went over to Tracy and Eric. Tracy was still sobbing. Eric stood sentry-like behind her chair.

Quinn squatted down in front of Tracy's chair and started to talk to her.

Richard, who had stayed near Eric and Tracy—had Quinn deputized him?—wandered off toward the bar. He spoke to the young woman on duty there. She poured from a bottle into a plastic glass and held it out to him. He tilted the glass back. Obviously he had found that little episode unnerving too.

Quinn got to his feet. The female officer took Tracy's arm and spoke to her. Tracy rose from her chair, her head down, her body limp. Eric threw a beseeching glance in Megan's direction. Then he hurried out after the three police officers and Tracy.

But Amos Baylor had reached Megan's side now. He patted her shoulder as he spoke to her. She smiled, but she seemed to be trying hard not to weep.

I had forgotten Joyce was standing beside me until she said, "Excuse me. I need some fortifying." She sauntered off toward the dessert table.

I looked back at Megan. She was nodding her head as she listened to Amos, but her attention was elsewhere. I followed the direction of her glance. Richard had been joined at the bar by Noah Webster, his grad assistant. The two of them were laughing. Probably in relief rather than in amusement. Or maybe they were discussing male displays of risk-taking behavior. Man, what that does to the old adrenaline.

And speaking of adrenaline, what exactly had been wrong with Quinn? He had spent his entire adult life in potentially dangerous situations, first as a military police officer and then as a Philadelphia detective. Did confrontations always hit him like that?

But, of course, most police officers went through their entire careers without ever having to use their guns except on the firing range. Maybe he had never been in a situation where he'd actually had to face down someone with a gun, particularly a drunken teenage girl. It must have been really frightening to think that she might shoot Eric, that he might have to shoot her.

But there had been something about the expression on his face . . . something about the way he had not quite met my glance as he passed. Had Quinn's reaction been about more than what had happened tonight? Did it have something to do with that "helluva bad year" that his ex-partner Janowitz had mentioned when we were in Cornwall?

I could always ask Quinn. But if he didn't think I trusted him, why would he tell me anything?

Chapter 13

I CAME OUT OF THE DRESSING ROOM carrying my jacket and purse and still thinking about whether I should try to call Quinn and see if he was all right. I could hear Claire in one of the other rooms issuing orders to her theater majors about the costumes and props they had used. But it was going on eleven o'clock, and I was not inclined to offer my help.

I stuck my head in the door. "Claire, I'm leaving if you don't need me."

She looked up from the costume she was folding and waved a hand. "Take off. We've got it under control."

Seasoned trouper that she was, Claire had carried on with aplomb after the Tracy incident. "I'm sure you will agree with me," she had told the party guests, "that under the circumstances, proceeding with tonight's festivities would be both frivolous and anticlimactic."

Several people tittered. Nervous laughter.

"Therefore, we will continue this on Sunday afternoon at four when you are all invited to join us for dessert, coffee, and the solution to our mystery. Remember, the solution that comes closest to the true one wins a to-die-for prize."

No one requested the price of the rather expensive ticket back. Not even the Sunday afternoon football fans who didn't intend to return for the finale.

"Why would they want their money back?" Claire had said. The proceeds of the evening were going to the scholarship fund. A good cause. And besides, they had gotten more entertainment than they could have hoped for. A real-life drama for the price of a party ticket.

Now the buffet tables were stripped. The lights lowered. Evening over. I started toward the stairs.

"Nice party, Professor Lizzie."

"Richard?"

Richard Colby stepped from the shadows. He looked rumpled.

"Richard, what are you— I thought you'd gone."

"Not yet. I could use a ride, please."

"A ride? Sure."

"Only as far as our parking lot. I left my car over there, and it's raining."

"Sure. Of course, I can give you a ride."

As we started down the stairs, I tried to think of something to say. Hey, what was your wife so upset about, other than the fact you could have gotten yourself killed? Or, don't you think you'd better watch out for Scott Novak? Neither question would endear me to the man.

The wind swooshed in when he pushed open the exit doors.

"The cold front must have moved through," I said.

Richard offered no response to that meteorological observation. Obviously he was not a fan of the Weather Channel.

We were both soaked by the time we'd splashed across the street to my car and gotten ourselves inside. Richard wiped his face with a handkerchief. Then he leaned his head back and closed his eyes.

"Are you okay?" I said.

"Offering stray men your sympathy can be misconstrued, Professor Lizzie."

"I wasn't offering sympathy. I was inquiring about your health."

"My health is fine."

"Great. I'm glad." I twisted the ignition key. The engine grated in response to my unnecessary force.

It was a five-minute drive back to Brewster Hall. I turned on the radio. The twang of an electric guitar faded out. Over the sound of clapping hands and catcalls, the DJ shrieked, "This is Jumpin' Jack Flash coming to you from the Campus Center Ballroom of the Piedmont Pirates. Yo ho ho, mateys. We're rockin' on down with a Halloween blast brought to you by the biggest, baddest station on your FM dial."

I punched the off button on the radio. And caught my breath as I looked up.

My foot slammed on the brake.

The black-masked figure that had leaped from the sidewalk did a jig and dashed off across the campus green. His companion, Tonto to his Lone Ranger, made a gesture of helplessness and followed in his wake.

"I love Halloween," I said.

"Don't we all?" Richard said.

Brewster Hall, the five-story Gothic building which housed the social sciences, loomed up. Massive gray stone with gargoyle rain spouts. I turned into the parking lot behind the building.

"Richard, look at that."

"Look at what?"

"That. Someone's hung a skeleton out of one of the windows on our floor."

"You have to have a sense of humor to be in criminal justice, Professor Lizzie."

"So it would seem. That's your car over there, isn't it?"

"That's it."

In the rain, the BMW was a blurred shape standing alone in a space near the front of the lot. I pulled up behind it.

Richard lifted his head from the headrest. "Thanks for the ride."

"You're welcome."

"And I apologize for my mood."

His mood? In the two months since we had met, his mood had ranged from aloof to arrogant to downright irritating. So why did I give a damn? Because the man managed to be vulnerable in spite of it all?

"Don't worry about it," I said. "We all have things to deal with sometimes."

In the dim light of the dashboard, I saw him smile. "Things to deal with? Tell me, Professor Lizzie, do you believe in ghosts?"

That got my attention. "Ghosts? That's a strange question."

"A completely appropriate question," Richard said. "Tonight is All Hallows' Eve. The night of the dead."

The wind swooped across the parking lot, shaking the car, sending rain slashing across the windshield. I shivered in my damp jacket.

"Do you believe in ghosts, Richard?"

"The ghosts of misdeeds," he said. "Of wrongs done and mistakes made. Those are the ghosts that come back to haunt you."

"Yes."

"Do you have any old ghosts, Lizzie?"

"I don't think so. Unless it's a generational thing. The sins of the—" I pulled my jacket closer. "Why don't we change the subject?"

"Okay." And that was when Richard Colby leaned across the seat and kissed me.

I shoved him away. "Richard, what are you doing?"

"I must really be losing my touch if you couldn't tell. Let me guess. You don't fool around with married men."

"No, I don't. And even if I did," I said, "I would think if you were going to fool around it would be with Clovis."

He stared at me. "With Clovis?" He almost seemed shocked.

"You did say that you love her. Or did I hear you wrong?"

Richard sighed. "Clovis and I were a long time ago. You can't go back with that kind of thing."

"Well, that's something you and Clovis and Diane are going to have to work out. If you don't mind, I would like to go home now."

The interior light came on as he opened his door. The rain sprayed in. "Thanks for the ride." He bent back down to smile at me. "And I apologize for my clumsy romantic overture."

"Just promise never to try it again."

"My word as a gentleman and a scholar. See you tomorrow."

I left him standing in the rain, watching me drive away.

Chapter 14

IT WOULD HAVE BEEN a stylish exit if I hadn't remembered the videotapes. Five of them, in a bag, sitting on my office desk. I'd taken the bag out of my car earlier in the day because it was so hot I thought the tapes might be damaged by the heat and sunlight. Very efficient. Except, when I'd left for home, I'd managed to leave the bag there on my desk. So it was either go back for them now, or drive back to campus in the morning, pick up the tapes, and then drive back to the video store before noon. That or pay $12.50 in late charges because I was forgetful.

I groaned and made a U-turn. I splashed back into the lot and stopped beside Richard's car. He rolled down his window as I opened my door and jumped out of my car.

"I've got to run upstairs," I called to him. "I left something in my office." The wind snatched my words away. I plunged through the puddle blocking my way and darted toward the shelter of the building.

The rain ran down my neck from the eaves as I pulled my ID card from my wallet and swiped it once, twice, and a third time before the green light came on and the outer door lock disengaged, admitting me through the double glass doors leading into the basement.

As I stepped inside the foyer, the automatic doors into the hallway glided open. I was wiping my feet on the black plastic doormat when someone ran up behind me. I spun around.

"Just me," Richard said. "If you're going upstairs, I might as well go too. My cell phone's not working. I should call home."

"You and E.T.," I said. "It's always a good idea to check in." I took off my wet jacket and shook it. Then I tried to squeeze out the water that was managing to drip from the inch-long hair that was plastered to my skull.

"What did you forget?" Richard asked as he took off his own jacket. The tweed gave off the odors of wet wool and smoke. I hadn't realized he smoked.

A shadow flickered in the dimly lit hall.

"What?" I said.

"I said, what did you forget?"

"Videos."

Our voices and footsteps echoed down the empty hallway. In the basement, at the other end of the hall, there was a small cafeteria and vending machines. Halfway down the corridor there was a computer lab for students. In the adjoining corridor by the elevator there were several classroom. The maintenance crew also had a break room down here.

But tonight—now—the building felt empty. There were no sounds from the floors above. No fire doors slamming shut, followed by feet pounding down the stairs. No laughter or voices.

I glanced at my watch. It was nine minutes after eleven.

"Why is it so quiet in here tonight?" I asked Richard.

It was even darker in the side corridor leading to the elevator. Richard pushed the button and leaned back against the wall. "Didn't you read the memo, Professor Lizzie? They locked all academic buildings down at ten o'clock tonight. Worried about Halloween vandalism."

"I did read that," I said, remembering the university-wide electronic memo. "But people are usually here in the building even when it's locked."

"It's Halloween," Richard said. "Everyone's out having a good time. The faculty went home to take their kids trick-or-treating. The students went out to get drunk." He smiled. "Unlike you, Professor Lizzie, most people don't hang around this place when they have an excuse not to."

"I don't hang around here either," I said, surprised that he had noticed my comings and goings. "I just have work to do, and it's easier to come in than to cart everything home."

"Good story," Richard said.

"It's the truth. I actually do have a life."

Of sorts, anyway. And I made it a practice not to hang around at the office late at night. I tried to be out of here by at least eight every evening. Although, two or three times I had stayed later to finish something I was working on, and sometimes I did come in on weekends. But so did some other faculty. Including Richard.

I was about to point that out to him when the elevator came. The doors creaked open.

"Boo!" Richard said in my ear.

"Richard!"

"You jumped." He grinned and then tried to look repentant. "Sorry. I've been messing with you all day, haven't I?"

"Yes, you have," I said. "So cut it out. Let's both go do what we came to do and get out of here."

"Sounds good to me."

I looked at him in the bright light of the elevator cage. "You seem to be in a better mood than you were a little while ago."

"That's because I had a sudden, blinding revelation," he replied.

"About what?"

"About the folly of giving two hoots. I am about to go home and instruct my wife on that very subject."

"I'm sure she'll enjoy that," I said.

"I doubt it."

I didn't touch that one. Richard begin to hum off-key.

The elevator jerked and shuddered as it climbed upward. I glanced at the instructions on the emergency call box. But we made it to the fifth floor and bumped to a stop.

The elevator doors opened halfway. I punched at the OPEN DOOR button. "Don't you dare get stuck now," I told it.

Richard laughed.

The doors slid open as if they had never intended to stick. The foyer and the corridors on each side were in shadow.

"Where are the light switches?" I asked.

"End of the hall," Richard said. "But neither one of us is going to be here that long."

"No, we aren't," I said. "I'm going to retrieve my videos. And then I'm headed home to a hot shower, a cup of tea, and a good book."

"Better make that a so-so book," Richard said as he turned toward his office in the opposite corridor. "Tomorrow's a workday."

The videos were on my desk where I'd left them. I picked up the plastic bag and started back out the door. I was almost out, my hand was on the knob. But I was too well-programmed. I walked back to my desk and hit the switch for my computer. E-mail. I had just enough time to give it a quick look.

It was a sign of being a borderline obsessive personality. But there it was. I felt obliged to make frequent checks of my E-mail in case there was someone out there who felt the urgent need to communicate with me.

Mumbling to myself, I read the almost verbatim messages from two students in my undergrad seminar about the problems they were having with my research assignment. Of course, the real problem was that these two students tended toward the conservative end of the continuum, and they didn't approve of the uninhibited discussion that had been taking place in the class. They also didn't approve of some of their fellow students and certainly not of me. And it was too late to drop the course without penalty, so they had decided to be pains in my posterior.

I took a leaf from Greta's handling of the caterers that afternoon. Addressing my response to both of them, I sympathized with their personal difficulties with work and family. And then I reiterated my expectation that the assignment would be completed and turned in on time at our next class meeting on Monday afternoon. Two lines sufficient.

I flicked through the rest of my E-mails. I took another minute to type out a response to a request from a colleague for the title of a book I had mentioned the last time we talked. I also sent my "yes, thank you" in response to an invitation to a brunch/women's gathering at the home of an African-American-studies professor I had met soon after I arrived in Gallagher.

I was about to turn off the computer when I thought of something else.

Quinn.

I stared at the screen, considering. It felt a bit like invasion of privacy. But if information was on the Internet, then—in the outlaw territory of cyberspace—it was public information. And it was unlikely he had anything to hide that I could find this easily, or he wouldn't have gotten the position of university police chief. So I was probably wasting my time anyway.

I pointed my mouse arrow. When the search box came up, I typed in "John Quinn Philadelphia police."

I leaned forward, scanning the list of matches—Web sites where both the names *John* and *Quinn* and the words *Philadelphia* and *police* appeared.

There were several Web pages for the Philadelphia PD. I already knew about those. When Quinn and I had begun to e-mail, I had taken a look at his police department and the district he worked in. But I had never done a search that included Quinn's name. Maybe because it was a part of keeping my distance from him. Don't know too much. Don't get too involved.

But now I was curious. His reaction to the girl with the gun tonight had made me want to know.

I heard a door slam shut. Richard. He was going to leave me up here if I didn't get a move on. I could do this at home.

I began to move my mouse arrow toward the exit symbol. The computer screen blinked and went black. My office went black. The lights were out.

I sat there for a moment in the dark. The drapes at my window were open, but there was no light outside, either. Only the sound of the rain striking the window and the wind whistling around Brewster Hall's Gothic bulk.

I hadn't noticed those sounds when the lights were on.

I let out my breath and stood up.

I was too old to be afraid of the dark. Bending down, I felt along the side of my desk until I found the bottom drawer. I reached inside and dug around until my hand closed on the flashlight I kept there.

At the end of the corridor, the red emergency light glowed like a one-eyed Cyclops from its perch on the wall.

"Richard," I called out as I started down the corridor. "Hey,

Richard, are you still here?"

Had he left me up here alone? I hadn't asked him to wait, but I had assumed we would walk back out together. Of course, I had stopped to read E-mail. Maybe he had finished his call home and left.

"Richard?" His door was closed. So were all the other doors on that side. My yellow flashlight beam washed over them and reflected back from the beige wood. "Richard?" I knocked on his door. "Are you in there?"

I turned the knob. The door opened under my hand. "Richard, if you're playing hide-and-seek. . . ."

My shaky attempt at humor fell into the silence. Richard was on the floor beside his desk. His eyes were wide open. His uncle's molasses skimmer and the stack of newspapers from his bookcase had tumbled onto the carpet beside him. But it was the gleaming, black-handled knife sticking out of his chest that my flashlight fastened on. The flashlight jumped in my hand, zigzagging over the red blood soaking his white shirt, darting back to his wide-open eyes.

I heard a whispering echo of my own harsh breaths, coming from behind the door that I had pushed ajar.

I took a step back. Another. I whirled and ran toward the foyer and the elevator. The elevator that was not going to take me anywhere because the power was out.

I turned and swept the flashlight beam back up the corridor. There was no movement. No other sounds but my own gasps. I began to edge sideways toward the fire door and the stairs. I snatched open the door and half-fell onto the fifth-floor landing, bruising my knees. Then I was up, taking the stairs two at a time, tumbling and banging off the walls as I skidded around corners with the flashlight beam ricocheting in front of me.

I burst through the first-floor fire door and into the front lobby. There was no one there. "Help! Are you here? Help!"

A gray-haired man in uniform came around the corner. "It's all right," he said. "Just a power failure. A problem with the—"

"Someone's dead," I said, trying to slow my breathing so that I could focus on the man in front of me. Had I ever seen him before? Was he the real building security officer?

"Dead?" he said. His small blue eyes had widened in his broad, flat face. "Who's dead?"

"Professor Richard Colby. Upstairs. In his office. He's been stabbed. I think the person who— I think someone is still up there."

"Stabbed?" He jerked his radio from his belt. "What floor?" he asked me as he begin to talk to the dispatcher on the other end. "We got an emergency here, Casey. What floor, lady?"

"Fifth," I said and sunk down on the black and white tile floor. Sitting down was a stupid thing to do. In horror movies, the monster was never stopped by one lone guard. I should run out the door and keep running.

The building security officer told me to stay there while he went upstairs to see what was happening. He didn't look as if he wanted to go.

The security officer came back pale and shaking, then went outside to wait for the police. He must have communicated with the maintenance crew in the basement, because just as the sirens sounded in the distance, they came up the stairs and into the lobby. There were four of them, two men and two women, in blue smocks and jeans. The flashlights they had brought with them and the one I was holding provided us with a half-circle of light. The maintenance crew stood off to the edge of the circle, stealing glances in my direction and whispering among themselves.

Outside we could see the security officer. He stood in the rain and wind, waving the campus cops in as their cars screeched to a stop in front of the building.

I leaned back against the wall and tried to make my mind blank. To blank out that picture of Richard with a knife in his chest.

I seemed to have my very own crime wave going on. First, Dee in Cornwall, now Richard here in Gallagher. John Quinn was going to love this.

Chapter 15

BUT IT WASN'T QUINN WHO CAME. The first university police officer through the door was African-American, golden-skinned in the cold light cast by the flashlights. He had sergeant stripes and a frown on his face. He ordered the other campus cops to search the building. His name was Petrie, he told me. And then he listened, with one eye on the activity around him, as I told him what had happened upstairs. When we were done, he went off to look at something a young officer, who looked like a rookie, wanted him to see.

I sat back down on the floor. The maintenance crew had been escorted down to their break room by two officers who were supposed to get their statements. They had looked relieved to get away from me.

Petrie came back to the front lobby. He was still frowning. He glanced over at me on the floor and told the building security officer, who had been fidgeting in the background, to "get her a damn chair."

The outside door opened again, bringing in a burst of storm-chilled air and a man in a belted raincoat. Petrie went to meet him. As Petrie talked, the man shrugged out of his wet raincoat, folding it inside out as he draped it over his arm. He flicked a glance in my direction. Then he motioned for Petrie to follow him down the hall. Petrie was still talking, his voice pitched too low for me to hear what he was saying, but the man he was talking to seemed more interested in finding something behind the doors he was opening. Finally, he opened a door and seemed to be satisfied with what he saw.

He looked back toward the foyer, where I was sitting in my chair. He said something to Petrie. Maybe it was "get the damn lights on," because they came on at that moment.

I blinked and turned off the flashlight I had been clutching.

The security guard, who had brought himself a chair when he brought mine, said, "About time they got some lights on."

"Yes," I said.

Petrie was back, standing over me. "Professor Stuart, Detective De Angelo is the senior investigator. He'll be in charge of the case. He'd like to speak to you now."

"All right," I said.

That was when it dawned on me that even though this was a homicide, John Quinn would not be the person who would conduct the investigation. Quinn was a police chief now, in charge of the overall operation of a university police department. Piedmont State was a big university, the equivalent of a small city when one considered all the people who came and went on the campus each day. The university police department was structured like those in many cities. Quinn had a small squad of investigators, plainclothes detectives, who handled serious cases. Serious on a university campus usually meant robbery or assault or date rape. Drug offenses too. In this case, serious was murder. But Quinn's investigators would investigate. And they would report back to him.

So Quinn was probably not going to come charging through the door. He was probably not going to come here to the crime scene at all. By now, word of what had happened would be getting out, and he would have media fallout and administration hysteria to deal with. Easier to handle that from a command post at the police station.

Besides, he would probably choose to stay off his investigators' turf. To let them do their jobs while he did his.

So I would be dealing with this Detective De Angelo. And that might be all right. All I had to do was tell him what had happened. Except Petrie's deadpan tone when he said De Angelo was in charge didn't exactly fill me with confidence.

We walked down the hall to the seminar room De Angelo had gone into.

Detective De Angelo didn't look tough. He looked like a dandy. He had discarded his suit jacket and rolled up his sleeves. He was wearing dark blue suspenders—Noah would have approved—and a pale blue shirt. He had thick dark hair, brushed back from his forehead, and the hint of a cleft in his chin. He was sitting on the edge of the table in the seminar room swinging his leg back and forth when Petrie escorted me in.

Petrie introduced us.

De Angelo nodded his head. "Good to meet you, Professor Stuart. That's all for now, Petrie."

Petrie left without comment or even a glance in my direction.

"Have a seat, Professor," De Angelo said. He pushed out a chair for me with the toe of an expensive-looking black loafer.

I sat down, and he left his perch on the edge of the table and pulled out another chair for himself. We sat facing each other.

He laddered his fingers under his chin. "So, I understand you barely escaped with your life tonight," he said.

"I don't know if that's true," I said. "As I told Sergeant Petrie, I saw Richard's body on the floor, and I thought there was someone behind the door."

"And that was when you took off running." He smiled, a pleasant smile that dimpled his left cheek. "'Feets, don't fail me now,'" he said. "Right?"

He might have been referring to the blues melody or to the title of Herbie Hancock's album. But given the hint of "negro dialect" in his reading, I would have bet he was seeing an image of Charlie Chan's chauffeur, Birmingham Brown.

"And they didn't," I said, smiling right back at him while I digested his little racial slur and persuaded myself that now was not the moment to share with him my initial assessment of his character. *Choose your battles,* my grandfather said in my head. "At the time," I said, "running seemed well-advised."

"Well, it probably was," he said. He reached for his jacket on the chair behind him. He took a pack of cinnamon gum out of a side pocket. "Have some?" he asked, holding it out toward me.

"No, thanks."

"Smoking," he said as he unwrapped a stick for himself. "I'm trying to quit. But people keep telling me that giving up cigarettes is doing nothing at all for my disposition."

"Thank you for warning me."

He smiled. He moved the gum around in his jaw and then re-steepled his fingers beneath his chin. "So, tell me how you and Professor Colby came to be here in the building at this time of night. You seem to have been the only two people in the place."

"Other than the maintenance crew and the building security officer," I said. "And, of course, the killer."

"Absolutely. We mustn't forget about the killer. Him—or her." De Angelo's dark eyes held my gaze. "I've got to go upstairs and have a look at the knife. I hear it's a big one. That's the way to do it, huh? Big knife, right in the chest?"

I did an internal five count. "I'm surprised you stopped to talk to me before going upstairs," I said.

"Not the way they do it on television, right? But I thought we could chat first and then go upstairs together. You don't mind going upstairs again, do you?"

"Yes," I said. "I do. But if you think it's necessary." As I said that, it occurred to me that it might not be a particularly bright thing to do. "Unless, of course, you consider me a suspect. In that case, perhaps I should call an attorney before I—"

"An attorney?" De Angelo smiled. "That's the problem with dealing with people who know something about the law. The first thing they want to do is call an attorney." He leaned forward and touched my arm. "Come on, I just want you to show me what happened, okay? I'll try not to upset you."

I looked into the brown eyes that had suddenly gone all sincere. "I understand, Detective, that as a witness, my cooperation is important, but—" I wasn't sure how I was going to finish that sentence.

I didn't have to finish it. De Angelo frowned and took his hand from my arm. I turned around, half expecting to see Quinn in the doorway.

But the person standing there was female. A slender, blonde woman wearing a navy pantsuit and navy flats. Her curly, unruly hair was caught back on each side with no-nonsense clips. She looked as competent as the sleek, burgundy leather attaché case she had in her hand.

De Angelo got to his feet. "Well, Marcia, honey. This is an unexpected pleasure."

The woman did not return his smile. She gave him an account-auditor's look and said, "Your boss called mine to ask for a liaison from the Gallagher PD. My boss sent me."

"And I can tell you're just plumb thrilled about that," De Angelo said. "You must have really burnt rubber getting over here."

"Chief Quinn said he wanted us in on this case from the beginning," she said. "And I know how fast you like to work, Ron. So I thought I should just get myself on over here real quick."

Her drawl mocked his. De Angelo, his mouth tight, turned to me. "Professor Lizabeth Stuart, Detective Marcia Williams of the Gallagher PD."

I stood up to shake the hand that Williams was holding out to me. "Detective Williams," I said.

"Professor Stuart," she said. "A pleasure to meet you."

She waved a hand at De Angelo. "Don't let me interrupt, Ron." She went around the table and took a seat on the other side. "I'll just be a fly on the wall. Here to provide the support of my department if you should need it."

"That's mighty kind of you, Marcia, honey," De Angelo said, his drawl back in full force. "Lending me your support."

Their gazes locked. Her hand hovered for a moment over her attaché case. Then she looked away. She took out a legal pad and a pen. In another moment, she seemed calm and in control again. But De Angelo had won that round, and his smile said he knew it.

If he hadn't turned his attention back to me, I would have pondered that little exchange. But I had other things to worry about.

"Now, Professor Stuart," he said as he sat down in his chair. "This is not a custodial interrogation. At the moment, I consider you a witness. However, if you consider it in your best interests to call an attorney. . . ."

I glanced over at Williams. She said, "That is your right, Professor. As I'm sure you know."

My right. But Richard was dead upstairs. If I wanted to help the police find his killer, sooner or later I was going to have to answer their questions. If I called an attorney, they would think I had something to hide. If I didn't. . . .

Of course, I would have to find an attorney before I could call one. What would I do? Open the telephone book? Call someone—Joyce Fielding or one of the other faculty members—and say, "Richard is dead. Can you recommend a good attorney?"

"I think I'll wait on that call," I said. "I have nothing to hide, and I want to be as helpful as I can to the police."

"And we certainly appreciate that, Professor," De Angelo said. "Don't we, Marcia, honey? Getting back to my question about why you and Professor Colby were here in the building so late. . . ."

I told him—starting with the murder mystery party at the Performing Arts Center that we had both attended. When I got to Tracy's abrupt arrival, De Angelo nodded. "Yeah, I heard about that. We'll come back to that later if we need to. Let's fast-forward to how you came to be here with Professor Colby."

I bit my lip and thought again of calling an attorney. Instead, I went on with my story. I told him about how Richard had asked for a ride. De Angelo let me go on uninterrupted until I got to the part about coming back for the forgotten videos.

"Let's back up a moment, Professor, if you wouldn't mind. You say you gave Professor Colby a ride over to the parking lot to pick up his car." De Angelo was sitting on the edge of the table again, staring down at me. "Tell me—" He glanced at Williams. "Sorry, Marcia, honey. Tell us again about that."

"Tell you what about it?" I said.

"You see, what I'm puzzled about, Professor Stuart, is why Professor Colby would have hung around there at the Performing Arts Center waiting for you. There must have been quite a few other people there that he knew. People who would have been happy to swing by Brewster Hall and drop him off. So why did he wait for you and ask you to bring him over here?"

I hadn't thought of that. Now was not the time to think about that. Not when I had deliberately skipped right over that kiss in the car.

"I don't know why he waited for me," I said. "Maybe he . . . maybe he stayed when everyone else was leaving because he wanted to have a snack or another drink as the caterers were packing up."

"And while he was snacking and drinking, everyone else left? Well, yeah, that's possible." De Angelo slid off the table and slumped back down in the chair across from me. "Of course, he might have had something he wanted to talk to you about. Except you say you and Professor Colby didn't talk about anything in particular."

"No," I said. "We didn't."

"But you must have talked about something. Think about it for a moment. What did you talk about?"

I resisted the temptation to shift in my own chair. "We talked about the weather—and about Halloween. A young man in a Lone Ranger costume had dashed in front of the car as we were on our way over. I almost hit him. And then when we were turning into the parking lot, I saw the skeleton someone had hung out of the window on the fifth floor. I pointed it out to Richard."

De Angelo nodded. "The wind ripped up that skeleton. I stepped over a piece of plastic rib cage as I came in. Who do you think put it there?"

"I don't know. Maybe a student. Today we had a rash of Halloween pranks."

De Angelo straightened in his chair. "What kind of pranks would those be?"

I told him about the pranks on the faculty that day. The paper skeleton with a dagger in its heart that Carol had found under her door. Joyce's rubber scorpion and Pete's voice-mail call with the *Halloween* theme music. And my cartoon tombstone.

"You say one of the faculty received a skeleton with a dagger through its heart?"

"That was what I heard," I said. "I didn't see it. I heard about all this—except my cartoon—secondhand from another faculty member."

"Who would that be? This other faculty member?"

"I don't think— I would rather you speak to the other faculty members about that. About what they received or saw."

"Don't want to be a squealer, huh?"

"I would rather not drag anyone else into this," I said. "Especially when it's probably completely unrelated. As far as I know, Richard didn't receive anything."

"Nope. He just ended up dead up there with a real knife in his chest."

"You think the Halloween pranks and Richard's murder are linked?"

"You tell me," he said. "Do you think they are?"

"I've told you what I think. I think the pranks today were probably just a student—"

"Maybe it was a whole bunch of students. A reign of terror on the faculty," De Angelo said. "So, I gather you don't think a student might have killed Professor Colby?"

I thought of the kid who had almost knocked me over as he came charging out of Richard's office. But killing Richard would hardly get him into the graduate program. Let De Angelo find out about that kid for himself. "It's rather a leap from Halloween pranks to murder," I said.

"But not an implausible leap, given the right psycho." He turned and smiled at Williams. "Marcia, honey, could I have a sheet of paper from your pad?"

She tore off a sheet of paper and pushed it across the table. He nodded his head at her. Then he took his gum out of his mouth and put it in the paper. "All the flavor's gone," he said. "No point chewing on it."

Williams said nothing. She had been taking sporadic notes as De Angelo and I talked. But she was maintaining a silence that might have been because she was on De Angelo's turf and he was the lead investigator. Or it might have had something to do with whatever was between her and De Angelo. Or maybe both.

De Angelo turned back to me. "So, leaving this student who was pulling these pranks aside for the moment, let's go back to your driving Professor Colby over here."

"All right," I said.

"So you drove him over and dropped him off and started to leave—"

Let it go, the smart cells in my brain said. But my mouth popped open anyway. "Actually, we talked for a few minutes before he got out of the car," I said. "Not long. No more than five minutes."

"Still talking about nothing in particular?"

"Richard asked me if I believed in ghosts."

"Ghosts? Now why would he ask you a question like that."

"Because it was Halloween," I said, "and a wild, rainy night." I hesitated. De Angelo was the senior investigator. He might even know something about being a detective. "I think he was depressed about something. He mentioned old ghosts."

"What did he mean by that?" De Angelo asked. He was unwrapping another stick of gum.

"He seemed to be thinking about something in his past—something that depressed him, made him sad."

"Uh-huh," De Angelo said as he pushed the gum into his mouth. "Did he tell you what that might be?"

"No. He just seemed to be in a strange mood. And then when I came back to get the videos, he said he would come in with me—"

"Because his cell phone wasn't working, and he wanted to call home. Now, I'm wondering why he just didn't drive on home. Why come all the way in here to call if he was on his way there anyway?"

I shook my head. "He— I think maybe he wanted to ask his wife to wait up for him. He said he wanted to talk to her."

"And his wife was there at the party, right? I think you told Sergeant Petrie that. You were concerned about someone calling her and letting her know what had happened."

"Yes. I mean, yes, I did tell Sergeant Petrie that Diane Colby had been at the party, and, yes, I did ask if anyone had called her."

"But instead of leaving the party with his wife, Professor Colby waited for you."

"He— I told you about what happened. I mean, you had already heard about that—about the girl with the gun. Diane left right after that was over. And Richard stayed."

"To wait for you. What else did the two of you talk about when you were sitting out there in the parking lot? Besides ghosts?"

And why in the devil had I even told him that much. Maybe I should blurt out something about Diane and Scott leaving together and send De Angelo ferreting off in their direction. "I don't remember what else we talked about. I think that was about all. And then he thanked me for the ride and got out of the car."

"And you drove away. But then you came back. And then the two of you came into the building."

"Yes."

"And then what happened?"

I told him about the shadowed hallway and the elevator ride upstairs. About going to my office while Richard went to his. I told him about stopping to read my E-mails and hearing a door slam. And then the lights going out. I told him about going around to Richard's office and finding his body.

"And that was when you ran down here," De Angelo said. "You say you heard a door slam. Was your own door open or closed?"

"It . . . it was not quite closed. Ajar."

"So the noise you heard—when this door slammed—it was loud enough for you to hear around in the other corridor."

"Yes," I said.

"Did you hear anything else? Professor Colby calling for help? An argument? Any other sounds?"

I shook my head. "Only the door slamming."

"Was it Professor Colby's door?" De Angelo asked.

"It— I don't know. I don't think it was one of the fire doors. There's a kind of metallic sound when they close. It sounded like an office door."

"But you aren't sure it was Professor Colby's door?"

"No," I said. "But I'm sure it was in that corridor. So unless someone else was in one of the other offices—" I came to a stop as I thought about that.

De Angelo smiled. "Exactly. If you didn't do him in, and unless Professor Colby managed to stab himself in the chest, our killer had to be hanging around somewhere. . . ."

"Did anyone else come into the building? I had to use my ID to get in. Wouldn't there be a computer record of some sort showing who entered the building after it was locked."

"Now you're thinking, Professor. But, of course, our killer could have hidden in the building before it was locked."

"But you said— You suggested the killer might have come out of one of the other offices. Richard and I were talking when we got off the elevator. This person—he or she must have heard us and known I was there. Why slam a door? Why make enough noise to attract my attention?"

"The door slamming like that might have been an accident," De Angelo said, displaying his dimple again. "I heard you had one of those at your party."

"What?"

"The tray you dropped. You weren't supposed to drop it, were you?"

That caught me completely off balance. "You're very well-informed for someone who wasn't there."

De Angelo steepled his fingers again. "Tell me about your relationship with Professor Colby."

My leg was cramping from the way I was sitting. I shifted in my chair, trying not to look as if I were squirming. "I . . . we didn't have a relationship," I said. "We had never socialized at all until today when we went to lunch together."

"To lunch? He invited you, did he?"

"Yes. I'm here as a visiting professor. He invited me to lunch to talk about my impressions of the university and the school. And to talk about the research I'm doing."

"What research would that be?"

"On crime and justice in Gallagher in the 1920s. My grandmother came from Gallagher. She saw a lynching here when she was twelve. Richard and I talked about that."

"So it was a working lunch, so to speak?"

"Yes."

"Where did you go?"

"Downtown to the Orleans Café," I said.

Had anyone told Clovis? Had she heard it somehow already?

"They serve some first-rate gumbo at the Orleans," De Angelo said. "Superior gumbo."

"I had the chicken wings and potato salad."

"Then you got to go back and try the gumbo. Of course, you'll need to find yourself another lunch date, won't you?"

"Yes," I said.

De Angelo stood up. He stretched. Then he tugged down his shirt sleeves and reached for his jacket. "Ladies, shall we go upstairs and have ourselves a look at the crime scene."

I got up in a jerky motion that he probably interpreted as fear or guilt. Or both.

While we were waiting for the elevator, he said, "I wouldn't have taken Chief Quinn for a party animal. I wonder why he was at your party tonight, Professor Stuart."

And there came the other shoe.

I said, "Perhaps you should ask Chief Quinn about that, Detective De Angelo. But don't police chiefs and other university officials occasionally do that? Put in appearances at university events as a part of their official role?"

De Angelo said, "Yeah, I guess they do. But the thing is, the way I heard the story, you were the only one the chief talked to at that party."

"Where did you hear that?" I asked.

"One of our dispatchers has a son who's a major in the theater department. After the party tonight, he dropped by to see his mom during her break."

"Did he?" I said.

"Yeah. He was the one who mentioned that Chief Quinn had been at the party even before all the fuss started. And the chief had been talking to the new female professor from criminal justice."

"Yes, we did exchange a few words," I said.

"So you and the chief know each other, do you?"

"Does it matter?" I said.

"Matter? Not to me. I'm just a cop trying to do his job." De Angelo glanced over at Williams. "But that would explain why Detective Williams was sent over here double quick. Wouldn't it, Marcia, honey?"

Neither Williams nor I said anything.

The elevator doors were standing open. "After you, ladies," De Angelo said.

Had Quinn really asked to have Williams assigned to this case because of me? To protect me from De Angelo? When De Angelo had made that "Feets, don't fail me now" crack, he had known then that I knew his boss. He had known that I had been seen talking to Quinn at the murder mystery party earlier in the evening. He didn't care that I might complain to Quinn about his behavior. And he seemed to find Williams's presence more amusing than anything else. De Angelo felt safe.

"Something on your mind, Professor?" he asked.

"Yes," I said. "I was wondering if I should have called a lawyer."

"Why would you be wondering about that, Professor? You aren't guilty of anything, are you?"

"No," I said. "But sometimes that doesn't matter, does it?"

"Only in bad places with bad cops," De Angelo said. "Now, Chief Quinn—he's told us all that we have to be real good. He doesn't approve of bad cops." That smile. "Hasn't he ever told you that?"

Oh, lord, what had I walked into?

The elevator doors opened onto the fifth floor, where now there was light and bustle.

"Hey, Ron, they're ready to move the body. You want to come have a look?" The question came from another detective. He was older than De Angelo, balding, his badge on display, attached to his belt.

"Exactly why we're here, my man," De Angelo said.

"Excuse me," I said. "I don't see any reason why I should look at Professor Colby's body again. I've already described to you what I saw and heard and did. If you have no more questions for me, I am going to leave now."

De Angelo turned to me. He was smiling.

"May I leave now, Detective?" I said. "Unless I am in custody. . . ."

He gestured toward the elevator. "Yes, ma'am, if you no longer wish to cooperate with us, then please feel free to go on home. Would you like a police escort to your car?" Before I could speak, he turned and called to one of the uniformed officers. "Leave that for somebody else to do, Officer. I want you to escort Professor Stuart, our star witness, down to her car. In fact, why don't you follow her home to make sure she gets there safely."

De Angelo turned back to me. "I'm sure Chief Quinn would want us to do that. Don't you think so, Marcia—pardon me—Detective Williams?"

Detective Marcia Williams was looking at him with an unreadable expression on her face. She said, "Yes, I think providing Professor Stuart with an escort home would be a good idea."

"There you go, then. We'll see you tomorrow, Professor. After you've had a good night's sleep." He walked off down the hall toward Richard's office.

Williams glanced at me, her expression still unreadable. "Good night," she said. She followed De Angelo.

"Ready to go, ma'am?" the young officer asked.

"Yes," I said. "More than ready."

"Do you have a jacket, ma'am?" the young officer asked as we rode down in the elevator. "You're shaking."

Shaking, was I? Hadn't he noticed the rage behind De Angelo's smile? Or was that just for me because I had crossed him? Or because Quinn had.

"I have a jacket," I said. "It's upstairs in my office. I really don't want to go back for it."

Chapter 16

WHEN WE GOT TO MY HOUSE, the young officer, whose name was Zimmer, got out of his patrol car and escorted me to the door. He offered to come inside and make sure everything was all right. I accepted.

He checked all of the rooms, including the closets. Then I saw him to the door and locked up behind him. After that I stood in the middle of the living room trying to decide what to do next. I wanted to talk to Quinn, but I wasn't sure I should call him. He would probably rather I didn't. As police chief, he would need to keep his distance from a woman who might be a suspect in a murder case. Especially if De Angelo, the lead investigator, thought that Quinn was trying to run interference or to protect me. So it was probably not a good idea to call Quinn. Then neither of us would ever have to lie if we were asked if we had discussed the case.

I thought of calling Joyce Fielding. But it was late, and I wasn't sure what I would say to her. Even if she had already heard about Richard, the conversation would be awkward. De Angelo was not going to be the only person who would wonder why Richard and I had been together after the party. It was simple enough to say that I had given him a ride and then both of us had needed to go into the building. But as De Angelo had said, the underlying question—the question people would wonder about—was why Richard had hung around waiting for me to drive him to his car when there were other people there he might have asked.

I sat down on the flowered sofa that had come with the furnished house. The fabric was a poppy pattern, huge red flowers that I normally find cheerful but that tonight reminded me of the blood on Richard's shirt. I got up again and walked out to the kitchen and put on the kettle. It was 1:19, according to the sunburst wall clock. Time for bed.

I carried my mug of hot chocolate into the bedroom and sipped it while I undressed. Then I climbed into bed and turned out the light. I closed my eyes and willed myself to sleep.

After a while, I switched on the lamp and reached for the novel on my night table. *The Great Gatsby* had been on my college reading list. I was reading it again because of my research on the 1920s. The world of Jay Gatsby was far enough removed from what I had seen tonight to be safe to inhabit for a while.

I nodded off, falling asleep with my arm twisted under me and the book beneath my cheek.

The ringing telephone brought me upright, sluggish and groping for the receiver. And then I remembered Richard and drew my hand back. I glanced at my clock radio. 3:25.

"Hello," I said, cutting into my own recorded message. "Hello?"

I could hear someone breathing. And then the click of a receiver being replaced.

I got up and checked the doors and windows again. When I got back to the bedroom, I closed the door and locked it. Then I pulled over a chair and propped it beneath the knob.

I didn't have a gun. Even though I had grown up in a house with a grandfather who was a hunter of small game and who had enjoyed nothing more than a tramp through the woods with his hounds, even though I had loved spending time with him in the woods and had learned at his insistence to load and fire his shotgun and rifle, I did not like guns and I did not own one.

I reminded myself of my well-thought-out ethical position as I opened the night table drawer and took out the claw-headed hammer I kept there. I slid it under my pillow and curled up in the bed with the lamp still on. Sometimes ethical positions sucked.

Chapter 17

WEDNESDAY, NOVEMBER 1

I came awake to the sound of rain pounding on the roof and the telephone on the night table ringing. The palest hint of daylight had seeped between the miniblinds and the curtains.

I picked up a pillow and covered my head with it. Whoever it was could leave a message—unless he or she had called to breathe some more.

My recorded message ended. A familiar voice said, "Lizzie? Lizabeth, wake up and pick up the phone."

I rolled over and grabbed up the receiver. "Quinn?"

He said, "I'm standing in a telephone booth making a call that I shouldn't be making. Are you all right?"

"Yes," I said. "I— Are you?"

"I'm not the one who managed to land myself in— Dammit, Lizzie, do you walk around wearing a sign?"

Before I could frame an appropriate response to that, he said, "You know I have to stay away from you while this is going on."

"I know," I said. "I had already figured that out. Speaking of which, do you think it was a good idea to call? Not that I don't appreciate your calling. But suppose someone should ask if we've communicated about the case. What will we—"

"Lizzie, will you— Just stop talking and listen to me."

"I am listening. How can I not be listening when you're shouting."

"I am not shouting. I am trying to get you to focus on what I'm about to say."

"Say it," I said.

"De Angelo is the senior investigator in the department."

"I know that. Sergeant Petrie told me."

"Did he also tell you—" Quinn paused and started again. "De Angelo is a good detective. He knows what he's doing. But sometimes he comes on a little strong."

"I've noticed. He—"

"Listen to me, Lizzie."

"Dammit, Quinn, I said I was listening."

"I want you pay attention to what I'm saying because I'm not going to have a chance to say this again. De Angelo is not someone you can play games with."

"Me play games? He's the one who— The man's a—"

"I know what he is. But you've got to deal with him. This is his case. So don't do anything to get his back up."

"Do you really think you helped matters when you sent Marcia Williams over?"

"I didn't send Williams anywhere. I asked for a Gallagher PD liaison. Her chief proposed Williams. I've met her, and I know she's a good cop. I said fine."

"De Angelo didn't interpret it that way. He thought having Williams there was some kind of ploy on your part to protect me."

"To protect you? He thought I—"

"He knows we know each other. One of the dispatchers has a son in the theater department." I told him what De Angelo had said.

Quinn said, "All right. I'll deal with that. You try not to add fuel to the fire."

"De Angelo is the problem here, not me."

"No, the problem is that you were running around in an empty building when you should have been at home. What the hell were you doing there, anyway? First, you have lunch with Colby, and then you—"

"Find him dead? If you must know, Quinn, I asked Richard over lunch if he would mind getting murdered last night and letting me find his body. I had such a good time in Cornwall with Dee that I thought—"

"I'm going to hang up now before I say something I'll regret."

"Do that," I said.

"Lizzie, dammit," he said. "This isn't— If you need me, call me. Do you understand?"

"I understand," I said. "But I won't need you." I hung up.

And sat there for a while with my arms wrapped around my knees, feeling sorry for myself and mad at Quinn for making me lose my temper. He had gone out in the rain and found a telephone booth and called me at seven o'clock in the morning when he shouldn't have been calling me at all. Then he had gone and spoiled it by blaming me because he had De Angelo in his police department. Of course, according to him, it was all my fault, anyway, because I had been there when Richard was murdered instead of at home where I belonged.

Did he think I was getting a major thrill out of this new habit I seemed to have developed of being at murder scenes?

It was just as well we were going to be keeping our distance from each other until this was over. By the time it was over, I would have gotten control of whatever form of temporary insanity seemed to affect me when I was around John Quinn. I would go on with my life, and he would go on with his—the way I had said we should when we said good-bye in Cornwall. Because there were any number of good and sufficient reasons I should get John Quinn out of my life and keep him out. One of them was that he was downright annoying when he started snapping out orders.

I got up and shrugged into my robe. Now that I was awake, I might as well get dressed. It was a safe bet that I was not going to be left in peace today. And, even if De Angelo didn't come looking for me with an arrest warrant in hand, there were things I needed to do. First on the list was to have a talk with Clovis.

I was in the shower when my second call of the morning came. By the time I grabbed a towel and stepped dripping out of the tub, the answering machine had come on. I heard a disembodied voice leaving a message, and I opened the bathroom door to listen. It was Amos Baylor. I finished drying off, and then I went into the bedroom to play back what he had said:

"I've scheduled a faculty meeting at nine tomorrow morning. Please try to make it. It's vital that we discuss this matter as a faculty." Amos paused. "Also, we have a request from the president's office that faculty in our school not give interviews to the press. All comments about Richard's death and the investigation are to come from Chief Quinn or the president's office." Another pause and a bit of throat clearing. "I'm afraid the press will be especially eager to talk to you, Lizzie. Aside from the fact that you found Richard's body last night, you are the only other African-American faculty member in the school. There are already some rumors that this was a hate crime."

Richard's murder a hate crime? That had not occurred to me. But, of course, it was possible. It was possible that Richard had been killed because someone didn't like him because he was black. Or because he was black and arrogant. Or black, arrogant, and married to a white woman. That was possible.

Except, if it had been a hate crime, the killer had certainly gone to a lot of trouble. Unless the killer had been hiding in the building when it was locked or had a university ID, then he or she would have to get hold of one to gain entry to Brewster Hall.

And why bother to follow Richard inside and kill him in his own office? Why not just stab him out there in the parking lot? Why not shoot him and send a note claiming to have killed another nigger?

Unless personal hatred counted. Maybe the person who had killed Richard was someone who had watched and brooded and stewed and finally acted. That was possible. Not a hate group, but one lone, up-close-and-personal hater.

I had missed the rest of what Amos was saying. I played it back again:

"The press will be eager to hear your opinion. But, please, do try to avoid saying anything that might inflame the situation. Brewster Hall will be closed until eight tomorrow morning, but I need to spend some time on campus today. I'll be using Claire's office in the theater department. Call me there if you have questions." A pause. "I am sorry about all this, my dear. I'll see you in the morning at the faculty meeting."

And how did one behave at a faculty meeting where one of the people at the table might be a murderer?

Chapter 18

IT TOOK ME A WHILE to get out of the house. Since my landlords, Piper and Sonny, had left their big-screen television in the living room, I had relegated my portable to the kitchen. I turned it on as I was making myself a cup of peppermint tea—and had a hard time pulling myself away from the five-minute local news spots "at the top and bottom of the hour." The morning anchor, his expression solemn, described Richard's murder as "sending shock waves through the campus community at Piedmont State University." He cut to a reporter on campus, "live at the scene." I sat down hard when I heard her identify me by name as the faculty member who had found the body of the victim.

I was still sitting there twenty minutes later, waiting for the promised "update" in the next segment. When the doorbell rang, I froze, imaging hordes of reporters on my front porch waiting to thrust their microphones at me when I opened the door. I tiptoed out into the hallway. I peeped out and saw Mrs. Cavendish's dyed blonde hair above her wrinkled face. She was carrying a basket. "Lizzie," she called out as if she could see me on the other side of the door.

I unlocked the door and opened it. She sailed past me. "I brought your breakfast," she said. "Hash browns and bacon. Real bacon. I didn't have any of that turkey stuff you buy. Brought some hot biscuits and strawberry jam too." Her voice floated back to me as she trotted down the hall toward my kitchen. "You need to keep up your strength. From what they're saying on the television, you're going to need it. Oh, good, you have your set on. I started to call and see if you did."

She turned and pointed her finger at the closed kitchen cabinet. "Get yourself one of those plates. And I need a mug." She held up the thermos in her hand. "I brought my own coffee. No offense, sweetie, but you do need to work on your coffee-making. Your young man drinks coffee, doesn't he? He looks like a coffee drinker. What does he think of this mess you're in? Being university police chief and all. No offense, sweetie, but it is a mess. I know you didn't kill this Colby guy, and your young man knows you didn't do it. But it looks suspicious. There you were in that building practically alone with him when he was killed. Opportunity, as they always say in my mystery novels. Now, motive is another question. They have to establish that, don't they?"

She sat down at the table and with a sigh of relief stretched out her legs in their ankle socks and sneakers. "Walked three miles this morning. In the rain yet." She nodded at the television screen where Katie Couric was conducting an interview. "That little hunk's an awful actor. Did you see his last movie? But he is cute, isn't he? The little girls love him. Not that we're forgetting your problem, sweetie, but sometimes things come to you if you don't think about them too hard. Of course, the other question is how this is going to affect your young man's job. Being new at it and everything. And the two of you being an interracial couple."

I found my voice that had been temporarily overwhelmed by Mrs. Cavendish's onslaught. "If you mean Chief Quinn, he isn't my young— We don't have that kind of relationship. We're just acquaintances."

She gave me one of her wicked looks from mascared eyes. "Oh, come on now, sweetie. I may be ancient but I'm not senile." Her eyes narrowed. "Good grief, that might give him a motive too, mightn't it? This black professor being offed. If he was jealous . . . and, of course, it would be easy enough for the university police chief to get in and out of one of his own buildings."

I sat down in the kitchen chair that I had been occupying before Mrs. Cavendish's arrival.

She gave me a surprised look. Then she bobbed back up to her feet. "That's right, sweetie, you just sit there. I'll get what we need. You must be tired out. Did you sleep last night with all this on your mind? You do look tired, circles under your eyes. And frankly, you do tend to look washed out when you're tired. I never thought about that with a black woman, but it's true—not that you're all that light-skinned, but enough so that you can't afford to lose too much sleep. Especially with those reporters poking around with cameras. You don't want people thinking you're guilty of something because you didn't get your rest."

"I need to go out," I said. "I was on my way out."

"Eat your breakfast first," Mrs. Cavendish said.

She sat there sipping at her coffee and nibbling on one of her biscuits while I picked at the hashed browns she had put on one of Piper and Sonny's huge flower-shaped plates. But at some point my throat stopped trying to close and realized the food sliding down it was delicious. I finished the biscuit on my plate and reached for another.

Mrs. Cavendish pushed the jar of homemade strawberry jam toward me. "That's better," she said.

She refilled her cup and turned her attention to the television. The promised update had produced nothing more than the news that

John Quinn would hold a press conference at noon. The object of Mrs. Cavendish's attention now was an actress who had written a book about her decades-long struggle with depression. Mrs. Cavendish seemed fascinated.

When the interview was over, she turned to me. "All right, give me your version of what happened last night."

"I'm sorry. I really do appreciate the breakfast. But we—the faculty in criminal justice—have been told not to discuss the case."

"But you're not discussing it. You're just telling me. I don't gossip."

Well, as far as I knew, she didn't. She simply seemed to like to collect information.

It is hard to tell a woman in her seventies that she is a pushy busybody. Especially when she has offered you aid and comfort in the form of food. Especially when she is sitting there with an expectant expression on her face. I finally gave her an abbreviated version—minus the kiss—of what had happened. It was the only way to get her out of my kitchen.

"Like I said," she concluded when I was done. "A mess. But never fear, it'll all come right in the end."

"I hope so," I said. "But I really do have to leave now."

"Where are you off to?"

"Errands," I said and picked up her cup and my plate.

Mrs. Cavendish nodded. "First, go put some makeup on. I wasn't kidding about those circles."

"I know. I saw them. But I don't have any makeup."

"Then get some while you're out. War paint, my husband, God rest his soul, used to call it. Adele's war paint. Of course, you don't want to overdo it. Looking too stylish was one of the reasons Ruth Snyder got the chair back in 1928."

"Maybe I should hire you as my media consultant," I said. I ran water over the dishes and put them into the dishwater.

"People believe what they think they see," Mrs. Cavendish said. "You can commit serial murder and get away with it as long as you look like a cuddly little old lady like me." She patted her dyed hair and smiled.

I laughed. And then I was crying.

"Good grief, sweetie," Mrs. Cavendish said as she grabbed a paper towel from the roll and pressed it into my hand. "Do I look that bad? Well, never mind. You probably need to get it out of your system. Don't want to break down when someone's got a camera on you."

"Excuse me, I need to go wash my face."

She stayed until I had washed my face and scolded me again when I came out with my face bare of makeup. "Even when you're not dealing with the media, it wouldn't hurt you to wear a little. Men like it."

She followed me out to my car. As I got behind the wheel, she waved and trotted off back toward her house across the street. Why was she in such a hurry? On her way to call one of the local television stations and give them an "inside scoop"?

That would be all I needed.

When I walked into the Orleans Café, there was no sign of Clovis, but the young man with the ponytail was on duty behind the counter. It was around 10:15, and about half of the tables were occupied—presumably for a late breakfast or a very early lunch. Miss Alice's was not the kind of place that would call that in-between meal "brunch."

The young man came over with menu in hand. "Hi," he said. "We're still serving breakfast until eleven o'clock, but if you'd like the gumbo, it's ready."

"Thank you," I said. "But what I'd really like is to speak to Clovis."

His expression became cautious. "Sorry, she's not here."

"Will she be in later today?"

He shrugged. "I dunno."

So much for that. I could try going to her house if I knew where it was, but. . . .

"Miss Alice," I said, glancing toward the table by the kitchen where Richard had said she always sat. "Is she going to be in today?"

"She's already here. She's out in the kitchen."

"Oh, then do you think I could speak to her? My name is Lizzie Stuart. She won't know me, but she may remember my grandmother. I asked Clovis to mention me to her."

"Hold on a minute," he said and retreated through the double doors leading into the kitchen.

I looked around as I was waiting. Nothing had changed since yesterday. The Halloween decorations were still on the wall—black cats and witches on brooms.

"And put a little more bacon grease in those collards," a strong voice, slightly querulous with age, instructed as the kitchen doors opened outward.

A woman—a small woman, no taller than my grandmother had been, clad in a clean gingham dress, white braids wound around her head—stopped beside the counter to look me over. She was leaning on her cane.

"Miss Alice? Thank you for seeing me. I'm Lizabeth Stuart. I believe you might have known my grandmother. She was Hester Robinson when she lived here."

Miss Alice cackled. There was no other way to describe the sound. "Hester? Lord, yes, I knew Hester! We was girls together. She was about three years older than me, but we used to play together." Miss Alice gestured toward the table with the end of her cane. "Sit down there, child."

"Thank you, ma'am."

She eased herself into the chair across from me. "How is Hester?"

"She died last year."

"It's getting so about everybody I used to know is dead."

"You seem to be in good health, ma'am."

"I weren't talking about me. I'm tough as old shoe leather." She shook her head. "Not like young people nowadays. You children don't know how to deal with tribulation."

Did she mean Clovis?

One thing at a time. First, Mose Davenport. Then I would ask about Clovis.

Or maybe Clovis would put in an appearance before I had to ask.

"Miss Alice, the reason I'm here. . . . My grandmother sometimes talked about Gallagher. About why she had to leave."

"She told you what happened?"

"Yes, ma'am. About Mose Davenport being lynched. Please, would you tell me what you remember?"

Miss Alice was studying my face. "Tell you about it?"

"What you remember about that day. About the lynching."

"How come you want me to tell you about it, if Hester already told you?"

"Because I— The truth is, Miss Alice, I'm writing a book, and—"

"A book, you say?"

"Yes, ma'am. I'm a crime historian. I'm here in Gallagher for the year, teaching at Piedmont State—"

"You're there at the university, are you? Then you knew that boy? You knew Clovis's Richard?"

Clovis's Richard?

"Yes, ma'am, I knew him. He— Actually, yesterday Richard brought me here for lunch. I met Clovis then."

Miss Alice said, "She's taking it mighty hard. Would that mama of his had let them alone."

"Richard's mother?" I said, confused.

"Elise was her name. Snotty as she could be. Thought she was better than most folks 'cause she had a little white blood in her. Thought Clovis weren't good enough for her boy. Too dark and too big-breasted. She wanted a 'refined' girl for her boy."

"So that was one of the reasons she sent Richard away?"

"That was the only reason."

"But wasn't Richard getting into trouble—"

"All boys get into trouble. That's part of being a boy."

"Yes, but a black boy in a Southern town—"

"The trouble he was getting into weren't no trouble white folks worried themselves about. Just teenage boy shenanigans. Pranks. Most of them on colored folks. Besides, they all know—the white folks know it too—they know that boy was special. Smart. Going to be somebody. And Elise, she worked as housekeeper for Judge Matthews. The judge was a real important man."

"Aah," I said.

"You see, do you? Fact, she used to brag about how the judge would tell her weren't nothing to worry about. That Richard was just 'sowing his wild oats.' The judge said someday a boy as smart as Richard would be a fine lawyer—"

"A lawyer?"

"That's what Elise was planning for him to be. The judge promised to help her get him into a real good school."

"But then she sent Richard away."

"She played her weak heart on him."

"She what?"

"Elise was born with something wrong with her heart. Weren't nothing to keep her from doing everything she wanted to do. But whenever she wanted to get her way with somebody—"

"I see."

"And that boy adored her. Worshiped her. So when she saw he was getting real serious about Clovis, she started with him about how he was shaming her with his behavior. Kept at him until he said he'd go stay with his aunt and uncle in Texas."

"So that was the way it happened."

"That was it. She thought my girl weren't good enough for her Richard." Miss Alice glared at her cane. "Well, you see what he's come to now. First, he married that woman in Baltimore. Then he married him a white woman. And now he's dead."

"Yes, ma'am. Clovis—is she all right?"

"She's taking it hard, like I said. I left her there at the house, sitting at the kitchen table staring into space."

"Are you sure she— I mean, do you think it's all right for her to be alone?"

"My granddaughter's got her good sense. She ain't gonna hurt herself over this."

"No, ma'am."

"I told her not to go counting on nothing," Miss Alice said. "She been telling herself Richard was going to leave that woman—"

"Leave Diane?'

"That white woman he was married to. Clovis was building her hopes up—"

"Had Richard told her that he was going to divorce Diane?"

"Didn't have to tell her. When he started coming in here all the time, she told herself."

"Then they were seeing each other—" I stopped when Miss Alice glared at me.

"My Clovis is a good girl," she said.

"Yes, ma'am. I didn't mean— But you said—"

"I said he started coming in here. Sometimes three or four times a week. And he would talk with her and tease her. They would play like they used to do. And she started building her hopes on that."

"Oh," I said.

None of the other questions that came to mind were questions I could ask Miss Alice.

She tapped her cane against the tile floor. "But that ain't what you came to talk to me about, is it? You just want to talk to me about Clovis and that boy being dead?"

"No, ma'am," I said. "I also wanted to talk to you about—"

"Your grandma?" Miss Alice said. "Where did she go to when she left here? I never heard no more about her."

"She ended up in Kentucky. That was where they found her hiding in one of the boxcars and put her off the train."

"Kentucky. I never been out that way." Miss Alice propped her cane against her leg. "Been to New York and several times down to New Orleans, but never to Kentucky. Got lots of race horses out there, don't you?"

"Yes, ma'am."

But something else was on Miss Alice's mind. "Hester did all right then?"

"Yes, ma'am. She found a job in one of the hotels in Lexington. She worked there for years."

"And she got married. Was your grandfather a good man?"

I smiled. "Yes, ma'am, he was. He died about seven years ago."

"How did Hester come to meet him?"

"He saw her washing the front steps of the hotel one day when he was passing. He worked for the railroad."

"They travel a lot, don't they? Men who work for the railroad."

"Yes, ma'am. When they were first married, he did. He was a sleeping-car porter."

Miss Alice nodded to herself. "I'm glad he was a good man."

"Miss Alice, why—"

"You wanted to know about Mose Davenport, you said."

"Yes, ma'am. But about my grandmother—why did you ask if my grandfather was a good man?"

"Your grandma had a hard time of it when she lived here. I was just hoping she'd ended up with a good man."

Yes. Except there was something else there.

But Miss Alice was saying, "Mose Davenport. Now, that one weren't what you'd call a good man."

"But my grandmother seemed to like him," I said.

"She liked him 'cause Ophelia liked him. But Mose Davenport

weren't nothing but trouble coming. The first time he came in here, my daddy say, 'That boy gonna be trouble.' He was too big and too sure of himself. Not the way no colored man was supposed to be in those days."

I reached for the microcassette recorder that I'd stuck in my shoulder bag because I didn't want to leave it in the car. "Do you mind if I record this, ma'am?" I said. "I should ask you to sign a consent form before we talk because, technically, this is an interview. And I should ask you to sign a form saying that you are talking to me of your own free will and specifying how and where I can use the information from this interview."

"Well, where's your form?" Miss Alice said.

"That's what I was about to say, ma'am. I don't have a form with me. But if we could talk now, I promise I'll bring one for you to sign as soon as I get back by here."

"So you're saying you need me to sign before you can put what I'm telling you in that book you're writing," she said.

"Yes, ma'am, I do need your permission."

Miss Alice eyed the recorder. "I heard myself on one of those things once. I didn't sound like myself."

"No one ever does. But I won't play it for anyone else."

She grinned. "You get my permission before you do that too."

"Yes, ma'am, I will. May I turn it on?"

"Go on, then."

"You were saying about Mose. . . ."

I leaned back in my chair as Miss Alice began to talk about Mose Davenport and his free and easy ways and his gambling in Jessup's Alley where there was illegal liquor and loose women, and where, every now and then, the police raided the houses just to say they were doing their job. But nobody cared much as long as the "dens" were operating in the colored part of town.

So men like Mose drifted through. And they settled for a while in one of the rooming houses. And they drank and gambled. And then they drifted on.

And Mose would have, too. But then he met Ophelia. Met her downtown one Saturday afternoon. There he was, grinning and talking and fancy-walking around her. And she trying to get past him, shy as she was, half scared to death of him.

But then, sudden-like, he caught her hand and carried it to his chest and smiled real sweet at her.

And next thing you know, next day after church, there was Ophelia walking with him down by the river. And him talking and grinning. And she just looking up at him with her big brown eyes.

And so Mose stayed in town. The other fancy men came and went. But Mose stayed on. Hanging around Dr. Stevens's house some days, waiting to walk Ophelia home.

And Ophelia—she wouldn't hear nothing bad nobody had to say about him. Would just turn away so the women were talking to her deaf ears.

Even closed the door on the preacher when he came to talk to her about him. Stopped coming to church after that.

"But your grandma Hester Rose, she was always over at Ophelia's little house. Ophelia helped to nurse Hester's folks when they was sick. Hester told you, didn't she, about how her daddy and mama died during the flu epidemic?"

"Yes, ma'am."

"Well, after they died, Hester just about adopted Ophelia as her big sister. Hester was living with one of her mama's friends and helping with her children. But every other moment she could get, she'd be over at Ophelia's. Then she'd come back and tell us girls the stories Mose used to tell. He claimed he was from New Orleans too—like my daddy was. And he said he had traveled all about. Even been down to Mexico, he said. And to Canada once. Told lots of stories, and laughed as he told them."

"Miss Alice, in one of the newspaper articles I read, the article said the police thought that Mose was selling cocaine to the local colored people."

"I expect he was," she said. "Or if he wasn't, he wouldn't have had no problem getting some."

"It said in the newspaper that the police thought that was why he killed Dr. Stevens. To steal the drugs in Dr. Stevens's office."

"That was what they say at the time. Said someone came in the doctor's office and smashed him over the head with that statue he had on his desk, and then ransacked his office. And if it wasn't Mose who done it, who was it? That woman 'cross the street saw him and Ophelia going in the house, and she hadn't seen nobody else go in there all day."

"The doctor hadn't seen any patients that day?"

"Some folks had come by. But he had his sign on the door saying he was out. Mose and Ophelia was the only two anybody saw go inside. Ophelia let herself and him in through the back door with her key."

"And you really do think Mose did it?"

"He shot that policeman. He got Ophelia killed—"

"Got her killed? The newspaper report said that she hanged herself in her jail cell. Do you think it happened some other way?"

Miss Alice was silent for so long that I thought she wasn't going to answer. I was about to offer to turn off the recorder, when she said softly, "The women said Ophelia was carrying a child."

"A baby? Mose's baby?"

"Well, who else's would it have been? And there she was in that jail cell. And her child's daddy was dead, and she never been married to him. And on top of all that, there was that white man—that policeman who had been a hero in the war—and he'd been shot dead there in her front yard. And he had a wife, a young, scrawny thing with eyes as big as Ophelia's and her stomach all swollen up with his child." Miss Alice shook her head. "Ophelia was in a heap of trouble. Trouble in more ways than one. They would have sent her off to prison and taken that baby when it was born."

"So you think she killed herself?"

"I think it. It was a sin before God, but I think she did it. After Lawyer Caulder went to see her, she must have known—"

"Lawyer Caulder?" I sat up straight in my chair. "Jonathan Caulder?"

"That was him. Him and Dr. Stevens was almost as close as brothers. And Dr. Stevens was crazy about that sister of his."

I had out my pen and pad. "What was his sister's name?"

"Name was Laura. Full of life, that girl was. And so pretty all the men would trip over their feet when she walked into a room."

"Daniel Stevens too?"

"No, not him. He would just stand there and look at her. Watch her flirt with the others. You see, he was the quiet type. Real soft-spoken and serious. And she couldn't sit still for more than a moment, to save herself. Always laughing and dashing about to them socials and skating parties and what all." Miss Alice shook her head, smiling. "My sister used to keep house for them—for Miss Laura and her brother. She said it near 'bout killed Miss Laura when she had to wear that back brace. She should have been grateful she was alive."

"What happened? How was she hurt?"

"A car accident. It happened early that spring. On one of the first fine days. Miss Laura went out driving with one of her beaus. And he went around a curve too fast and ran them off the road. The car flipped over. The boy weren't hurt. But Miss Laura was hurt some. They had to take her to the hospital. She didn't want nobody but Dr. Stevens to examine her, so they sent for him. He came and examined her, and he wanted her to stay in the hospital. But she weren't having none of that. So finally he told her she could go home, but that she had to stay in bed for a week. Then after that, she had to wear a brace on her back till it was healed. Well, she didn't like that at all. Said the brace messed up her nice silk dresses."

"Miss Alice, if we could go back to the day Mose Davenport—" The outer door opened. Lunchtime customers were beginning to arrive. I really would have to keep this short. "Miss Alice, you said Jonathan Caulder went to see Ophelia in jail."

She raised her hand in greeting to the man and woman her waiter was showing to a table. She turned back to me. "He went over to the jail," she said. "I guess he thought Dr. Stevens would have wanted him to try to help Ophelia. Dr. Stevens was real fond of her."

"And she was still alive when he got there?"

"She was. He told my daddy later, she was sitting there in that cell on her cot. Her dress was all torn, and she had smudges on her face and blisters on her arms from the fire. He tried to talk to her, but she wouldn't even look at him. So he squatted down in front of her so that she could read his lips. But she turned her head away and closed her eyes. Finally he wrote her a note on a piece of paper and left it there on the cot."

"Did he tell your father what the note said?"

"It said that he would be back to see her and that he would do everything he could to help her and for her not to despair."

"But she did despair, if she killed herself."

"She must have known that even Lawyer Caulder, as sharp as he was, would have had a hard time talking them into letting her walk out of there scot-free. The next thing any of us heard, they had found her hanging there in her cell when they went to take her supper."

The outer door to the café opened again.

I said, "Just one more question, Miss Alice. Do you know what happened to the Caulders?"

"Both of them took what happened to Dr. Stevens real hard. Especially Miss Laura. She couldn't even come to the funeral. For two, three weeks she wouldn't even leave the house. Her brother told my sister not to come over to do for them. He said Miss Laura didn't want to see nobody, didn't want nobody except him in the house." Miss Alice shook her head as she remembered. "Lord, when he finally did get her to come out again, she looked like a ghost of herself. All pale and quiet. Moving like she was in a dream. And she weren't getting no better. He finally decided he needed to send her back down to Atlanta."

"Atlanta?" I said.

Richard had been in Atlanta. But lots of people went to Atlanta. I was missing what Miss Alice was saying.

"I'm sorry, ma'am. Did you say they had family there?"

"They come from there originally," Miss Alice said. "Still had some cousins there. Lawyer Caulder stopped in here for his dinner that afternoon after he'd put her on the train. He told my daddy he was hoping that being with her own people would bring her back to herself."

"And did she ever come back here to Gallagher?"

"They say she had to go into one of them places."

"One of what places?"

"The places they used to send rich white women to. The places they went to when they was having trouble with their nerves."

"Laura had a nervous breakdown?"

"That's what they call it now," Miss Alice said. "The cousins sent her to that place, and she still weren't getting no better. So her brother went down to Atlanta to see to her. He came back here about a month later to arrange to sell their house and to wrap up his business and say good-bye to everybody. That was the last anybody I know saw of either of them. Though I reckon some of the white folks around here probably did visit with them when they traveled down that way."

"But you never heard anything else about Laura? Or her brother?"

"No, I never did."

"Excuse me, Miss Alice." It was the waiter. "Mrs. Jenkins wants to say hello."

"Tell her I'll be done in a little while."

"No, ma'am," I said as I switched off the recorder. "Please don't let me keep you from your customers. Maybe I could come back another day and have lunch, and we could talk some more. Maybe by then I'll have thought of what else I want to ask you."

"That'll be fine." Miss Alice looked me up and down as I rose from my chair. "You're too thin, child. You better come back by here and let me get some meat on your bones."

I smiled. "Yes, ma'am. Thank you so much for taking the time to talk to me."

She grinned, displaying her false teeth. "At my age, what else I got to do but talk."

I hesitated. "Miss Alice, do you think if I stopped by, Clovis would speak to me? I don't want to disturb her, but it is rather urgent that I— You see, I was the person who found Richard last night, and the police—"

Miss Alice nodded. "I wondered when you'd get around to mentioning that. Go on by there. She might talk to you."

"Could you give me the address, please?"

"She lives with me, in my house," Clovis's grandmother said. She gave me the address and told the young waiter to tell me how to get there.

"Thank you, ma'am."

Miss Alice nodded her head and gestured to the woman who had wanted to say hello. The woman got up from her table and started over. The young waiter told me to come with him to the counter and he would draw me a map.

"Hit the deck!" a voice boomed as the front door flew open. "Hit the damn deck!"

I spun around, ready to throw myself to the floor. But chuckles and catcalls were coming from the patrons scattered around the tables.

The young waiter said, “Excuse me,” as he started toward the door.

Miss Alice called out, “Parnell, you take yourself on round back if you want your lunch. Don’t be coming through my door disturbing my customers.”

“Yes’m,” the man in the doorway said, as the waiter herded him back out. He was wearing a bright red scarf around his neck. A brown paper bag stuck out of the pocket of his ragged fatigue jacket. The man I had seen when I came to lunch yesterday. The man who had been sitting on the steps of the building that had been Andrew Clark’s general store.

The young waiter came back. “He was in Nam,” he said. “Screwed up his head.”

I mouthed a “good-bye” to Miss Alice as I was leaving. She raised her hand in a regal gesture and went on with what she was saying to the enthralled Mrs. Jenkins.

I had left my car across the street in the municipal parking lot. I paused outside the door to open my umbrella. The day was grey and cold, yesterday’s heat wave broken by last night’s storm.

“Hit the deck.”

I stepped away from the door and looked around the corner. Parnell was making his way down the alley between the café and the barber shop next door. He was kicking a tin can that must have fallen from the garbage cans. He was chuckling to himself as he mumbled over and over in a singsong, “Hit the deck. Hit the damn deck.”

And I had more than enough trouble of my own without thinking too hard about Parnell’s.

Chapter 19

MISS ALICE'S HOUSE, white shingled with black shutters, stood on a side street. Like its neighbors, the house had a well-groomed yard. Unlike some of the other houses, there were no bikes or wagons or other signs that children lived there.

But there was a red Pontiac, waxed and shining, in the driveway.

I walked up the steps and rang the doorbell. No one came.

The house was too quiet. Miss Alice had said Clovis was there. Was she inside peering out at me? Or was there some other reason she wasn't answering the door. Miss Alice had said Clovis was all right, but. . . .

"Clovis," I called out and banged on the door frame. "Clovis, it's Lizzie Stuart. Clovis!"

"Will you shut the hell up?" The woman standing on the porch of the house next door, holding her bathrobe together, was not happy with me. "I'm trying to get some sleep over here."

"I'm sorry," I said. "I'm here to see Clovis. Her grandmother said she was here, and I saw the car—"

"The car belongs to one of Miss Alice's nephews. Clovis drives a truck. She went tearing out of here in that thing about twenty minutes ago."

"I don't suppose you have any idea where she was going."

"No, and I don't give a—" She said quite explicitly what she didn't give.

"I'm sorry," I said. "I really do need to find her. But I didn't mean to disturb you."

She tightened the belt of her robe and frowned. "I got to work third shift tonight, and my kids are going to be home before I even get to sleep," she said. "I already had to get up out of my bed and come over there because of all that racket Clovis was making. Over there yelling her head off and throwing things around."

"Throwing things?" I said.

"I thought she was fighting with somebody." The woman put her hands on her narrow hips. "And I get over there, and ain't nobody there but Clovis. Her grandma's gonna pitch a fit when she sees that living room."

"Did Clovis tell you why she was so upset?"

"No, and I didn't ask. Clovis been had a temper on her as long as I known her. Back when we were in school together, she was always ready to go upside somebody's head."

"You went to school with Clovis?" I moved closer to the edge of the porch, so that I could see her better. "Did you happen to know Richard Colby?"

"Him. Yeah, I knew him. Everybody knew him. He thought he was hot stuff." The woman sniffed. "And Clovis thought he was her personal property. Tried to jump me one day 'cause he was looking me over. All that, and she still didn't get him. Served her right, I say."

The woman turned toward her door. I said before she could go inside, "Have you heard what happened last night?"

"I ain't heard nothing, and I don't want to hear nothing. Just shut the hell up and let me get some sleep before my kids get back here." She went inside and slammed her door.

I sat in my car looking at Miss Alice's house. I could wait, hoping that wherever Clovis had gone, she would be back soon. But given the kind of mood her neighbor said she was in, maybe I really didn't want to talk to her right now.

Clovis had a temper. Back in high school, she had considered Richard her personal property and had not hesitated to defend her claim. According to her grandmother, since Richard had returned to Gallagher, Clovis had begun to "get her hopes up." What if Richard had done or said something to shatter those hopes? Would Clovis have responded violently?

I caught my breath as I remembered that kiss in my car.

But that was ridiculous. Clovis had not been at the party. Why would she have been lurking in the Brewster Hall parking lot? Unless she had come there and seen Richard's car and waited to see if he would come back for it.

No, the person who had killed Richard would have had to be able to get into Brewster Hall. Where would Clovis have gotten an ID card?

My mouth felt like the Sahara. I reached for the bottle of water that I had bought yesterday and left in the beverage holder. Was it safe to drink after sitting in yesterday's heat?

A glint of metal on the floorboard caught my eye. I reached over and plucked up a gold coin—or, at least, a fake gold coin, pierced with a hole. It looked as if it had come from a bracelet or necklace. But how had it gotten into my car? No one had ridden on the passenger side of my car in months. No one except Richard last night. Of course, it could have fallen from his pocket. But why would he have had it in the first place? It certainly didn't look like something Diane would wear.

I unscrewed the water bottle and took a half swallow of the tepid liquid. Then I dropped the coin into the side pocket of my shoulder bag to think about later.

Time to go. I would call Clovis.

I decided not to go back to my house. I wanted to avoid any and all media encounters. And the best way to do that might be to stay away from home a while longer.

The question was where to go. As I turned onto Main Street, I answered my own question. The library. Ever since I was a child, the library had been the one place I could go when I wanted to hide out.

Public library, not university.

The periodicals room was located in the basement of Gallagher's public library. There were five microfilm machines. All were in use.

I crossed the hall to the archives room. "Hello," I said to the woman at the desk. "I came in a couple of weeks ago to do some research on Gallagher—"

"Well, here you are!" A series of expressions rippled across the woman's face. "I misplaced the card you gave me, and I was sitting here the other day wondering how to get in touch with you. I knew you were at the university, but I put your card down before I read it, and I couldn't remember what department." She paused. "Then this morning, I heard your name on the news. But with the trouble you all are having over there—"

"Yes," I said. "Actually, I'm hiding out. I'm afraid reporters are looking for me."

The woman nodded. "Well, I can understand that. I won't tell anyone you're here, if you want to have a little quiet for a while."

"Thank you," I said. "Why was it that you wanted to get in touch with me?"

"Oh, yes, goodness, I'd almost forgotten." The woman—Miriam Lockwood, her name plate reminded me—reached into a drawer of her desk. She brought out a white cardboard box. "We acquired this last week," she said as she opened the box.

I moved closer. "A scrapbook?"

Miriam nodded. "A patron found it among his great-aunt's things. His great-aunt Sophie was a member of the debutante set, and as you can see, she saved newspaper clippings and photographs."

"And party favors and ribbons," I said as the woman turned a yellowed page of the book.

Miriam pointed at the elegant script below each item. "And she captioned each with a pithy comment."

"May I look through this?"

"Certainly. That was why I wanted to reach you. I was sure you'd want to see it."

* * *

I paused over a page midway through the scrapbook.

Below a newspaper clipping about a Valentine's Day ball at the home of Mr. James Brighton and his wife Estelle, great-aunt Sophie had written: "Estelle Brighton spent the evening flirting with Dan Stevens—which prevented him from keeping an eye on Laura."

Dr. Daniel Stevens? Yes, there it was. The *Gazette* reporter had listed him by title and identified Laura as Laura Caulder.

Why had he been keeping an eye on Laura? Because he was in love with her?

Hester Rose had said very little about Daniel Stevens. She had spoken of him only as Ophelia's employer and as the man Mose Davenport was supposed to have killed.

I stared down at the yellowed clipping and the faded script. Then I dug into my shoulder bag for paper and a pencil. The question, of course, was who was going to be important in the social network I was constructing for Daniel Stevens. Constructing slowly because I had spent my first two-and-a-half months in Gallagher learning about the city. That had meant reading everything I could find about the city's history, including city council minutes and the annual reports of the chiefs of police.

My research thus far had been sandwiched in among the tasks related to getting settled in a new place and preparing for the two classes I was teaching. Not to mention helping Claire plan her murder mystery party.

And now there was Richard's murder.

If and when I was ever able to finish constructing the network of social, business, and political connections that linked Daniel Stevens to the people in his sphere, I might have a better idea why someone had wanted him dead.

Unless the killer really had been a thief, someone Dr. Stevens had caught in his office. Not Mose Davenport, as the police had premised, but someone else.

A passing stranger? No; for now, I would assume I could identify the suspects.

I turned to the next page of great-aunt Sophie's scrapbook. The Gallagher young set had been active that spring and summer of 1921. Parties, picnics, afternoon teas, book discussions, concerts. I had known that much from my earlier scanning of *The Gallagher Gazette.*

What hadn't been clear at a glance was how involved a busy doctor on the municipal payroll as the official "city physician" had been in such activities.

I would have to go back through all the newspaper's "society notes" and look for his name and Laura's.

Chapter 20

I HAD FOUR MESSAGES on my answering machine when I got home. Three were from reporters—the *Gazette*, a Martinsville paper, and Channel 13. They all said more or less the same thing. They wanted to talk to me. The fourth message was from Joyce. She asked me to call her when I came in. I glanced at my watch. It was almost nine-thirty. I had stayed at the library until it closed.

"Give me a few minutes, Joyce," I said to the machine.

After I made myself a chicken-salad sandwich, I checked the clock again and then went to call Joyce. I had erased her message, so I reached for my pocket phone book. As I was flipping through it, I saw another name and number.

Tess answered on the fourth ring, just as I was expecting her answering machine to come on. I could hear Elena, her baby daughter, gurgling near the receiver.

"Hi," I said. "It's Lizzie. Am I calling too late?"

"No, we were both awake," Tess said. A pause. "What's up?"

"A mess, according to my neighbor, Mrs. Cavendish. I almost didn't call, but then I thought you might see something about it on the news."

Another pause. Elena gurgled. Her mother said with great caution, "The news?"

"A faculty member in my school was murdered last night in his office."

"Murdered?" Tess said, her voice rising.

"I know. That's why I almost didn't call."

What neither of us was saying was that after what had happened in Cornwall, the last thing Tess wanted to discuss with me was another murder. In fact, it had been a while before we could talk about anything.

She said, "Are you all right?"

"Yes." I straightened the alignment of the salt and pepper shakers on the counter. "But it's messy."

"How so?" Tess said, still cautious.

"The faculty person who was murdered was Richard Colby, the only other black faculty member in the School of Criminal Justice. I was the one who found him in his office."

As I told her about that, she groaned and offered her opinion in Spanish too fast for me to follow.

"Tess, if you're insulting my intelligence—"

"Would it help?" she said. "What does John Quinn say about all this?"

"He's not happy with me."

"I don't blame him."

"Thanks," I said, changing my mind about telling her what had happened in the car.

Elena's gurgles were turning to irritated whimpers.

I said, "Anyway, I wanted to let you know what's happening. In case . . . well, just in case you hear something about it."

"Just make sure that what I hear isn't an announcement about your funeral arrangements."

"What I'm more concerned about is staying out of jail."

Tess said, "I've got to go. The baby's hungry."

"Okay," I said. "Is everything all right there?"

"Busy. Things are always hectic on a television show. I'm working on a segment about Venice."

"Italy?"

"California." Elena began to bawl. "I've got to go—as you can hear."

"Bye," I said. "Kiss Elena for me."

"First I need to change her," Tess said. "A word of advice, pal. At the rate you're going, you'd better give serious thought to finding yourself a live-in cop."

"What?"

"Quinn. Bye." She hung up.

Lousy advice, Tess. As you ought to know better than anyone.

But I hadn't called for advice. I had wanted to hear a friendly voice. My friend's voice.

One of these days, it might really be all right between us again. At least she sent me pictures of Elena now and then. But I still hadn't been invited to visit her in Chicago, and she said she was too busy with her new job on the cable television travel show to visit me.

I didn't feel like talking to anyone else tonight. I would talk to Joyce when I saw her tomorrow.

It had rained that morning in Drucilla, Kentucky. A damp breeze came through the screen door. It wafted the tilled earth smells of the garden into the kitchen to mingle with the odors of the yeasty dough my grandmother was kneading and the beef stock simmering on the back of the stove. I filled my lungs with the smells. My stomach growled in response.

I hooked my bare toes around the rung of my chair and leaned my bony elbows on the table as I watched my grandmother sift more flour into the bowl, scrunch down the dough, then flop it over.

Hester Rose spoke without looking up, "Lizabeth, pass me that butter dish, girl."

I stretched forward and pushed the yellow plastic dish across the red and white oilcloth. I sat back in my chair and tugged at the too-tight braid dangling over my left ear. "Grandma?" I said.

"What?"

"I've been thinking about it, and I don't understand. If Mose Davenport wasn't a bad man, then why did he shoot that policeman?"

"I already told you that. 'Cause he thought one of them was getting ready to shoot him."

"But when they came looking for him, how come he didn't give himself up and explain he didn't do it?"

Hester Rose's hands paused in their work. Her heavy-lidded gaze fastened on my face.

"You think it was that easy, do you? Weren't you watching that TV program last night 'bout back during the civil rights demonstrations, with them police using dogs and tear gas and beating on people with their sticks? Well, it was a whole lot worse back in 1921. Back then, didn't no colored man just give hisself up."

"Then why didn't he run away?"

"Him and Ophelia did intend to run away. What they didn't know was that the old biddy who lived across the street from Dr. Stevens's house had seen them go in there and then come sliding back out again." Hester Rose turned the wooden bowl over the dough on the bread board and set it to rise.

I said, "What did the woman do, Grandma?"

"She went over there and found Dr. Stevens's body."

"And she thought Mose and Ophelia had killed him?"

"Course that's what she thought."

"But, Grandma, even if they didn't know she'd gone over there, didn't they think somebody would find him?"

"They thought they could be gone before he was found."

"But why didn't they just run? Why'd they go back to Ophelia's house?"

"Because there was things that they needed to get." Hester Rose wiped her hands on a damp towel and reached for the sack of potatoes. "Ophelia wanted her mama's stuff, and Mose had some money he'd been hiding under a floorboard—"

"But if the police were after them—"

"I told you, girl, they didn't expect the police to be coming that fast. They didn't know that old biddy'd been spying. Now, you go look in the oven and see how my pie's browning. I don't want that pie to burn. Reverend Thomas and Sister Briscoe are coming by this evening."

"They are? Why they coming, Grandma?"

"To talk about doing a chicken fry. We got to raise money for the choir's new summer robes. Go check on my pie, now."

"Yes, ma'am." I scraped back my chair and went to do as I was told.

I opened the oven door. The heat rushed out. I leaned over to look inside. . . .

"A toast! I propose a toast," Richard Colby said.

He was at the head of the banquet table. He held a glass aloft in his hand. Blood ran down his arm and dripped onto the table. Blood covered the front of his once-white shirt.

"To Lizzie," John Quinn said.

But when he turned his head and looked at me, I saw it was not Quinn. It was Thomas Kincaid. And there was a gaping hole in his chest.

"To Lizzie," Richard echoed.

"To Lizzie," the ghastly wraiths seated around the table repeated.

"I told her not to come here," a voice said behind me.

I twisted around in my chair. Hester Rose was standing there. Hester Rose, wasted and withered.

"I told her not to come," she said. "But the girl's just like her mama was."

"No!" I sprang up from my chair. It toppled to the floor. "No, I'm not like her."

"Slut!" Hester Rose screamed at me.

"Slut," Richard said.

"Slut," Thomas Kincaid echoed.

"No!"

"Richard is dead," Diane Price Colby said from the doorway. "It's your fault, Lizzie. Why did you come here?"

"I didn't know. I didn't—"

"I'm going to kill you, you slut," Diane said. She pointed her gun at me and pulled the trigger.

"No!"

The only good thing about having a nightmare was waking up from it. I sat up and turned on the light and settled in with my copy of *The Great Gatsby.*

Chapter 21

THURSDAY, NOVEMBER 2

John Quinn was on the morning news. The tape was of the press conference he had held the evening before. Quinn was behind the podium in a university conference room, surrounded by reporters, all with their hands in the air to ask questions.

That weary look I had first noticed in Cornwall was on his face again. He was not getting enough rest. But Quinn was an adult, and this was his job. He had wanted to be a university police chief, so obviously he had been prepared to handle any of the headaches that went along with the position.

However, he had probably been thinking more of brawls at the student center than of a faculty member murdered or of a scorned female student turning up at a Halloween party with a gun. The reporters were asking about both. Asking if there was a link between the two.

Quinn said there was no obvious link, other than the fact Professor Colby had been involved in the earlier episode when he helped to disarm the young woman at the party. Yes, the young woman had been in police custody at the time when Professor Colby was murdered. She had been taken to a healthcare facility. The university administration would make a decision about how to proceed in her case after her mental and physical state had been evaluated.

A reporter from *The Gallagher Gazette* asked about security on campus. What assurance could Chief Quinn give concerned parents about their children's safety?

"The university police department, in cooperation with Student Life, has enacted a number of heightened security procedures to ensure the safety of the dormitories and classrooms here on campus," Quinn said. "Additional security measures also are in place in the parking lots and other public areas. We have done everything possible to ensure the well-being of all our students, faculty, and staff." He paused, then continued, "However, at this time, we have no reason to believe Professor Colby's homicide was anything other than an isolated event."

"Are you saying that Professor Colby was the target of a killer with personal grievances against him?" the *Gazette* reporter wanted to know.

"Then you don't believe this is a hate crime?" another reporter called out. "Are you saying there is no reason to think other minority faculty or students are in danger?"

Quinn responded, "We have no reason at this time to believe this is a hate crime. We are following up all leads in the case. I will provide you with daily updates regarding our progress. Thank you. That's all for now."

Other questions were called out to him as he left the podium. He paused long enough to repeat the hotline number that those with questions about campus security measures should call. He paused long enough to confirm that the university police were working closely with the Gallagher PD with assistance from the state police labs. And then he was gone.

I went to finish dressing. I had a faculty meeting to attend.

In the first-floor lobby of Brewster Hall, two building security officers were examining student and faculty IDs as we entered. From the grumbles of the students and the faculty who were waiting to get in, no one was happy about having to queue up.

I saw Pete Murphy up ahead of me in the line and lifted my hand in greeting. He waved back. At least one member of the faculty was willing to acknowledge me in public.

By the time I got inside the building, Pete was out of sight.

I made it to the fifth floor with twelve minutes to spare before the faculty meeting. My first stop was the mail room. I always stopped in the mail room first. As I reached into my box, it occurred to me that the police had probably not allowed university mail delivery to our floor yesterday. Maybe they hadn't even let the carrier into the building.

But there was something in my box. I turned the white envelope—identical to the one I had received on Tuesday—over in my hand. No return address. Only "Professor Lizzie Stuart" typed across the front.

I pulled the flap open and slid out the single sheet of paper inside. The message was typed too, this time in caps: BET YOU DIDN'T TELL THE COPS WHAT YOU AND RICHARD WERE DOING IN YOUR CAR. SHAME ON YOU, LIZZIE. RICHARD WAS A MARRIED MAN.

"Lizzie?"

I bumped into the table as I whirled around.

Joyce Fielding was in the mail room doorway. She was wearing a black caftan-like dress and holding a paper cup of coffee. She looked like she had been crying.

"Joyce—hi! Sorry I didn't call you back last night. I—" I opened my briefcase and slid the sheet of paper in my hand into it. Joyce's eyes followed my furtive movement.

"Is something wrong?" she asked, raising her glance to my face.

"No, everything's fine," I said. "Would you excuse me? I need to get a pad and pen from my office before the faculty meeting begins."

She stepped back to let me out of the mail room. I swallowed hard as the smell of her cappuccino filled my nostrils. My stomach always reacted badly to shocks. It was a wonder I hadn't thrown up in the hallway after finding Richard dead in his office. But of course, I had been too busy running.

"Lizzie, are you sure you're all right?" Joyce called after me.

"Fine. I'll see you in a moment."

I had made it almost to my office door when Eric Walsh hailed me. "Professor Stuart? Professor, could I speak to you?"

"Eric—" I stuck my key into the lock. "I really don't have time right now. I have to go to a faculty meeting."

"I know, Professor. I have to be there too."

Of course he did. Eric Walsh and Megan Reed were the two representatives from the Graduate Student Association who sat in on faculty meetings. More proof that my brain had stopped functioning.

"All right, Eric. But this will have to be fast." I went around to the chair behind my desk.

He sat down in the blue imitation-leather armchair that had been unearthed from a storage room when I arrived.

"What can I do for you?" I asked him.

"Professor Stuart, I saw you standing with Chief Quinn at the Halloween party before everything happened."

Did everyone at the party have nothing better to do than watch me and who I was talking to? "Yes?" I said.

"I was wondering if you could tell me anything about Tracy."

"I'm sorry— Tell you anything about her?"

"About what happened to her. How she is," Eric said.

"Don't you know how she is? I thought you went with them when they took her away."

"I did. I went with the police when they took her to the infirmary. But then she got upset again, and they made me leave. Yesterday I tried to check on her, but all they would tell me was that her parents had come for her."

"If her parents came for her, she's probably being cared for by her family doctor," I said. "Eric, I don't know how I can—"

"I read in the newspaper that she'd withdrawn from school," he said, leaning forward in his chair. "But no one will tell me anything else, Professor. So I thought I'd ask you."

"Why do you think I would know how Tracy is?"

"Because you—" Eric had the look of someone on uncertain ground. "You and Chief Quinn seemed to know each other. I thought maybe if you had spoken to him since the party— I know you must be upset about Professor Colby, but I thought maybe Chief Quinn might have said something about Tracy."

"Chief Quinn and I have not talked about Tracy, Eric. Chief Quinn and I do not discuss university police—" My tongue stumbled on the last part of that. "I need to get ready for the faculty meeting, Eric."

"Okay. I'm sorry." He stood up. "I was just hoping you might know something. Megan is really upset about this Tracy thing."

"I can imagine she would be," I said, standing too.

"Halloween night, when I got to her—Megan's—apartment—" Eric dug his hands into his jean pockets. "I swear to you, Professor Stuart, I didn't mean to hurt Tracy."

I nodded. "When three people are involved. . . ."

"Yeah," Eric said. "With me and Megan, it just happened between us. When Megan came, I was still seeing Tracy. But it wasn't the way Tracy wants to believe it was, Professor."

"Wasn't it?" I said, holding onto my patience by a thread. I wanted him out of my office so that I could have another look at that sheet of paper in my briefcase.

"No, it wasn't," he said, all earnestness. "Tracy's an undergrad and really too young for me. I know I shouldn't have started anything with her in the first place—"

"But you did."

Eric had the grace to look embarrassed. "But I kept telling her that we couldn't get serious."

"You told her you wanted to be friends?" I said.

"But then she wanted it to be something else, and she started pursuing me. I know I shouldn't have gotten involved with her. But there was no one else in my life at the time."

Did they teach Soap Opera 101 here?

"Until Megan came?" I said, playing my role of confessor.

"Yes. But we didn't start out to— We were both in Professor Fielding's theories seminar, and we had white-collar crime with Professor Colby. I was trying to show Megan the ropes, to help her get settled in. Then we started spending time together. As friends."

"But it became more?" I said.

"We were attracted to each other," Eric said. "But we never meant to hurt Tracy."

I nodded. "I'm sure you didn't. In situations like this, it's probably impossible for someone not to get hurt."

"Yes. But Megan feels awful about it. So do I."

"Eric, I'm sorry. As I said, I don't know what I can do to help you with this. And I really do need to—"

I broke off at the knock on my door.

"Lizzie? It's Joyce. You ready to go?"

"Coming," I called back. "Eric. . . ." I gestured him toward the door as I scooped up my briefcase.

Joyce raised her eyebrows as she saw Eric.

"Good morning, Professor Fielding," he said and flashed her a wan smile.

"Good morning, Eric," Joyce said.

"Thank you for your help, Professor Stuart," Eric said and walked away down the hall.

"What did you help him with?" Joyce asked.

"I didn't," I said. "But it seems both he and Megan are really upset about the Tracy thing."

Joyce made an inelegant sound. "She may be. But I bet our boy Eric is sopping up all the attention."

"Sopping up?"

"Haven't you realized yet what a con artist that kid is? Charming and likable, yes. But a real con artist."

"You'll have to explain that one to me. But right now, we're about to be late for the faculty meeting." I turned in the direction of the seminar room.

"Wait a minute," Joyce said. "I wanted to ask you something about Richard."

"Can it wait until after the meeting?" I said, throwing her a glance over my shoulder.

"I'll ask you later," Joyce said. "Let's go get this over with."

When we got to the seminar room, I found a seat and sat down.

The rest of the faculty were still standing. Britt Davis heaved a sigh of relief as he dashed through the door and saw that. "I've got time to get coffee," he said.

"You should have done that before you left home," Pete Murphy called after Britt as he dashed back out again.

"With a three-month-old baby in the house, that young man's lucky to find his pants before he leaves home," Joe Larsen said in his soft voice.

Carol Yeager glanced at her sports watch. "Amos, can we get started as soon as Britt gets back? I've got a ten-thirty meeting over at the jail about our interns."

"You mean the inmates haven't eaten them alive already?" Ray Abruzzo said.

"The inmates in county jail?" Kate Vincent said. "The only thing that happens in that particular facility is that the sheriff spends his time coming up with ways to obstruct research."

Kate was a medical sociologist with a joint appointment in sociology and criminal justice. I was surprised she had shown up for this faculty meeting. It was the first criminal justice faculty meeting I'd seen her attend. But maybe she thought this one was going to be interesting.

Well, it probably would be.

Carol shook her head in response to Kate's comment about the sheriff. "That old goat still stonewalling you?"

"Including dodging my phone calls. What I want to know is, why is he so worried about my interviewing women about domestic violence?"

"Could be he knocks his own significant other around," Pete said. "I hear tell the guy's temper—"

Ray said, "I hear that too. Last spring, I had one of the county deputies in my seminar. He was telling me this story about what the sheriff did to this kid who fouled up his lunch order—"

Amos clapped his hands to get our attention. "Let's all take our seats."

"And try to remember why we're here," Joyce said.

"What do you want us to do, Joyce?" Pete said as he sat down in the chair across from me. "Put on sackcloth and ashes and speak in mournful tones?"

"Or you could try acting as if you give a damn," Joyce said.

"I do give a damn. I liked Richard. We got along." Pete brushed his hand over his beard. "At least, we did until he stopped getting along with anyone."

Ray said, "Pete's right, Joyce. Even you have to admit that for the past few months Richard had been walking around with a monumental chip on his shoulder."

Carol said, "And when I asked him what was wrong, he looked right through me."

"Yes," Joe said. "I'm afraid he'd been that way with everyone."

Pete grinned. "So," he said, "which one of us was pissed off enough about his attitude problem to kill him?"

Joyce said to Pete, "Common sense if not common decency should tell you that this is nothing to joke about."

Amos said, his voice crisp, "Joyce is right, Pete. Aside from being inappropriate, remarks like that—"

"Will have that campus cop, De Angelo, back up here sniffing around," Carol said. "And I've already spent more than enough time answering questions that are none of his business. He actually wanted to know if I had an alibi for the time of Richard's death."

"He asked us all that," Ray said. "He also asked me about hate groups."

Pete frowned. "Hate groups? So he's considering that possibility. I thought I heard his boss say last night that they had no reason to believe that."

Ray said, "What else was Quinn going to say with the press breathing down his neck and the black students and faculty on campus ready to send for Jesse Jackson." Ray shot a glance in my direction. "Nothing personal, Lizzie."

Well, of course not, Ray. Why should I take that personally?

"Anyway," Ray said. "De Angelo had read an article I'd written about hate groups in prison."

De Angelo could read? Not nice, Lizzie. For all I knew, the man might have graduated magna cum laude and be even smarter than his boss.

Actually, Quinn did keep up on criminal justice research. Maybe he was encouraging his investigators to do the same. Or maybe De Angelo had an intellectual side.

"But nothing like that has been going on here in Gallagher," Pete was saying. "It's been years since I even heard about a cross-burning."

"And why would they wait so long?" Kate said. "Richard came in the same year I did. If they were going to kill him because he was married to a white woman, why would they wait three years to do it?"

"Kate—" Joyce said.

"Everyone," Amos said. "Let's get to our business."

"This is our business, Amos," Pete said. "We've got cops showing up at our houses. It's pretty obvious we're all suspects as far as De Angelo and his sidekick Marcia Williams are concerned."

Now, I really wouldn't have described Williams as De Angelo's sidekick. Not unless they'd gotten a lot more cordial than they were the last time I saw them.

Carol said, "I made the mistake of telling De Angelo that I'd once been married to a cop."

Ray said, "And he wormed out of you that you now have a distinct distaste for the species? I bet he'd be fascinated by those divorce horror stories you and Richard used to trade."

Carol bristled. "Richard had been through a divorce. He understood what I was going through. The fact that Richard and I talked now and then does not give me a motive for murder."

"Simmer down, Carol," Pete said. "We all used to talk to the guy. He was damn interesting to talk to."

"Yes," Amos said—and smiled at me. "Richard was both an excellent conversationalist and an excellent listener. Perhaps because he had pulled himself up from a difficult background and was therefore more tolerant of other people's foibles."

Kate nodded. "I always had the feeling that nothing you could tell Richard would really shock him. At least I did until a few months ago when he started to brush me off every time I tried to talk to him."

"So the question is," said Pete, "what caused the big change from Richard, affable friend and colleague, to Richard, militant black man or whatever it was he'd gotten into?"

"A better question," Joyce said, "is why we didn't make more of an effort to help him with whatever it was he was trying to deal with."

"Well," Pete said. "There's the fact he was married to a psychologist. And he didn't ask for our help. And although we may not have helped him, we sure as hell didn't kill him." He paused. "Of course, I'm speaking for myself, ladies."

Joyce and Carol were not amused. Kate—it was hard to tell about Kate.

Amos said, "I'm sure none of us at this table had anything to do with—"

Kate asked, "What about the book he said he was writing?"

"What book?" Joe asked.

She looked around the table. "Remember? It was a few days after the semester started. We were all in the faculty lounge—all, except you, Lizzie—and Richard was sitting at the table writing on a legal pad. And, Pete, remember you asked what he was working on, and he said his memoirs."

Pete shook his head. "Kate, the man was being sarcastic."

"Oh," Kate said, and her creamy cheeks flushed. "Well, it was hard to tell sometimes with Richard."

"Sorry!" Britt Davis skidded back into the room, his curly hair looking even more as if he had been raking his fingers through it. "Didn't mean to keep everyone waiting. Pam sends her apologies for not coming in. But the baby's whiny, and she's feeling a little nervous about him."

Kate gave Britt one of her wide-eyed looks. "I thought you two had hired a nanny."

"We did. And she's great, but, uh—"

"But this is their first child," Joe said. "I remember how antsy Marie and I were with our first. It takes a while to believe they won't break."

Britt grinned a boyish thank-you at Joe. Britt probably felt in need of that kind of show of support from senior faculty. From what I had seen at this university and my own, it was tricky being what was known as a "faculty couple," a married couple who worked at the same university and, in the case of Britt and Pam, in the same school.

The door Britt had closed behind him opened. "I'm sorry we're late, Dr. Baylor," Eric said as he and Megan came in. "It was my fault."

"You're excused," Amos said. "Come sit down. We're about to get started."

Megan pushed the door shut. She and Eric joined the faculty at the table.

I was not surprised when the faculty meeting hit a snag. That was to be expected in any faculty meeting. On this particular occasion, it happened when Amos Baylor announced his plan for coping with Richard's absence. Cries of protest swept around the table.

"Oh, come on, Amos." Pete ran his fingers through his beard. "You're kidding, right?"

"Why can't you hire an adjunct?" Carol wanted to know.

"Because Richard's class on environmental crimes requires specialized knowledge," Amos said.

"Richard was the only faculty member who had it," Ray said.

"Ray's right," Carol said. "I know about as much about environmental crimes as I know about Chinese philosophy."

"I'm not asking you to teach Richard's class, Carol. All I'm asking of any of you is that you each take on a couple of Richard's students—"

"For independent study," Ray said. "But if we don't know anything about the subject, how are we supposed to grade the papers that they write?"

"My point exactly," Pete said.

Eric Walsh's hand went up.

I hoped he was ready to be flayed alive. When threatened with demands that they considered unreasonable, faculty could be vicious.

"Yes, Eric," Amos said. "You have some thoughts about this?"

Eric looked around the table. "Megan and I are both in Professor Colby's environmental crimes seminar. And I wanted to say that if the faculty is worried about not knowing enough about the subject to supervise independent studies, all the students in the class have already developed reading lists for the topics we're researching."

Megan nodded in support of her man. Still by his side in spite of the Tracy episode. "Professor Colby reviewed our reading lists and gave them back to us with comments."

"So," Eric said, "it really wouldn't be as hard for the rest of the faculty to take over as you all seem to think. I'm sure I'm speaking for everyone else in the class when I say we really would appreciate it if you would."

Joyce sent me an amused look. I took it as a reference to her earlier remark about Eric as a con artist.

Joe said, "Eric, it isn't that we aren't concerned about the welfare of the students—"

"Then why don't we do what Amos has asked?" Joyce said.

Britt spoke up. "I agree with Joyce. Even if we could find another adjunct—"

"We'd be asking that person to plunge into someone else's class in the middle of the semester," Amos said. "We'd also have to come up with the money for his or her salary—"

"Come up with it?" Pete said. "We've lost a faculty member who was making more than a dozen adjuncts would cost us."

"Pete's right," Carol said. "Tell the administration to get up off some of the salary Richard would have gotten for the rest of the year."

Kate said, "I'm not sure if I'm involved in this."

Which would have been an odd comment since she was there. But Kate was effectively part-time in the school because of her joint appointment in both sociology and criminal justice.

"Feel free to put your two cents worth in, Kate," Joe said.

She blushed and returned his smile. "Well, my two cents worth is that I think it would be healthier for the students psychologically if this faculty did step in and pinch-hit for Richard."

"Amen," Joyce said.

"Wait a minute," Carol said. "We're missing three faculty members. Hank and Charlie are at that gang conference."

"And Kyle's in Tokyo," Ray added.

"But they'll all be back next week," Carol said. "If we agree to this independent study scheme—"

"They'll be assigned students too," Amos said.

"We've wasted enough time on this," Pete said. "Let's vote on it."

Amos's white brows drew together. Obviously he had thought he was informing them of his decision, not putting the matter up for a vote. But faculty tend to stand on their perceived right to a democratic process.

On that thought, I shifted my position in my chair and silently seconded Pete's request. Anything to get this over with.

"We've had a call for the question," Amos said. "All in favor."

To my surprise, everyone voted in favor of taking on Richard's students.

Then Carol opened another can of worms. "How are you going to assign them, Amos?"

"Good question," Pete said. "None of us want to get stuck with the class imbeciles."

Joe said, "Clearly with no reference to those students who are present."

Eric grinned. "Thank you, Professor."

He seemed to be in better shape than his visit to my office had suggested. Even though Megan still looked drawn, Eric seemed to be rising above his distress.

The room was too warm. I tried to keep my heavy eyelids open as opinions were exchanged about how Richard's students should be assigned.

Gripping my hands together in my lap to focus my attention, I glanced around the table.

Three female faculty members other than myself.

Joyce Fielding, flamboyant and earthy and blunt, dressed in mourning black today.

Carol Yeager, nervy and efficient, dressed in her usual style of attire, a pin-striped coat dress.

Kate Vincent, oval face and dark cap of hair, wearing a ruffled, high-necked blouse right out of a Victorian novel. But wearing it with a kicky little ruffled skirt.

What did clothes tell one about the woman? Did they tell you if she was capable of stabbing a man to death? And then of sending a poison-pen letter?

What about Megan? Brilliant, love-struck Megan. Or her beau, Eric? Eric of the roving eye.

What about the other five men sitting around the table? Could one of them have done it?

I shifted in my chair again and wished I could drink caffeine. My mind needed a jump start and so did my body.

"All right," Amos said. "If there are no objections, we will assign the students alphabetically."

Carol looked at her watch and started to gather up her things. "I've got to get out of here, Amos."

"One moment, Carol. The memorial service is tomorrow. I want you all to be there."

"Where else would we be?" Pete said.

"What about classes?" Joe said.

"Canceled here in the school today and tomorrow. Canceled campus-wide tomorrow."

Carol was poised for flight. "Anything else, Amos?"

He waved his hand. "Go. All of you go. I'll put anything else in a memo."

"Thank you, Amos," Joe said as he stood up. "Let us know if there's anything else we can do to help."

"Anything but taking on more students," Pete said.

"What else do you have to do, Pete?" Joyce said. "That's what you get paid for."

"Sanctimonious this morning, aren't we, Joyce?"

"I happen to think you're being a real pain about this. That's all."

"Joyce," Amos said. "Pete."

"Sorry, Amos," Joyce said. "We'll behave."

"I will if she will," Pete said.

Amos shook his head at them, indulgent father to naughty children. "Try. Both of you try."

But Amos looked unhappy. Being a dean was never easy. It must be especially difficult when one of your faculty members was murdered and everyone else was a suspect.

The person who had left the note in my box would have had to walk in past the building security officers in the lobby downstairs. Then he or she would have had to walk down the hall and into the mail room here on the fifth floor and leave the envelope in my box without attracting attention or comment. That meant someone connected to the university—faculty, student, staff. Or someone who knew how to blend in and—

But still there was the matter of getting into the building. Unless the person had entered as a delivery person or—

But would building security have permitted a nonuniversity person to enter? That I didn't know. The only way to find out if someone from the outside might have been allowed to come in was to ask a cop. I could call up De Angelo and say, "Guess what, Ron, I've got a poison-pen letter." And then he would come right on over, and I could tell him what I'd left out. The part about when Richard kissed me as we sat in my car.

The first thing I noticed when I unlocked my office door was that the message light on my telephone was on. I punched in my personal code.

The message was from Diane Colby. She wanted me to return her call. She said she was in her office. What was she doing here in her office when her husband had been murdered? The psychology department was on the fourth floor in this building. How could she come into this building two days after her husband had been murdered here?

And why did she want to talk to me?

Her voice when she answered was throatier than I remembered from our brief introduction a few weeks ago. She sounded like she had a cold. Or as if she had been crying for hours.

"Diane? It's Lizzie Stuart."

"Will you have lunch with me today?" she said without preamble. "At noon?"

"All right," I said. "Where should I meet you?"

"Please come down to my office. We'll go from here."

"All right," I said again.

But when I hung up, I sat there staring at the telephone. Why did Diane want to talk to me? Did she know about my lunch with Richard on Tuesday? She couldn't possibly know that Richard had kissed me, could she? Had she gotten an anonymous note too?

At ten minutes to twelve, I pushed aside the undergrad exams that I had been trying to force myself to focus on. I got up and went to the ladies' room.

Joyce was already there. She came out of one of the stalls as I walked in. "Want to go over to the Rathskeller for lunch?" she asked.

"Can't," I said. "I have another engagement."

"Male?" Joyce asked.

"Female. Diane Colby."

"Diane?" Joyce paused in the middle of drying her hands. "How did that happen? Did you call her?"

"She called me."

"Why does she want to have lunch?"

"No idea," I said as I chose one of the empty stalls.

"Tell me when you find out," Joyce said.

I stuck my head back out of the stall and caught her as she was leaving. "Joyce, what did you want to ask me about Richard?"

She came back inside and closed the door. "Did Richard happen to say anything to you about having an offer?"

"An offer?" I stepped back out of the stall. "A job offer from another university? No, why? Did he said something to you?"

Joyce shook her head. "No, but when we were talking at the party, he was going on about how much he liked Atlanta."

"He mentioned that at lunch. His friend Ted is there. In the political science department at Emory. He enjoyed seeing him again."

"Hmm," Joyce said. "Well, that's probably all it was. I just thought maybe if things were as bad between him and Diane as they seemed to be at the party, maybe he had started looking around."

"But in that case, wouldn't she be the one to go? Gallagher is—was—Richard's hometown."

"But maybe he thought Diane would be staying here to be with Scott," Joyce said.

"Maybe," I said. "But he didn't mention a job offer to me."

She shook her head, "It's a moot point now anyway, isn't it? See you later."

She went out the door, and I went back into the stall. I had forgotten to ask Joyce if she had seen Richard after the party. I would have given a lot to know why he had still been there when I came out. Had he deliberately waited for me, or had there been some other reason he had stayed when everyone else was leaving?

I had never been to Diane's office. But I had checked her office number in the faculty directory before coming down.

The door opened when I knocked. Diane must have been standing beside it.

Her face was colorless above her black dress. She wore a single, tasteful strand of pearls. She gave me a fleeting glance. "Thank you for coming, Lizzie. Let me get my purse and jacket."

She left the door open. I assumed I was invited to enter.

Our office spaces were identical in that we both had white walls and yellowish-brown carpets. But in Diane's office, there were miniature white blinds at the window. Sunshine slanted through them and spilled over the crystal vase filled with pink rosebuds that stood on her work table. A Matisse print hung on the wall.

On the maple desk facing that wall was a silver picture frame. Was it a photograph of Richard?

And there was a small leather-bound book facedown on the flower-bordered desk blotter. A diary? What did a woman write in her diary at a time like this?

Diane picked up the book and dropped it into her briefcase. She gathered up a slender, black clutch bag and the jacket to her dress.

"I'm ready. Shall we go?"

"Yes," I said. "Where are we going?"

"Off campus, if you don't mind. I'll drive."

"All right," I said.

As we reached the elevator, a woman wearing jeans, a work shirt, and cowboy boots stepped out. She came to an abrupt stop. "Diane? What are you doing here?"

Diane ignored her question. She waved a hand toward the woman and then back in my direction. "Lizzie, this is Vivian Womack, also of the psych department. Vivian, Lizzie Stuart, one of Richard's colleagues."

"Hello," Vivian said. "Diane, why are you here? We—some of us—were planning to come over later."

"I appreciate the thought, Vivian," Diane said. "But I need some time alone."

"But there must be something we can do. What about picking people up at the airport? That kind of thing?"

"If anyone from either my family or Richard's decides to come, I'll let you know."

"But surely, at a time like this—"

"Vivian, you'll have to excuse us now. Lizzie and I are on our way out to lunch."

Vivian nodded her head. "Diane, please, call if you need anything."

"I will," Diane said.

"Nice meeting you, Lizzie," Vivian said.

"You too, Vivian," I said as I followed Diane into the elevator.

Diane's blue Mercedes was parked not far from where her husband's car had been parked on Tuesday night. As I slid into the passenger seat, it occurred to me to wonder how well-off Diane and Richard had been. Did Diane have money of her own other than her salary? Had the two of them managed to live very well, thank you, on their combined incomes?

At any rate, it was unlikely that she had killed him for his money. And it would have been simpler to divorce him than to murder him. Wouldn't it?

Chapter 22

THE OLIVE TREE, a light-fare Italian restaurant, was on Riverside Drive, not far from the university. I was surprised Diane had chosen it. The food was good, but I had assumed we were going off campus so that we could avoid curious glances. This was not the place to do it. The restaurant was a popular lunchtime destination.

As we got out of the car, I tugged at my pullover sweater. It was warm again today. Not as warm as Tuesday before the rainstorm, but still warm for autumn.

"Indian summer seems to have settled in," I said to Diane as I joined her on the sidewalk.

She looked up at the blue sky. "Yes, and Richard seems to have been massacred by one of the local savages."

That observation was bitter enough to leave me silent. I followed Richard's widow into the restaurant.

After the hostess had seated us, a waiter came. Diane ordered a bourbon on the rocks and knocked it back while I was still sipping my club soda. She asked for another drink when the waiter came to take our lunch order.

We both ordered one of the lunch specials, linguine with shrimp. But I stuck with club soda. I have no head for alcohol, and the way things were going, I might have to drive Diane's Mercedes back to campus.

"Diane," I said, when the silence between us had stretched too long for my frayed nerves. "Is there some special reason why you wanted to have lunch?"

"Yes, there is." She took another long swallow of her drink. "You were with my husband just before he was murdered—"

"It was raining. He asked me to give him a ride to—"

"Were you and Richard lovers?"

It took me a moment to find my voice. "No, I—" I shook my head. "No, Diane, your husband and I were not lovers."

She drained her glass. "Then it was someone else."

"Why . . . what makes you think he was having an affair?"

"Richard liked sex. We hadn't made love in months."

"Oh."

Diane held up her glass as a waiter passed. "Another drink, please."
"Yes, ma'am."
"I thought it was Clovis," she said as the waiter left. "I believe you know Clovis. I think she said she'd met you when she was screaming at me yesterday."
Why had Clovis mentioned meeting me?
Then I actually heard the rest of what Diane had said. "When she was screaming at you? Clovis came to see you?"
"Clovis—my husband's high school sweetheart—arrived on my doorstep yesterday morning. She introduced herself and accused me of killing my husband because he was about to leave me."
So that was where Clovis had gone when she had torn out of her driveway in her truck. She had gone to confront Diane.
"Did Clovis say she and Richard weren't having an affair?" I asked.
Diane shook her head, making her sleek blonde bob sway against her chin. "That was the point." She took another sip of her drink.
"What was the point?" I said.
"Clovis didn't have him either. She thought he was going to leave me, and then he would turn to her. But in the meantime, she didn't have him either. So there must have been someone else."
"Are you sure about that?" I said. "Richard seemed depressed to me. Maybe he wasn't involved with anyone else, maybe he was too depressed to be interested in . . . romance."
Diane said, "And who knows? Maybe I'll find it easier to have been widowed than to have been divorced."
"You think Richard planned to divorce you?"
"Why would he have stayed married to someone he hated?" Diane rattled the ice cubes in her glass. "No, that's not true. He was indifferent to me. Indifference is worse, you know. There's nothing left when someone's indifferent."
"Diane, maybe Richard—"
"I did try to get his attention. Tit for tat. He was having other women. So I had another man."
I didn't want to hear this. But, at the same time, there was a certain morbid fascination in being the confidante of the murdered man's widow. "You had an affair?" I asked.
"I wanted to make him jealous," Diane said.
"With Scott Novak?"
"Scott has a crush on me."
"Yes, I gathered that Tuesday night at the party."
"Your drink, ma'am." Mario, our waiter, had appeared at Diane's side. "Ladies, your linguine with shrimp should be ready in about five minutes. Sorry for the delay, but our chef is preparing it fresh."
"Don't worry about it," Diane said and raised her glass.
Mario left. The animated conversation at the next table continued.

One of the women, who was relating a story to the other, made a sweeping gesture and they both laughed. Between the other conversations and the aria being piped through the sound system, it was impossible to hear the details of what the women were discussing.

Which meant it was unlikely they had heard Diane and me discussing Diane's dead husband and the sorry state of their marriage.

"Diane, about Scott. You said he has a crush on you. Is it possible that he— Could he have killed Richard?"

She threw back her head and laughed.

The two women at the next table gave her a questioning look.

"Scott? He couldn't even get it up."

And that was really a lot more than I wanted to know.

"I don't think the two things—" I took a swallow of my club soda. "Then you and Scott— You had been together?"

Diane focused an owlish glance on my face. "Just once. One trip to a motel. But I made sure Richard would find out."

"What did Richard do when he found out?"

"I told you. He didn't care. He said if I was going to have an affair, I could do better than Scott."

"But maybe Scott took that one time much more seriously than either you or Richard did. Especially if he . . . if it didn't go as he would have liked."

Diane smiled. "Trust me. Scott couldn't kill anyone. I'm a shrink. I should know." Diane's smile faded. "Except I didn't know what to do about my marriage, did I?"

"But don't you think Richard's depression over his son's death—"

"His suicide," Diane said.

"Richard said it was an overdose."

"An intentional overdose," Diane said. She pushed at the ice cubes in her glass with a manicured fingertip. "Kevin killed himself. Believe it or not, Richard blamed himself for that. Not me. Not Delores. Himself."

"Delores? Richard's first wife?"

"Delectable Delores. That's what he used to call her. I saw it on the back of a photograph. One of the photographs of the two of them that he'd saved." Diane smiled. "But he didn't trust her any more than he trusted me. He thought she married him because he was a black man with prospects. He thought I married him because he was my one act of defiance in my otherwise conforming life."

"Why did Richard blame himself for his son's death?"

Diane shrugged. "Because he divorced Delores when Kevin was nine. Because he wasn't there like a good daddy when Kevin was growing up."

"Did Richard know Kevin had a drug problem?"

Mario arrived with a flourish. "Here you are, ladies." He transferred the steaming plates from his tray to the table. "Would you like a little

Parmesan cheese?"

"No, we're fine," I said.

"Then enjoy, and I'll check back later to see if you need anything."

Diane twirled linguine between fork and spoon. She did not carry the food to her mouth.

"Diane, did Richard know Kevin was on drugs?"

"No, not until Kevin graduated from high school. Richard went back to Baltimore for the commencement. That was when he found out."

"What did he do when he—"

De Angelo and Williams were standing by the door. De Angelo said something to Williams, who looked across the room at our table. De Anglo smiled at me and lifted his hand in acknowledgment.

I didn't wave back.

"What?" Diane said and started to turn her head.

"Nothing," I said as De Angelo and Williams were shown into the adjoining room by the hostess. "What did Richard do about Kevin?"

"About Kevin? Richard got him into a rehab program."

"But it didn't work?"

"It worked about as long as it took Kevin to get back home with his mother. Then he shot himself up with heroin and died."

"Were they sure it was suicide? Couldn't it have been an accident? An overdose?"

Diane did not reply immediately. Instead she gave the linguine on her fork another twirl.

I took a bite of my own food. It was good. Too bad neither one of us was doing it justice.

"He left a note," Diane said.

"A suicide note?"

"An apology for killing himself. 'Sorry, Pops. I tried. I really did. But I couldn't do it. Love, Kevin.'" Diane put down her fork. "Richard found it when he went back to Baltimore."

"When he went back?"

"We had an argument a few months ago. He jumped into his car and drove to Baltimore to see his ex-wife. That was when he found the note. He picked up one of Kevin's books, and there it was, tucked between the pages."

"If it was a suicide note, wouldn't Kevin have left it out where his parents would be sure to see it?"

"You're assuming someone who is about to commit suicide is rational," Diane said.

"Yes, I suppose I am."

"Richard said they would have found the note if Delores hadn't insisted on leaving Kevin's room exactly as it was. If she'd packed up his things, the book was right there on his night table."

"What was the book?" I asked.

"A book Richard had given him," Diane said. *"The Souls of Black Folk."*

W. E. B. Du Bois essays.

"Did the book have some special meaning for Richard?"

Diane shook her head. "He liked to send Kevin books and reading lists. What he refused to acknowledge was that Kevin lacked both his brains and his ambition."

"You think Richard put too much pressure on Kevin?"

"I think," Diane said, pushing away her plate, "Richard put too much pressure on everyone, including himself. I think Richard make it his personal mission in life to make us all—Delores, Clovis, Kevin, and me—and himself, of course—crazy. That's what I think." She reached for her clutch bag. "Let's get the hell out of here."

I signaled to Mario as he passed.

"Yes? What can I get for you?"

"The check, please."

He looked at our plates. "Is there a problem with your lunches?"

"The problem," Diane said, "is that my damn husband was murdered."

Mario's mouth fell open with an unrehearsed lack of grace. He quickly closed it.

"The check, please," I said and handed him my credit card.

"No, Lizzie," Diane said. "It's my treat. I can afford it. Richard left me a wealthy widow. Richard knew how to invest."

"You can get it next time," I said. "We need to get going."

Mario made it back with the check in record time. He eyed Diane with a certain fascination as I signed the receipt. I had the feeling he had figured out who she was. The woman whose husband had been murdered on campus.

As we were walking toward the exit, I prayed that Diane would not stumble and that De Angelo and Williams would not pop out of the other dining room to intercept us. I'd had enough for one lunch hour.

The Mercedes was where we had left it. No marked police cars were in sight. Was it coincidence that De Angelo and Williams had been there? The Olive Tree was convenient and close to campus. They might have been hungry.

Or they might have been following Diane and me. Had Quinn given his okay to keep the suspects under surveillance?

"Thanks for having lunch with me, Lizzie," Diane said. She was fumbling for her car key.

"We'll have to do it again sometime," I said. "Why don't you let me drive?"

Diane blinked at me. "Why? Do you think I'm drunk?"

"No. But I think you've had enough to be DUI if we happen to be stopped. Let me drive, okay?"

"Okay." Diane dropped her keys into my hand. "I wouldn't want to get you killed too."

When we were both inside, doors closed, I said. "What did you mean, you wouldn't want to get me killed too?"

"Richard." Diane looked at me. "I shouldn't have left him there at the party. I should have stayed and driven him to his car. And then he wouldn't have gotten killed. I was his wife. I was supposed to take care of him."

"Diane, whoever killed Richard— There was no way you could have protected him."

She scrunched down in the cream leather seat. "I was a bad wife, Lizzie."

I turned the key in the ignition and gave thanks that I had learned to drive in my grandfather's old Ford with the stick shift. The last thing I needed to do was strip Diane's expensive transmission. "I'm going to take you home. But you have to stay awake and give me directions."

"I'm awake. Wide awake. Too awake."

I edged the Mercedes into the flow of traffic. Then I glanced over at Diane, who had her eyes closed and who looked beautiful and tired and vulnerable. And like a world-class actress?

"Diane, wake up. I need your address."

She mumbled something.

"Diane." I shoved at her shoulder. "Wake up."

Chapter 23

I WAS MAKING ANOTHER TURN, trying to follow Diane's semi-coherent directions, when I saw the car again. It was a white sedan, and I had been catching glimpses of it in my rearview mirror since we left the restaurant.

Who was in the driver's seat? A man or a woman? It looked like a man.

"Diane? Diane, what color is Scott's car?"

"White," she said and turned sideways in her seat, curling up.

I made another turn. This one unnecessary and unexpected. The driver of the sedan was caught off guard and drove past.

But a few minutes later, as I circled back to where I wanted to be, I saw the car again. He must know the way to Diane's house. I should offer to follow him.

"Diane?"

"Huh?"

"Where did you and Scott go when you left the party Tuesday night?"

"Coffee shop," she said.

"How long did you stay?"

She didn't reply.

"Diane, how long did you stay at the coffee shop?"

"Cup of coffee, then I left. Went home to wait for Richard. But he didn't come." She began to sob. Hiccuping little sobs. If she was acting, she really was world-class.

I blew the horn when I pulled into Diane's driveway. If Scott was on our tail, I wanted a witness in case he showed up at the door before I could deposit Diane in her bed and get out of there. I continued to blow on the horn until one of Diane's neighbors came to her door. Then I got out of the car and called to her that I needed help.

The neighbor, tan and slender, with the look of someone who went on expensive vacations with a businessman husband, came over and peered into the car. She shook her head. Then she reached out and grasped Diane's other arm and helped me haul her from the passenger seat of the Mercedes. Together we got Diane up the walk to her door. I found the house key in Diane's purse while her neighbor propped her up.

When we had gotten her inside and into the master bedroom, I tugged down the linen sheets, and the neighbor and I poured Diane into the king-size bed that she might or might not still have been sharing with her husband. I wanted to linger and look around, but the neighbor was leading the way back into the living room. She introduced herself as Lenore Shannon. I gave her my name and explained my connection to Richard.

"Such a tragedy," Lenore said. She picked up a section of newspaper from the low coffee table and folded it and reached down to scoop up an overturned wine glass that would have stained the Oriental rug if it hadn't been empty. "I feel so awful about what's happened. They were such a lovely couple."

"Yes," I said, but my glance had been captured by what looked like mail piled on the kitchen counter.

"I'll stay here with her until she wakes up," Lenore said. "She shouldn't have tried to go into her office today."

"No," I said. I glanced at the kitchen counter once more. "Actually, I do need to call a taxi," I said. "I don't have my car."

I went over to the telephone on the wall above the counter. Lenore went back to her tidying. She started to pick up the rose petals that had fallen from their crystal vase onto the glossy lacquer of the piano, which stood by the French doors in the living room.

Half turning to shield my movements, I nudged the unopened mail toward me.

Bills. Credit card bill for Richard. Department store for Diane. Cable. A dentist's office.

A solicitation letter from an environmental group addressed to Richard.

And another envelope for Richard, this one hand-addressed. I glanced over my shoulder at Diane's neighbor. She was emptying an ashtray into a wastebasket.

The envelope had a return address. D. Colby in Baltimore. D as in Delores? Had Delores Colby written to her ex-husband?

The envelope had not been opened. Diane had probably brought it in with the rest of that morning's mail and dropped it there on the counter. Maybe she hadn't even noticed it. Probably hadn't, or she would have wanted to know what was inside. Delores seemed not to be one of her favorite people.

It was all I could do not to slip that envelope off the counter and into my shoulder bag. But I resisted temptation and replaced the telephone receiver as the recorded message asked me to "hang up and dial again."

I reached for the telephone book and flipped to the yellow pages.

"The taxi should be here in about twenty minutes," I told Lenore when I hung up the telephone for the second time.

"Why don't I make us a pot of tea while you're waiting?" she said as she came into the kitchen. "I'm sure Diane wouldn't mind."

She made the tea and we talked—nothing useful. Nothing I hadn't known before about Richard and Diane. The only other thing I learned from Lenore was that Richard was a good neighbor. When her husband was out of town on business, she could always call Richard to come over if something went wrong with anything about the house.

I had the feeling that was one of the reasons Lenore considered Richard's death a tragedy. But perhaps I wasn't being fair to her.

When the taxi driver blew his horn, I said my good-bye and headed to the door. Lenore followed behind me—a good hostess in her neighbor's stead. I thanked her for her help and left her there on the doorstep of that beautifully decorated house.

I asked the taxi driver to take me back to campus. Then I took out my note pad and scribbled down Delores Colby's address in Baltimore before I could forget it.

I glanced back behind us several times, but no white sedan. Maybe it hadn't been Scott after all. Or maybe he had stayed behind at Diane's house. Her would-be knight-errant, there to protect her as she slept off her liquid lunch.

As soon as I got back to my office, I called information for Delores Colby's telephone number in Baltimore. But Delores was either out or not answering her telephone. When her answering machine came on, a female voice with a hint of a lilting Caribbean accent informed me that I had reached "Delores's Delectables—Down Home Catering for Every Occasion." Was that why Richard had called her Delectable Delores? Because of her cooking? From what I was learning about Richard, I doubted it.

I waited for the sound of the beep and left a message identifying myself and asking her to please return my call. I said it was urgent that I speak to her. I left both numbers. I invited her to call me collect at my home telephone number that evening or in the morning.

All right. Next I'd try Richard's friend at Emory. What was his name? Ted something. I went to the university Web page and then to the political science department. There he was. Ted James—that was the name. I considered sending him an E-mail, and then decided it would be better to call. I printed out his Web page so that I would have both telephone number and E-mail address on hand. Then I called his office number. And had no more luck than I'd had with Delores Colby. I left another message including my office and home telephone numbers.

And then I considered my options. I could sit there and wait patiently for Delores Colby and/or Ted James to get back to me. But if I tried to do that, I would probably end up pacing liked a caged animal. And then I'd start to scream and throw things like Clovis had, alone in her grandmother's house. And then someone would call the men in white coats, and they would come and take me away to the loony bin.

My problem was that sheet of paper in my briefcase. That message which had been left in my mailbox. Someone had seen Richard kiss me as we sat in my car. Someone was confident I had not told the police about that kiss. And if I hadn't told the police about the kiss, then it would be difficult to tell them about the poison-pen letter I had received referring to it.

Gotcha, Lizzie! Now what are you going to do?

I was standing there in the middle of my office. What I needed to do was to get out of my office and go do something until I could think of what to do about the letter. As Mrs. Cavendish had said, sometimes it was better not to think about a problem and hope the solution would come while you were doing something else.

Of course, I knew what the solution was. I should fess up to De Angelo about that kiss.

If I didn't, I would be at the mercy of my letter writer. At the mercy of the person who had probably killed Richard. Which did I care about more? My reputation or my life?

But there was another side of this, wasn't there? If I told De Angelo about the kiss, I also gave myself a motive for killing Richard. The scorned woman. A fatal attraction.

There was always the possibility that De Angelo might believe me. But as Quinn had said, De Angelo wasn't the kind of cop with whom one played games. He would undoubtedly consider the information I had withheld from him the equivalent of a lie.

I caught myself in mid-pace. All right. Get out of this office and hope Scott wasn't lurking around out there somewhere. But he was probably interested in Diane, not me. Unless he was the one who had killed Richard. But even if he had, why would he be after me? If I knew who the killer was, I would have told the police by now.

I sat down at my desk and found the number I needed in the telephone book.

If Clovis was at home, she was not answering her telephone. I hung up and called the café. The young woman who answered said that neither Clovis nor her grandmother was there. But Miss Alice would be in later. I called the house again and waited for the answering machine. I left a message asking Clovis to call me.

I would talk to De Angelo later, after I had talked to Clovis.

In the meantime, get up and go do something useful.

I went back to the public library. The last time I was there, I had spent over an hour with great-aunt Sophie's scrapbook, donated by her nephew. I had started to look again at the *Gazette*'s coverage of events in Gallagher in 1921 to see what else I could find about the Caulders.

This time I managed to claim a microfilm machine as the kid using it stacked up his books and walked away. I spent the next four hours going through the *Gazette*. The problem was that old newspapers lacked organization. There was no designated section of the paper where you could always expect to find society notes or crime stories or even editorials and obituaries. So to find what you were looking for, you often had to go through a daily newspaper page by page.

But what I found made my eyestrain worth the effort. From one of the copied articles that I'd had in my folder, I'd already learned that Jonathan Caulder had served as a pallbearer at the funeral for Daniel Stevens. Now, going through the newspaper again, I was finding records of a number of appearances by Attorney Jonathan Caulder in the police and corporation courts. His clients included both blacks and whites, and ranged from speeding drivers to the proprietors of illegal gambling houses. Obviously, Jonathan Caulder had either preferred to practice criminal law or, as a transplant to Gallagher, had found that he couldn't compete with more established attorneys for corporate and estate clients. At any rate, in early August he had been preparing to defend a man who had shot his business partner following an altercation in the tobacco warehouse they owned.

And in spite of his busy law practice, Jonathan Caulder seemed to have been as involved as his sister, Laura, in the city's social whirl. The Caulders were everywhere. Especially Laura. Laura had hosted a skating party. Laura had attended a gala with the visiting male cousin of another young woman. Laura had gone to Charleston, South Carolina, during the summer on a visit to friends.

What I still didn't know was whether or not Daniel Stevens had been in love with Laura Caulder. If he had been, did Laura, the social butterfly, return his affection? And how had Laura's brother felt about a match between his friend and his sister?

Only three of the questions I still needed to answer.

Later that evening, as I stood by my kitchen sink doing stretches, I thought some more about what else I needed to find out. As usual, after a session in front of a microfilm machine, the muscles in my back and neck were knotted.

When I had stretched away the worst of the ache (what I wouldn't give to have an expert neck massager on call) I picked up the kettle and filled it. A cup of hot chocolate and then a shower. That would make me feel better.

I was emptying a packet of hot chocolate into my mug when the telephone rang. Had De Angelo picked up my thought waves? Or maybe it was Clovis finally getting back to me. I had calls out to Ted

James and Delores Colby too.

"Hello," I said.

The kettle on the stove started to whistle. But the music on the other side of the line was much more insistent in its demand for my attention. The theme music from the movie *Halloween.* The music our Halloween prankster had played on Pete's voice mail. I listened and then I replaced the receiver.

The kettle was still whistling. I snatched it from the burner and poured the water out in the sink.

I made sure the front and back doors were locked, and then I went through the house checking all the windows. When that was done, I went into my bedroom and locked the door and propped the chair underneath the knob as I had the night before.

Chapter 24

FRIDAY, NOVEMBER 3

"This is Delores Colby," the woman on the telephone said with the islands lilt I'd heard on her answering machine. "I'm returning a call from Professor Lizabeth Stuart."

"Oh, Mrs. Colby, thank you so much for getting back to me." I nudged out a chair at the kitchen table and sat down. I was still half asleep.

"What was it you wanted?" she said. "You mentioned Richard. Is this about his funeral arrangements? Because if it is, I'm not coming."

"No, it isn't about the funeral arrangements. Richard and I taught in the same school."

"And why are you calling me?"

My carefully rehearsed speech had disappeared from my brain during the night. "I— Because I think my life may be in danger. I think the same person who killed Richard may have turned his or her attention to me."

"Then I suggest you call the police, Professor Stuart."

"Wait, Mrs. Colby, if you could tell me—do you know if Richard had enemies?"

"Other than me?"

"But you— Was your relationship that bad? He came to see you, and you wrote to him recently."

"How do you know that?"

"Diane told me that Richard drove to Baltimore to see you a few months ago. And yesterday when I was at their house, I happened to see an envelope addressed to Richard with your name and address."

"I was sending back his check."

"What check?"

"The check," Delores said, "that Richard sent me as his contribution to the fellowship I established in my son's name."

"He—" I tried to find the right question. "You didn't want him to contribute?"

"If it wasn't for him, our son wouldn't be dead. Why would I want Richard's money?"

"Could I ask why you blame Richard for your son's death?" I said, anticipating the receiver banging down in my ear. "I thought your son died of a drug overdose."

"An overdose that he took because of his father. Richard never let up on him. He couldn't bother to be here to raise him, but he thought that support check he sent every month gave him the right to tell Kevin where he was going to college and what he was going to study. He gave him that car that he almost killed himself in."

"What car?"

"A Mustang. A vintage, red Mustang. Richard always wanted one himself, so he gave one to Kevin the week before he graduated from high school. And the night of his graduation, Kevin went out with his friends and got high and almost killed himself driving home."

"He had an accident?"

"Smashed in the side of his car on a streetlight. And came running into my house all bloody and wild-eyed. And Richard telling me there was nothing to get upset about."

"Richard was at your house when—"

"More fool me. I was sitting there listening to that bastard sweet-talk as if I didn't know his lies. If Kevin hadn't come running in—" Delores paused. "That was the night that Richard decided his son was going to go to a drug rehab program. He shipped him off the next day. To a private clinic. It cost a fortune. And little good it did." Her voice cracked on her final words.

"Mrs. Colby—"

"I don't know why I'm standing here on this telephone talking to you. It's none of your business."

"But, please, I just want to know if—"

"Go ask Diane what you want to know. I'm the ex-wife."

This time the telephone receiver did bang down in my ear.

Well, the day was getting off to a flying start. And there was still Richard's memorial service scheduled for the afternoon.

I got to campus at a little after ten. The memorial service was scheduled for two.

In my office, I sat down at my desk and checked my voice-mail messages. One message.

The caller was a man—young and very serious. "I want to let you know you have the full support of SAR," he said.

What on earth was SAR? And why were they supporting me? Why did I need support?

"We've received an anonymous tip that the police have been harassing you about Professor Colby's murder," the caller said. "As students of color, we stand united with you against police racism. Please call me, Professor Stuart, and let us meet with you to discuss strategy in anticipation of their next move. We are here for you." He left his name—Ralph Martin—and his campus telephone number.

Good grief. Did he know something I didn't know? Was I about to be arrested and taken off to jail?

My hand hovered over the telephone as I thought of calling Quinn. Bad idea. If De Angelo showed up with an arrest warrant, I would call a lawyer. In the meantime, I would probably also do well not to return Ralph Martin's call. He sounded as if he were ready to call out his troops for a sixties-style protest in my name. That I did not need.

It was comforting to know that students still had enough passion left to get worked up about perceived injustice. But I'd just as soon not be their reason for marching.

On the other hand, if I didn't call, would Ralph Martin think I was being prevented from doing so by the police and/or the administration? Maybe I should call back and explain to him that right now everything seemed to be under control and. . . .

No, better to leave it alone.

I found the printout with Ted James's office number and tried calling him again. He was still not in his office. I left another message.

Maybe he was on his way here. Richard had said they were old friends, college buddies. Had Diane thought to call Ted and tell him about Richard's murder?

If she hadn't, I really didn't want to be the one to break the news.

I switched on my computer to check my E-mail. There was a campus-wide security memo from Quinn's office with a reminder about the blue emergency phones located strategically across campus in buildings and parking lots. The "Don't Walk Alone" program had been supplemented with additional escorts who would be available at the library and on-call. University police officers had increased their coverage of parking areas and other locations on campus. Those needing additional information should call the number provided.

I deleted that message and read through the several I had from grad students in my historical research methods seminar about the research proposals they were doing. I replied to each and then to an undergrad who wanted to know—and he was just getting around to contacting me—if he could make up the midterm he had missed. He had taken cold medication that made him sleep, and his roommate had turned off the alarm clock.

There was also a brief message from the African-American Studies professor I'd met. "Call if I can help." That was nice of her. I typed back "thank you."

Then I clicked onto Netscape. Delores Colby lived in Baltimore. Did she have a Web page for Delores's Delectables? She did. It came complete with price list and comments from satisfied customers.

I typed in Kevin Colby. And came up with nothing useful. It had been a long shot. All right, I could trek back to the library and have a look at the Baltimore newspapers on microfilm. Except I didn't know the year Kevin had graduated. Richard said he had died four years ago. So assume graduation in June of that year.

I jumped as my office door was flung open.

Pete Murphy filled the doorway. "What is this? What the hell does this mean?" He waved a piece of paper at me.

I took a deep breath. "If you'll show me what it is, maybe I can answer your question, Pete."

I got to my feet. He was a big man and he was angry, and I, at least, wanted to be standing for this conversation.

"This," he said as he shoved the white, letter-size sheet of paper toward me. I looked up at him and then down at it. A one-line message, in caps, was typed in the center of the page: I KNOW WHAT YOU DID ON TUESDAY NIGHT. It was signed LIZZIE.

"Pete, you don't really think I wrote this. Why would I do that?"

"You tell me why."

"I didn't write it, Pete. I don't know anything about it." I looked down at the page. "When did you receive this?"

"I found it in my mailbox when I came in a few minutes ago."

"So anyone could have left it there," I said. "It wasn't me."

He let out his breath. "Okay, maybe I overreacted."

"A little," I said.

And what had he done on Tuesday night that he didn't want anyone to know about? Was the message intended to imply that he was the killer? That Pete had killed Richard? A note like that, signed with my name. . . . What had the sender expected Pete to do?

"I think you should show this to De Angelo," I said.

Pete tugged at his beard. "Do you? It's got your name on it."

"I know that. But I didn't send it."

He folded the sheet of paper. "I'll mention it to him the next time I see him."

"Pete—"

"I'm going to go have some lunch before the memorial service." He left as abruptly as he had arrived.

I locked my office door. It seemed my poison-pen pal had just upped the ante. Now I not only had to worry about him or her, but about the people he or she made angry enough to punch my face in.

The university chapel stood at the north end of the drill field where cadets had once marched. Now that expanse of grass—the campus green—was crisscrossed by cement walks connecting one side of the campus with the other. On fine days the drill field attracted sunbathers and Frisbee players. But today most of the student body seemed to have opted for alternative activities. Some of them were drifting into the chapel now in couples or in small groups. Whispering to each other as they found seats.

It was unlikely that most of them had known Richard Colby. Much more likely that they were drawn there by curiosity about his death. And by the sight of the campus police cars and a couple of Gallagher PD vehicles and three television mobile vans. Camera crews were taping outside the chapel from behind a rope barricade.

From where I sat in the back of the chapel, I watched Amos Baylor confer with President Sorenson and the Protestant chaplain, Reverend Todd. They were standing in front of an altar bedecked with bronze chrysanthemums, a flower that was appropriate for November and that always reminded me of death.

"I'm back." Joyce picked up my shoulder bag and dropped it into my lap. "Thanks for holding my seat."

She had gone up to speak to Diane, who was sitting in the front pew. Not knowing how Diane felt about our lunch together, I had decided not to risk upsetting her.

"Who are those people with Diane?" I asked Joyce. A short, barrel-chested man sat on Diane's left. She was flanked on her other side by a blonde woman.

"Her sister and brother-in-law," Joyce said.

But my attention had been caught by someone else. Inez Buchanan was making her way up the middle aisle. She stopped at a pew near the front and waited for the people already occupying it to slide over a bit more to make room for her. Inez was wearing a black suit today.

But on Tuesday night she had worn a gypsy fortune-teller's costume to the murder mystery party. A costume with a belt of gold coins that matched the one I had found in my car. Somehow, Richard must have come by one of Inez's coins. That was the only way it could have gotten into my locked car.

"Did they misspell somebody's name?" Joyce said.

"What?"

"The program." Joyce flipped open her own. "What's wrong with it?"

And I realized that I had been scowling down at the one in my hand. "Nothing's wrong with it. I was wondering why they don't get started."

I was wondering how I could have forgotten about Inez's gypsy costume.

A few minutes later, Reverend Todd rose and moved to the podium. In the middle of his invocation, the chapel doors—heavy and Gothic in design—opened, admitting a shaft of sunlight. De Angelo and Williams stepped inside.

Amos Baylor followed Reverend Todd to the podium. He spoke of Richard as "gentleman, scholar, friend, husband, inspiration." After Amos came President Sorenson, a tall blond Viking with political aspirations. He spoke of the "tragedy" that had struck our campus but would bring us together.

In the front pew, Diane's head—in a wide-brimmed black hat—was held high. No weeping. No hysterics.

Reverend Todd rose again as President Sorenson returned to his seat. "Richard Colby loved African-American spirituals," he said. "His wife, Diane, has asked that the choir perform a medley of his favorites. As we listen, we know that Richard is here with us in spirit, a part of this beautiful music."

There was a moment of silence followed by a note from the organ. The members of the university choir, clad in green and gold robes, came to their feet.

It was "Swing Low, Sweet Chariot" that moved Joyce to tears. In her pew near the front, Inez Buchanan was also sobbing. She had a lace handkerchief pressed to her eyes.

After we'd run to my car in the rain, Richard had taken a handkerchief from his pocket to wipe his wet face. If Inez's coin had been in his pocket. . . .

Someone was staring at me. I could feel the force of that stare. I turned to look behind me. De Angelo nodded his head and smiled at me.

Wonderful. Smack in the middle between the devil and the deep blue sea.

When the service ended, De Angelo and Williams were the first back out the door. Most of the mourners followed, looking subdued. But Joyce had gone up front again. She was speaking to Amos about the gathering at his house that night. Not really a wake, Amos had said in his E-mail. Simply an opportunity for the people in the school to come together and remember Richard. Our own private memorial service.

Inez had gone over to speak to Diane. I wanted to speak to Inez.

"Coming, Lizzie?" Amos asked as he and Joyce came up the aisle.

"In a moment," I said. "I want to light a candle."

President Sorenson and Reverend Todd were escorting Diane toward the door. Her head was bent, as if she had wilted after her brave performance during the service. Or was she preparing for another performance outside for the cameras?

I waited until they had passed, and then I stepped out into the aisle. Inez did not turn as I approached her. Her head was bowed as she stood in front of the altar by the candle she had lit.

"Inez?"

Her head snapped up, her blue eyes skidded over me.

"Lizzie Stuart," I said. "We met on Halloween night at the murder mystery party."

"Oh, yes. How are you?"

I held out the gold coin I had taken from my shoulder bag. "I believe this belongs to you."

She frowned. "It looks like a coin from my costume."

"It is," I said. "Richard Colby dropped it in my car when I gave him a ride to Brewster Hall. What I can't quite figure out is how he came to have it."

Inez drew back as if I had slapped her. She darted a glance toward the open chapel doors.

The fact that those doors were open and that people—including police officers—were within screaming distance was the only reason I had dared to confront her like this.

"How did Richard get your coin, Inez?"

She stared at me. "Do you think I killed him? Is that what you think?"

"I don't know what to think," I said. "I'm waiting for you to explain."

"And if I don't choose to explain?"

"Then I'll give this to Detective De Angelo and let him ask the questions."

Inez went over to the front pew Diane had been occupying and sat down. I went over and sat down beside her. She didn't look dangerous. She looked tired and alone.

"I made a fool of myself," she said. "Nothing new for me. But this time I thought—Pete Murphy always seemed to be such a nice guy—I thought the worst I would get was a "no, thanks." She dabbed at her nose with her crumpled handkerchief. "Instead, he told me in elaborate detail exactly why he wasn't interested."

"Maybe you caught him at a bad moment," I said. "I did warn you that he was busy when you said you were going to talk to him."

"It wasn't then. It was later when I saw him leaving," Inez said. "I asked if he'd like some company. That was when he let me have it with both barrels right in my ego. I ran off and found a rehearsal room downstairs to hide in while I licked my wounds."

"Where does Richard come into this?" I said.

Her blue gaze flickered in my direction and away. "He heard me licking my wounds rather loudly. Bawling my head off, in fact, and—" Inez lowered her face into her handkerchief. "And he was really nice. He came in and put his arms around me and held me while I cried." She lifted her head. "Of course, I felt like a fool afterwards, but Richard said sometimes he hated that grown men weren't supposed to cry. He'd be bawling his head off right alongside me."

"And then what?" I said.

"And then I pulled myself together, and he walked me out to the door. And we said good-night, and that was the last time I ever saw him." She nodded toward the gold coin in my hand. "I don't know when I lost that. He must have found it." She told her story as if it was the truth. If it wasn't, she was an excellent liar.

"Did you see anyone else around when you were leaving?" I asked.

She shook her head. "The place had pretty much cleared out. I could hear you all upstairs. The people who were cleaning up. But there was no one down in the lobby."

"No one except you and Richard," I said. "You're sure?"

"I didn't see anyone else," Inez said. She held her hand out. "May I have that back?"

I stood up. "If you don't mind, I'll hold onto it for now."

"I do mind," Inez said. "I want that back."

"Not yet," I said.

She ran after me and grabbed my arm. "You give that to me, you bitch!"

I shook her off and backed away. "Don't touch me like that. I'm going to give this to a friend for safekeeping."

Her eyes blazed at me, and I got myself out of there.

The sun was shining outside the chapel doors. There was a pleasant breeze.

And a barrage of reporters. Actually, it began with one, who asked if I was Professor Stuart. As he spoke, the others turned from President Sorenson toward me.

The first reporter stepped over the rope barricade and in front of me. A camerawoman was right behind him. "Professor Stuart, is it true that you were the last person to see Professor Colby alive?"

"No comment," I said. "Excuse me." I tried to step around him.

I saw two campus cops, who had been talking to students with signs, move toward us. Before they could get to me, another reporter moved into my path. "What was your relationship with Professor Colby?" she asked. "Why was he with you that night?"

"No comment," I said. "Please, let me by."

"You heard her! Let her by!" Two male students, muscular and African-American, were suddenly there, shoving at the reporters.

"Stop the harassment!" a young, apparently white, woman with blonde dreadlocks yelled. "Find Professor Colby's killer and stop harassing black faculty!"

The four or five campus cops who were running toward us found their way blocked by more students. One of the students waved his sign in a cop's face. The cop grabbed the sign and tossed it away. A cameraman trying to capture the melee for the 6:00 news took a shove that sent him and his camera flying. A circle of students, interested spectators, yelled and cheered. I could see Dean Baylor and Reverend Todd urging President Sorenson along a path two cops were clearing for him. Sorenson was resisting, trying to speak to the students.

I backed up against the chapel wall. I was about to retreat inside with Inez when a hand grabbed my arm. I turned, ready to strike out.

De Angelo grinned at me. "Now, you don't want to hit a cop, Professor. Come with me, please."

"Where?" I said.

"Away from here. Or would you rather stay and see how this mess turns out?"

I followed him, ducking through the bushes behind the chapel and running. A gray sedan was parked out on the street. Williams was sitting in the front passenger seat. I got in back as De Angelo slid behind the wheel.

I slumped back against the seat as he started the car. "Was that SAR?" I asked. "The students with the signs?"

"That was SAR," De Angelo said. "A brand-new group on campus formed on the occasion of Professor Colby's demise. Students Against Racism. Made up of members of the various and sundry multicultural and multiethnic organizations on our diverse campus."

"They obviously feel such a group is necessary," I said.

"Obviously." De Angelo glanced over his shoulder at me. "I gather you've been in communication with them."

"They left me a voice-mail message offering me their support," I said. "Where are we going?"

He glanced over at the silent Williams. "Now, where do you suggest we go, Detective Williams?"

She said, "We need to get away from the reporters. We could go downtown to my office."

"Now that's a grand plan," De Angelo said. "Thank you kindly for offering, Marcia, honey."

"You're completely welcome, Ron," Williams said through her teeth. If he hadn't yet gotten on her last nerve, he was obviously getting there.

"What are we going to do when we get to Detective Williams's office?" I asked from my place in the back of the car.

"Talk, Professor," De Angelo said. "It's time we had another talk."

Williams's office might best be described as functional. There was nothing of a personal nature, not even a photograph, on view. Unless one counted the plant that was wilting on the windowsill and the coffeemaker on the table beside a stack of files. She gestured me to a chair in front of her desk as she sat down behind it. De Angelo took the other chair.

He said, "What's been happening, Professor Stuart?"

"I should be asking you that," I said. "Have you made any progress in the investigation?"

"A bit," he said. "For example, we know the knife in Professor Colby's chest was stolen from the caterers who provided the food and beverages at the murder mystery party. We also know that you were probably telling the truth about someone being behind the door of Professor Colby's office."

I felt my heart flutter as the tension went out of me. "You— How do you know that?"

"The forensics guys say there was blood on the wall there as if someone with blood on his or her clothes had pressed against it. There was also a trace of blood on the doorknob." His brown gaze held mine. He was waiting to see what I would say.

"Of course, I could have stood behind the door," I said. "I could have been wearing a rain slicker or some other kind of covering and taken it off after I killed Richard."

De Angelo smiled. The smile that showed his dimple. "Now, I did suggest that. Problem is, we searched that whole building and we couldn't find a rain slicker or anything else you might have worn while you did the deed. You left your jacket right there in your office. No blood."

They had examined my jacket? Was that legal?

"And there was also the sunscreen lotion," Williams said from her chair behind her desk.

"The what?" I said, still back on the jacket question.

De Angelo answered. "It seems the killer must have used a tissue or a paper towel from a jacket pocket to hold the knife and the doorknob. This piece of paper had traces of sunscreen lotion on it."

I had two choices at that moment. I could have kept my mouth shut. I didn't. "I use sunscreen lotion," I said. "Black people do use sunscreen."

De Angelo said, "Exactly what I pointed out to my colleagues. I told them they were being downright racist to assume that people with darker skin didn't need to protect their hides from the sun just like the rest of us." He paused, watching me. "But then again, it could be that you were telling us the truth."

"That's entirely possible," I said.

"And that's a real shame, because I was hoping to get this wrapped up quick so I could get back to hanging out in donut shops."

"Sorry," I said. Relief was flooding through me so strongly I could barely speak.

"Don't worry about it," De Angelo said. He took a pack of gum from his pocket. "I might still find something to charge you with."

Williams stood up. "Would you like some coffee, Professor?" she asked.

"No, thank you," I said. "I don't drink coffee. What did you mean about finding something else to charge me with, Detective De Angelo?"

"How about obstruction of a police investigation?" he said. He shoved a stick of gum into his mouth. "I hear you been lying to us. In fact, I had an anonymous letter saying I ought to ask you about your relationship with Richard Colby. Is there something you haven't told us about that, Professor?"

"Do you believe anonymous letters?" I said. "It could have come from the killer."

"Now, that did occur me. In fact, I said that to Detective Williams, didn't I, Marcia, honey?" He shot a glance at Williams, who was pouring coffee into a Gallagher PD mug. "But you see, Professor, I'm thinking there must be something else we don't know about. Or else why would our letter writer have gone to all that trouble?"

"To misdirect your attention," I said. "To send you off on a wild-goose chase. Professor Colby and I had no relationship."

De Angelo smiled. "So you and him never did the nasty, huh?"

"No, we didn't," I said. "We did not have an intimate relationship." I cleared my throat. "But he— That night when we were sitting in my car, he did kiss me."

"Now, is that a fact? Did you forget to mention that before?"

"No," I said. "I didn't think it was important before."

"Why don't you tell us about it," De Angelo said. He slumped deeper in his chair, steepling his fingers under his chin.

I told them about the kiss from Richard. "So you see, it really was nothing. Professor Colby was depressed, maybe a little drunk. He apologized, and we both agreed to forget about it."

"Did you? Just forget it, huh?"

"Yes," I said. "And we would have if he hadn't been killed. I'm telling you about it now because I received a letter too."

"And what did your letter say?" De Angelo asked.

I opened my shoulder bag and took out the folded sheet of paper. I passed it over to him and said, "I found that in my mailbox yesterday morning."

De Angelo read it and passed it across the desk to Williams, who was sipping her coffee.

"It didn't occur to you to call us about this?" De Angelo said.

"It did," I said. "But I was afraid of what you would think. There was also another letter." I told them about the one Pete Murphy had received.

And I still had Inez Buchanan's gold coin.

"Is there anything else you haven't told us, Professor?" The question came from Williams, not De Angelo. Her blue eyes were as shrewd as his brown ones.

I looked away. There was no reason I should protect Inez. What if she had been attracted to Richard when he comforted her? What if she had followed us back to Brewster Hall? What if the woman was crazy?

I opened my shoulder bag again and fished out the gold coin from the side pocket. I held it out to De Angelo. "Richard dropped this in my car," I said. "It's from the belt of a costume."

"Any idea whose?" De Angelo asked.

"Inez Buchanan. She works in the vice president's office."

De Angelo smiled, his shark's smile. "Now, thank you, Professor. You're being real cooperative today. Anything else you care to share with us?"

"I've been getting telephone calls." I described the calls.

"Music?" De Angelo said when I was done. "Didn't I hear that before? Something about one of the other professors getting a musical call on Halloween."

"Pete Murphy," I said.

De Angelo said, "It was also Professor Murphy who received that letter about you knowing what he did on Tuesday night. What do you make of that, Professor Stuart?"

"I have no idea," I said.

"Me either," De Angelo said. "I'll have to think about it for a while. Anything else?"

I shook my head.

He stood up and stretched. "You have anything else, Detective Williams?"

"Not at the moment," she said.

"Then let's get you on back to campus, Professor Stuart," De Angelo said to me. "That little riot you accidentally started should be over by now. We'll drop you off at your car, and you can go on home. That sound okay to you?"

"Yes," I said.

"Good." He opened the door and gestured for me to precede him. "We'll get you back safe and sound, and then I'll go check in with Chief Quinn. By the way, Professor Stuart, does the chief know about Professor Colby kissing you? Or is that going to be news to him?"

I could have taken that smile right off his face. My grandfather had been a boxing fan. He had taught me how to throw a punch. But if I had hit De Angelo, it would have been another point in his column.

I told myself that as I walked by him and out into the hall.

Behind me, I heard Williams say, "You really work hard at being a bastard, don't you, Ron?"

De Angelo laughed. "Now, Marcia, honey, I was just asking so I'd know if I should be ready to duck."

We drove back to campus in silence. The two of them in front. Me in back. When we turned into the Brewster Hall parking lot, De Angelo asked which car was mine. I told him. He pulled up behind it. "You take care, now, Professor. Don't be talking to strangers. And you better watch your back with the people you know too."

Marcia Williams was right. He was a bastard. And a few other words I could think of.

And Quinn had the nerve to tell me De Angelo was a good detective. That De Angelo knew his job.

Did his job description include being a pitiful excuse for a human being? Or did Quinn use different criteria? Cop criteria? White male criteria?

Why did that surprise me? He was all of those things—cop, white, male.

So why should I care about what he might think when De Angelo told him that Richard had kissed me?

I went to the mall and bought a ticket for one of the movies showing at Cinema 18. It turned out to be a mindless comedy about two adolescent boys on a cross-country road trip. The people around me, most of them teenagers, fell over in their seats laughing. I stared at the screen and thought about Richard and De Angelo and Inez and Quinn and Clovis and Diane and the mess that my life was in.

I should have listened to Hester Rose and stayed away from Gallagher.

Chapter 25

THE BAYLORS LIVED in a white colonial at the end of a cul-de-sac. A young woman answered the door, probably a student they had hired for the evening. Dressed in blue jeans and sweater, she was wearing a white bib apron. "Good evening," she said. "Please come in."

I stepped into a foyer with a gleaming hardwood floor and a polished walnut side table. A curved staircase wound up to the second floor, but I couldn't quite imagine Claire making an entrance down those stairs. She was theatrical to the bone, but more character actor than glamour queen.

"Lizzie, here you are!" Amos Baylor came toward me, holding out his hands. "Forgive me, my dear, for not making an effort to come to your rescue at the chapel. I'm afraid Reverend Todd and I had our hands full persuading President Sorenson that he should leave."

"Yes, I saw," I said. "Actually, Detective De Angelo rescued me."

Amos frowned. "Not out of the goodness of his heart, I'm sure."

"He did want to talk. You have a beautiful home, Amos."

"Claire's handiwork," he said.

"Amos," Claire said from a doorway, "did you hear what—" She saw me and faltered for a moment. "Lizzie, you did make it, after all. Come into the living room. We're all gathered there."

A fireplace, fashioned from gray stone, dominated the living room. On the mantel, abstract paintings added splashes of color. Mirrors on the opposite wall reflected back the colors of the paintings. The stacked logs in the fireplace were not lit. In fact, someone had left the terrace doors ajar to compensate for the heat of bodies—faculty, grad students, and staff—crowded into the room. Some sitting. Some standing. All talking.

No one looked particularly grief-stricken.

"Please make yourself at home, my dear," Amos said.

"Yes, do," Claire said. "We have a buffet table and a bar set up in the dining room."

Joyce appeared at Claire's elbow and said, "I'll show Lizzie where everything is." She led me off. "So what happened when the fuzz took you away?"

"When the— If you mean De Angelo—"

"Who else would I mean?" she said. "Channel 13 caught it on camera. The two of you running to De Angelo's car. Didn't you see it?"

I shook my head. "I missed the news tonight. I hid out in the mall until it was time to come here."

Pete Murphy was at the buffet table helping himself to potato salad. "Lizzie! We thought you got busted."

"No, just taken in for questioning."

"No kidding," Pete said. "Do they really suspect you?"

"Well, I don't think I'm at the top of their list anymore. Apparently, De Angelo has decided to believe my story about someone being in Richard's office."

I stopped talking as I realized half the people in the room had turned in my direction.

"Does Detective De Angelo have any theories about the case?" Eric Walsh asked. He was holding a plate loaded with roast beef and fried chicken. Megan, at his side, had opted for fruit and veggies.

"None that he mentioned," I said. "He didn't share his thinking about the case with me."

I reached for a paper plate. "This casserole looks delicious. Anyone know what's in it?"

"Shrimp, pasta, and peas," Joe Larsen said. "It's really quite good." He handed me a napkin and plastic utensils. "You know, I wonder if the police will solve this. It seems to me that if there is physical evidence that would lead them to a suspect, they would have made an arrest by now."

Pete said, "Come on, Joe. Look at how many people they have to sift through. The killer used a stolen ID card to get into the building."

"He did?" I asked.

"One of the campus cops told me," Pete said. "Some biology major who attended the murder mystery party. He bought his ticket at the door, and he had to show his ID to get the student discount. He doesn't know what happened to it after that."

"So he might have left his ID there on the ticket counter," said a grad student whose name I couldn't remember. "Or maybe he shoved it into his pocket and it fell out upstairs during the party. And someone saw it and picked it up."

"Whatever happened," Pete said, "it's a pretty safe bet that the ID fell into someone else's hands during the party. So that means it could be anybody who was there."

"Do you really mean anybody, Professor?" Eric said. "I mean, can't we assume the killer is someone who had a reason to want Professor Colby dead? Unless we're talking about some kind of psycho."

"Maybe we are," Megan said. "Maybe this person is insane."

"And maybe," Ray Abruzzo said, "we're all going to be eliminated one by one like characters in an Agatha Christie novel."

"In that case," Pete said, "maybe we shouldn't be chowing down on this food. Anyone notice the strange, glazed look in our illustrious dean's eyes lately?"

"Pete—all of you," Joyce said. "Will you try to remember why we're here? This isn't a joke."

"But humor is sometimes a defense against the unthinkable," Joe said. "And Richard's murder is really rather unthinkable, isn't it?"

There was a moment of silence when no one could quite meet anyone else's eyes. And then Ray said, "Hey, Joe, you weren't still upset with Richard because he ruined your party by taking everyone off to the sports bar to watch the game, were you? Now, that's a motive. You must have spent quite a bit of money on that spread."

Pete laughed. "Yeah, Joe. Am I next on your hit list? It's always the quiet one who looks as if he wouldn't hurt a fly."

Joyce made a sound of exasperation. She grabbed my arm again and pulled me away toward the dessert table on the other side of the room.

"Lizzie, didn't De Angelo tell you anything?" she said as she reached for a plate.

"Tell me anything?" I said. "Does De Angelo strike you as the type who would share information with civilians?"

Joyce helped herself to a slice of the carrot cake. "Why in blue blazes doesn't Chief Quinn handle this himself?" she said. "He's the one with the experience as a homicide investigator."

"Yes. But his job now is to run the police department."

"Have you spoken to him since this started?"

I mentally crossed my fingers. "Police chiefs aren't supposed to fraternize with suspects in murder cases."

"But you said De Angelo doesn't really consider you a suspect anymore."

"No, what I said was that he believed me about someone else being in Richard's office. Excuse me, Joyce, I need to get something to drink."

I made good my escape, squeezing through the crush of grad students who were probably there as much to get a good meal as to remember Richard. Being a grad student is equivalent to living in poverty.

At the table that was serving as a bar, Carol Yeager was pouring herself a plastic glass of red wine. "Red or white?" she asked me. "Both excellent vintages, as you can see."

"Neither," I said. "I'm not much of a drinker."

"Neither am I," she said. "Except when the occasion calls for it. And this occasion does."

I put my plate down on the table and reached for the club soda. "Were you and Richard close friends, Carol?"

"We were fellow survivors of marriages to the wrong people," she said.

"Your husband and his wife Delores?" I said.

She smiled. "Not that he did much better when he married Diane. That lady could give an Eskimo frostbite. But then, according to my former husband, so could I." Carol set her half-full glass down on the table. "Excuse me. I'm going home now. I'm getting maudlin. You see, today is my anniversary. The day I made the mistake of saying 'I do.'"

"I'm sorry," I said. "It must be a difficult."

She patted my arm. "Just remember men are a waste of any intelligent woman's time and energy, and you'll be fine," Carol said and walked away.

I filled a glass, and then I spotted Noah Webster standing alone near the fireplace. He was watching the socializing going on around him with a brooding look on his dark face. I wouldn't have thought of Noah as the brooding type. But he had been Richard's grad assistant, and maybe he wasn't any more thrilled about being at this little gathering than I was.

"Hi, Noah," I said.

"Hello, Professor. How are you?"

"I've been better," I said.

"Me too."

"I was just thinking that all of this must be difficult for you. You and Richard worked together fairly closely, didn't you?"

Noah nodded. "I was helping him gather the data for the book he was working on about environmental crimes. He was also going to be my dissertation chair."

"Then this really is a tough break for you. Dissertation chairs are hard to replace. I remember back when I was in grad school, we would all pray that the professor we were working with wouldn't decide to pack up and move across the country to another university." I took a swallow of my club soda. "Richard hadn't said anything about leaving, had he?"

Noah looked down at me, frowning. "No. Did you hear that he had?"

"No. But he was telling me how much he'd enjoyed his visit with an old buddy of his in Atlanta—"

"But why would he want to move there?" Noah said. "This is one of the best schools of criminal justice in the country."

Another case of successful brainwashing.

"Yes, it is," I said. "If you'll excuse me, Noah, I—"

"Ladies and gentlemen," Claire said, clapping her hands for our attention. "My husband would like to make a toast. Your glasses, please."

We all raised our glasses as Amos stepped into the center of the room, in front of the fireplace. "To Richard Colby," he said. "May your journey be swift, your resting place Valhalla. Go in peace, dear friend."

"Go in peace," Joe echoed, and the echo was picked up by others, including me.

Noah turned and looked at me. A grim, cynical smile flickered across his dark face. Maybe the brainwashing hadn't been that successful after all.

The young woman in the white apron saw me out. It was after ten, and the gathering inside showed no sign of ending until the food and liquor ran out. I had made my excuses to my hosts—exhaustion, I explained.

I had gotten into my car and turned on the ignition before I saw the folded sheet of paper under my windshield wiper. I got out to get it. The message was brief and to the point: HAVE YOU EVER THOUGHT ABOUT BEING DEAD?

I dropped the sheet of paper onto the seat beside me.

I hit the bumper of the car in front of me and then shot back in reverse. Luckily, there was nothing behind me.

"Hello?" I could hear him yawning.

"Quinn, it's me. Lizzie."

"Lizzie? What's wrong?"

"I know I should call De Angelo, but I don't have his—" I took a deep, steadying breath. "Quinn, I got another letter. This one was on my car windshield. It asked if I had ever thought about being dead."

"Where are you?"

"I was going to call De Angelo. But there's no telephone book, and I couldn't remember the number for—" I glanced around as car lights swept over me. "I'm sorry. I had your number in my address book because you gave it to me when I first moved here, and I—"

"Lizzie, where are you?"

"In a phone booth."

"A phone booth where?"

I opened the door and checked the street sign in front of the convenience store parking lot. "Euclid Avenue and Fulton Street."

"All right. I'm going to tell you how to get to my house."

"No, I can't come there. What if someone sees me? I shouldn't have called—I'm all right—just give me the number for the university police, and I'll call De Angelo."

"Lizzie, you're near my house. I want you to come here."

"No, I'm all right. I'll go home and call De Angelo—"

"Dammit, woman, do you deliberately and with malice of forethought— Get in your car and come here. Do you hear me?"

"I don't want to come there. I'm going home."

"You—" I heard him mumble something. "I'll call De Angelo and tell him to come here."

I relaxed my grasp on the telephone receiver as the man who had gotten out of the pickup truck and glanced in my direction went into the store.

"Lizzie? Did you hear me?"

"Yes, all right. If De Angelo is there too, it should be— Quinn, I just don't want to get you into trouble."

"Thank you. I appreciate your concern for my job security. Do you have a piece of paper?"

I dug into my shoulder bag for my note pad. "Yes."

"Then write these directions down. I'm not that far away."

"Then I don't need to write down—"

"Lizzie, write down the damn directions. Will you just do that?"

"Can't we ever have a conversation when you don't curse?"

"Write down the directions," he said.

I wrote down what he told me. Then he said, "Lock your car doors and come straight here."

"I'm not a complete idiot, Quinn."

"And you're getting a cell phone. I don't care what your objections are to people who have them."

"Richard had one and it didn't work," I said.

"That's something else we're going to discuss when you get here. Why the hell didn't you tell me Colby kissed you?"

"I—"

"We'll talk about it when you get here." And with that he hung up. Given the fact that I had hung up on him the last time we talked, I could hardly complain about his bad manners.

But if it came down to who was making whom crazy. . . . I had been a reasonably well-adjusted woman before John Quinn came into my life. I did not run to a telephone booth and dial a man's number every time I was upset about something. I handled things on my own. If I hadn't been so scared right then, I would have gone home.

Chapter 26

QUINN'S HOUSE WAS SEPARATED from its neighbor on each side by a high wooden fence. From the street, only the garage and a section of the two-story, pale gray frame house were visible. I drove into the driveway and parked behind his black Bronco. Had the fence been there when he arrived, or had he added it later? A cop who believed that good fences made good neighbors?

Of course, from a crime-prevention perspective, being visible to the eyes of one's neighbors was more effective. Maybe Quinn's house was equipped with a high-tech security system. Computerized surveillance.

The light was on over the front door. I climbed the steps and rang the bell. Inside the house, a dog gave two growling barks in response.

Quinn had a dog?

He came to the door alone. "I thought I heard a dog," I said as I stepped into the hallway.

"You did," he said. He was wearing a wrinkled blue shirt. It hung out of faded jeans that had been washed so often they must feel like soft cotton. He was not wearing shoes.

I looked up from his bare toes. "Your dog—where is he? I didn't even know you had a dog."

"I didn't until a couple of weeks ago," Quinn said. "I found him on the highway—out in the middle of the highway, to be precise."

"And you brought him home?"

"No, I took him to the animal shelter. But nobody came for him, and his time was up."

"His time?" I said. "They were going to put him—"

"That's why I brought him home," Quinn said. "But I'm only going to keep him until I can find someone else to take him."

I nodded. "In the meantime, could I say hello?"

"If you want to," Quinn said. "He's down in the basement."

But he was sliding an uneasy glance over his shoulder. I looked too.

In the room behind him, a bookcase had overflowed onto the carpet. A blue bath towel was tossed over the arm of the brown leather recliner. Several manila folders and a pair of reading glasses were on the glass-topped coffee table. A newspaper was scattered across the beige and brown print sofa. A rubber bone was on the floor beside the red brick fireplace.

Quinn said, "I have this woman who comes in, but that's next week. I was trying to get the dishwasher loaded. I didn't have time to pick up in the living room."

I couldn't believe it. The man was actually embarrassed about his housekeeping. I had just gotten a letter from a killer, and he thought I would care that his living room wasn't tidy.

"You should see my house," I said, trying not to laugh.

"I have seen your house," he said. "It's always neat enough for a white-glove inspection."

"Since you're the one who was in the Army. Could I please meet your dog?"

"He isn't my dog. He's a stray dog. Come on out to the kitchen. I put on some water in case you wanted tea."

"That was thoughtful of you," I said.

I stopped in the kitchen doorway to look around me. Plants, lush and flowering, were suspended over a bay window with a cushioned and pillowed seat. A white wooden table with brightly cushioned chairs was adjacent to the window. The kitchen itself was painted sunshine yellow, with white and yellow cabinets. The effect was both cheerful and unexpected.

"I like this room," I said.

Quinn said, "The couple who lived here before me painted it yellow." He glanced around. "But I like kitchens."

"You do?"

"Not for cooking," he said, as he reached for the bright copper whistling kettle. "I'm not that great a cook. But I like sitting. Especially in the morning over a cup of coffee and the newspaper." He handed me a white mug and opened a cabinet door. "There are four or five different kinds of tea in there and a jar of honey."

"But you don't drink tea," I said as I inspected his collection. He had my favorite brand of peppermint tea. I reached for the red and white box.

"I'll go get George," Quinn said, ignoring my implied question.

"George? George, the dog?" I was teasing. It sounded like a name my grandfather might have given one of his beloved hounds.

"I had to call him something," Quinn said. "He looks like a George."

Well, that was a matter of opinion. The yellow Lab mix who bounded up the basement steps and into the kitchen a few minutes later looked as if he romped through life. He gave me two barks in greeting and was about to place his oversize paws on my lap when Quinn yelled, "George! Down!"

George glanced over his shoulder at him, woofed again, and then sat down beside my chair. He looked up at me, his mouth open and his pink tongue lolling as he beat his tail against the tile.

I reached down to pat him, and he washed my hand with his tongue.

"Did you call De Angelo?" I said before the silly, unexpected tears burning my eyes could start to fall. "Is he coming?"

"He's off-duty. I left messages on his answering machine and his beeper."

I held out the letter. Quinn read it and then carried it over to the counter and put it in a plastic freezer bag.

"Did De Angelo tell you about the other letters?" I asked him.

"He told me," Quinn said. He was pouring strong black coffee into a mug.

"I don't suppose that's decaf," I said, remembering the look on his face the first time I'd served him my version of coffee.

"No, it's not," he said. "I told you I never touch the stuff. Especially at night."

"I've heard tell that night is actually when most coffee drinkers switch over to decaf," I said. "Something about getting a good night's sleep."

"Either I sleep or I don't. I drink lousy station-house coffee all day. At night I want a decent—as in real—cup of coffee." He opened the refrigerator door and bent down to look inside. "Want something to eat?"

"No, thanks. I ate at the Baylors'. They had a buffet. It was a gathering in Richard's memory. And then I came back outside and found that little message on my windshield."

Quinn came back to the table carrying his coffee and a box of chocolate chip cookies.

George beat his tail harder. Quinn gave him a look, and George stretched out and put his head down on his paws.

Quinn gave me the same look, stern and slightly annoyed, as he sat down in the chair across from me.

"I'm not George," I said.

"What?" he said. He reached for a cookie and bit into it, scattering crumbs.

"Nothing," I said. "Now what?"

"If someone wants you dead, and it's someone in your school," Quinn said, "then the chances are this person has a good reason."

"A good reason?" I said. "A good reason for killing Richard and now—"

"From his or her perspective, Lizzie." Quinn took a sip of his coffee. Then he set the mug aside and squeezed the bridge of his nose in a weary gesture.

"Okay," he said, "go over what happened with Colby. Everything you can remember about Tuesday, including your lunch with him and driving him to the parking lot after the party. And this time, include the part about the kiss."

When I had finished describing the events of Tuesday, day and evening, in great detail, with occasional questions from Quinn, he sat back in his chair and shook his head. "There's something there. Something we're missing."

"How do you know that?" I said. "Maybe this person is just crazy."

"Even crazy people follow a certain logic. This person followed you and Colby into Brewster Hall using a stolen ID card and killed him with a stolen knife. Both items obtained at the murder mystery party. Premeditation, not impulse."

"Yes, but how did he or she know we would go into Brewster Hall?" I said. "We didn't even know that ourselves."

"Maybe Colby knew. You're assuming he was about to drive away. He said he had been trying to make a call on his cell phone. But maybe he had some other reason to go into the building."

"What? And how could the killer have known that in advance? Are you suggesting Richard had arranged to meet someone in the building?"

"I'm not suggesting anything, Lizzie," he said. "Just considering possibilities."

I rubbed at a tea stain on my mug with my finger. "Maybe something happened at the party. What about Tracy and her gun? I know you said at your press conference that there was no apparent connection, but are you sure?"

"The girl came gunning for Eric Walsh, not Colby," Quinn said.

"But did you ask her if she knew Richard when you questioned her?"

"We haven't been able to question her." Quinn looked irritated again. "Her parents have her in a private clinic in Martinsville. Her doctor says she's deeply depressed. The family lawyer is playing let's-make-a-deal with the charges against her."

"Are you going to make a deal?"

"That's not up to me," Quinn said. "But as far as we can tell without talking to her, she's just a mixed-up kid. There's nothing to tie her to Colby. She's an English major, not criminal justice."

"Quinn, while we're on the subject of what happened with Tracy—" I stopped. Now was not the time to get into that.

"What about it?" he said.

I hesitated, then said, "Well, you seemed rather upset when it was over. I wondered if it was— Was it knowing that you might have to shoot her if she tried to shoot Eric?"

Quinn stood up and reached for his mug. "Believe it or not, Lizabeth, this might not be the ideal time to discuss my reaction to Tracy and her gun."

He walked away from me and over to the coffeemaker on the counter. His back was half turned as he refilled his mug.

"I'm sorry," I said. "You're right. I'm here to discuss Richard's murder and the letter I received and—"

"But you've been wondering why I was upset," he said.

"Not upset," I said. "I mean, you just seemed—"

"Less than ice-cold and in control?" he said.

"If you had been ice-cold in that situation," I said, "there would be something wrong with you."

"But while we're on the subject, we might as well get this out of the way."

"Get what out of the way?" I said, watching what I could see of his face.

"I shot a fourteen-year-old boy," Quinn said. "He died."

"Fourteen?" The word popped out of me like an accusation. I would have taken it back if I could have.

Quinn said, "Just barely fourteen. He'd had a birthday the month before. He decided not to stay around for the next one."

"You make it sound as if he wanted to die."

Quinn came back to the table and sat down. His face was calm, his gray eyes shuttered. "He did want to die," he said. "But he decided to have someone else do it for him. Suicide by cop."

"Then you— If he intended—" I shook my head. "When we were in Cornwall, Janowitz told me that you'd had a 'helluva bad year.'" I wrapped my hands around my mug. "You mentioned your wife. That she'd died of cancer. Was killing—having to shoot the boy—another reason you'd had a bad year?"

It was a stupid question. The twitch of amusement on Quinn's lips said as much.

"Yes, Lizabeth, killing someone does tend to put a damper on the next few months," he said.

"I meant—"

"Of course, finding out my wife had been having an affair with her boss didn't do a lot for my morale either."

"An affair? She . . . your wife—"

"But getting back to the boy I killed. He was black."

"Black?"

"I did intend to tell you about that sooner or later. Preferably later."

He waited for what I would say, taking a sip of his coffee and reaching for another cookie.

George whined and stirred beside my feet. Dogs were supposed to be able to sense tension in the air. George's sensors were working just fine.

"But you must have been cleared of any wrongdoing," I said. "The shooting must have been ruled a justifiable homicide. They gave you a promotion."

"Brutal, violent, and/or racist cops sometimes get promotions," Quinn said.

"You aren't like that," I said. "You aren't brutal or violent or racist."

"You're sure about that, are you?"

That did it. "No, Quinn, I'm not sure about anything. Including you. But I'm willing to give you the benefit of a lot more doubt than I would give your star investigator De Angelo."

He laughed as if the sound had been jolted out of him. "Thank you, Lizabeth, for that rousing vote of confidence."

"You're welcome," I said. "Any time."

We looked at each other across the table until I cleared my throat and said, "So, shall we get back to the matter at hand? Who killed Richard and why."

"And how you fit into it," Quinn said. "Aside from being the tenderhearted type who didn't know better than to offer sympathy to a depressed man in a parked car on a rainy night."

I made a face at him. "Sounds like a country song."

He pushed the box of chocolate chip cookies toward me and I took one.

"Okay," he said. "Go over the conversation you and Colby had in the Orleans Café again."

"I told you we talked about my research on the lynching and his trip to Atlanta."

"And he told you he had always loved Clovis Durham."

"Yes. But that evening, when we were in the car, he said that was in the past and you couldn't go back with that kind of thing."

"But maybe Clovis Durham wanted to go back."

I hesitated. Then I said, "About that. . . ." I told him about my conversation with Miss Alice. About what she had said about Clovis and Richard and about his mother, Elise. I told him about what Clovis's neighbor had said too. "But when I had lunch with Diane, she said Clovis blamed her—Diane—for Richard's death. That doesn't sound like a woman who killed the man she loved."

"Unless she's a clever woman throwing down a smoke screen."

I shook my head. "I don't think she did it. I'd bet on Scott Novak. He has a crush on Diane."

"He also has an alibi. He was in his favorite bar drinking from around ten-thirty until closing time."

"So that's where he went when he left Diane," I said. "Does she have an alibi?"

"She says she went home after she parted company with Novak at the coffee shop."

"I know. But do you believe her?"

"De Angelo has his doubts," Quinn said. "But De Angelo doesn't trust attractive women. My conversation with the Widow Colby has been limited to a telephone call to express my sympathy and to assure her that my department will do all that it can to find her husband's killer."

"Don't you find it a little frustrating not being out in the field?" I asked. "Janowitz said you were a natural as a homicide detective."

"And now I'm trying to be a natural as a university police chief."

"I'm sorry. That question— I mean, if you wanted a change after what happened with—"

"I wanted a change for a lot of reasons," Quinn said. He stood up. "It's getting late."

I glanced behind me at the clock on the wall. "It's almost midnight. I didn't realize we had been talking so long."

"We had a lot to talk about." He arched his neck backward and cupped it with his hand.

"You need one too," I said without thinking.

"One what?"

"You— I noticed how you were— I always wish I had an expert neck massager. . . ." I trailed off and reached down to pat George's head.

There was a moment of silence, and then Quinn said, amusement in his voice, "The next time you need a neck massage, Lizabeth—"

I jumped up and reached for my shoulder bag. "It really is late. I'd better get moving."

"Hold on." Quinn picked up the two mugs on the table. "George and I will see you home."

"That isn't necessary," I said.

"Yes, Lizzie, it is necessary."

He put the mugs in the sink. Then he led the way back down the hall, with George padding along beside him. They went into the living room.

George picked up his bone and shook it. Quinn sat down on the sofa and put on his socks and running shoes. I stood in the doorway and waited.

"Okay," he said, picking up his keys from the coffee table. "Let's go."

George was more than eager to go out. He whined and woofed as Quinn reached for the leash hanging on the coatrack by the door.

That was when I really looked at the photographs I had noticed subconsciously when I came in. They were hanging, gallery fashion, along the white wall. Black-and-white photographs of the Southwest. One was of a rundown storefront. An old man with a hat tilted over his eyes sat in a rocker on the porch. In another, a small boy in a T-shirt and shorts kicked a soccer ball along a dusty, unpaved road.

"Did you take these?" I asked, moving closer to look at the one of a desert sunset.

"I wouldn't have them up there like that, except my sister, Marielle, had them framed as a gift."

"Marielle? That's the sister who owns an art gallery in Sante Fe? The one who sent you the painting you gave me as a housewarming gift."

"My only sister," Quinn said. "My only sibling." He had come to stand closer behind me. "That's Marielle," he said, pointing to the last photograph.

I stared at the young woman in the picture. She had dark eyes, high cheekbones, long silky black hair, and a mouth that looked as if it curved often in laughter. "She's beautiful," I said. "But she— Is she— Did your parents adopt—"

"No," he said.

"But she looks Native American. The clothes she's wearing—"

"Her father is full-blood Comanche," Quinn said.

"Oh," I said. "You didn't mention that your mother married again after she and your father divorced."

"But I did tell you that she went back to her people," Quinn said.

"Her people?" I said, turning to look at him. "Are you saying that your mother is Comanche too?"

"Her maternal grandmother was full-blood. That makes her one-fourth."

I stared at him. "That would mean that you—"

"Have Indian blood, Lizabeth."

"Why didn't you ever tell me?"

"I have a photograph of my family in my office," Quinn said. "If you had ever stopped by, you would have seen it."

"I did stop by," I said. "You weren't there. I bet De Angelo loves that. Having a boss with Native American blood."

"Actually, De Angelo claims that he has some Indian blood in his own family. Haven't you heard? These days, having Indian ancestors is chic."

"Really? Then why didn't you ever mention it to me? I mean if you told everyone else."

"What exactly should I have told you?" Quinn said.

"That you . . . that your mother—"

"Would that have made me more acceptable?" He reached out and opened the door. "Ready to go?"

"Okay," I said. "Let's go."

I stood inside the door while Quinn and George went through my house. Finally, George came thumping back into the hall, followed by his master.

"Find anyone hiding in the closet?" I asked.

"No," Quinn said. "So we're going home now. Get some sleep, Professor Stuart."

I opened the front door for him. "Thank you, Chief Quinn," I said.

He gave me his irritated look. "Lizzie, your locks are good. I called the Gallagher PD and asked them to have a car do a few extra drive-bys tonight. You'll be all right."

"I know that," I said.

"Then what's wrong?"

"Nothing's—" I stopped as my voice broke. "I'm fine."

"Would you feel safer if I left George here with you?"

"No, I'm fine. Just go."

"Will you stop saying you're fine? Tell me what's wrong."

"You called me a racist," I said.

He stared at me. "I what?"

"You said . . . you implied that I would have found you more acceptable if I had known you had Indian blood. That was the equivalent of calling me a racist."

"Dammit, Lizzie, if I thought that you—"

I opened the door wider. "Good night, Quinn."

He jerked the door out of my hand and slammed it shut. "I did not call you a racist."

"You said—"

I gave a startled squeak as he pulled me into his arms. His mouth came down toward mine. "I have been trying all evening not to do this," he said. "I don't want this when you're scared and— Oh, hell. . . ."

I slid my arms up around his neck.

When he released me, he said, "I don't kiss women I think are racists."

"And I don't kiss men I think are—" I stopped, not sure where that sentence was going. My head wasn't particularly clear. "I don't have a problem with your being white."

"Good," he said, studying my face. Then he reached out and touched my cheek. "Because, Lizabeth, it would be a real nuisance if you did have a problem with that." He grinned. "I'd never be able to take you home to meet my mother."

"Since your mother is Comanche. . . ."

But he wasn't listening. He had leaned closer and was sniffing at my neck.

"What is that?" he said. "The perfume you're wearing."

"It's—" I stepped back as his mouth nuzzled behind my ear.

"It's what?" he said, laughter in his eyes.

My shoulder bag was dangling from my arm. I opened it and found the spray bottle and held it up so that he could see it. "Healing therapy body mist," I said. "I bought it while I was hiding out in the mall today. It's supposed to increase positivity."

Quinn grinned. “It does wonders for my positivity. And on that note, I'd better get out of here.”

He snapped his fingers at George, who had sat down to stare at us. “Come on, dog. Lock the door behind us.” The second order was addressed to me.

Locking the barn door after the cow's been stolen, was the way Hester Rose would have described it.

Actually, Hester Rose would probably have had a lot to say about John Quinn. I just wasn't quite sure what.

I locked the door and went to bed. It had been a long and eventful day, and even the knowledge that someone might want me dead was not enough to keep my heavy eyelids from closing. Exhaustion kicked in, and I slept.

Chapter 27

SATURDAY, NOVEMBER 4

Hoping to avoid observation by Mrs. Cavendish, I dashed outside, snatched up my newspaper, and ran back inside again.

The story about the fracas at the chapel was on the front page of *The Gallagher Gazette*. No wonder Quinn had looked tired last night. I hadn't even thought to ask him about that. About how the administration had reacted. I read the story as I ate a bowl of fruit topped with vanilla yogurt.

President Sorenson was quoted as saying that the incident had been unfortunate, but that he and other university officials, including Chief Quinn, were meeting with SAR and other student groups on campus to assure them that the investigation of Professor Colby's homicide was being conducted in a thorough and fair manner. No charges were being brought against the students involved in the brawl. Quinn was quoted as saying that university police officers had been reminded not to use physical force to respond to provocation by student demonstrators unless there was imminent danger to life or property.

I cringed when I saw my name in print. But it was only a mention of the fact that I was the faculty member the reporters had been questioning when the altercation began. "Lizabeth Stuart, a visiting scholar in the School of Criminal Justice." It might have been worse.

Thank goodness I had not seen Channel 13 news last night. I did not want to know what the reporter had said as they showed that video of me, running behind De Angelo to his car.

But I had other things on my mind. The phrase Quinn had used—"suicide by cop"—kept running through my mind. I knew what it was. Someone who wanted to die created a situation in which a police officer was forced to shoot him or her. But I hadn't given such incidents a great deal of thought.

After I finished washing my breakfast dishes, I went into the second bedroom that I was using as a home office. The manuscript for my historical murder mystery that I was supposed to be editing was sitting there, neglected for the past week and more. I picked it up, put a rubber band around it, and put it in the desk drawer. I had too much on my mind to concentrate on my fictional account of a 19th-century murder in Kentucky.

I turned on my computer and went to the Internet. First, I searched for Quinn's name as I had started to do on Halloween night in my office before the lights went out. His name appeared in various places in connection with the Philadelphia police. I found a newspaper article about a robbery-homicide case he had cleared.

Was that it? No, the perpetrator in that one had been arrested, not killed.

Another article, cop receives commendation. For what?

"'Article no longer available.' Wonderful!"

Reaching for a sheet of paper, I scribbled down the date and title. I would have to go to the library and get the newspaper on microfilm. But first I might as well see what I could find about "suicide by cop." I typed in the phrase and clicked "search."

I found much more than I expected. Including a Web site maintained by a psychologist dealing with the traumatic impact of such incidents on the police officer involved. Nightmares, anxiety attacks, insomnia, irritability, flashbacks—in short, post-traumatic stress syndrome. Well, Quinn was probably through the worst of that by now.

Except he had resigned his job in Philadelphia and moved to Gallagher, Virginia, to be a university police chief. And the look on his face on Tuesday night after his encounter with Tracy and her gun. . . .

I switched off the computer. Add to that the fact that his wife had betrayed him with another man and then hung around so that he had to watch her die. . . .

And why would I even want to get mixed up with a man who carried a gun and occasionally shot people? People probably sometimes shot at him too. First, he was a soldier, now a cop. I didn't need this.

Of course, he hadn't asked me if I wanted it. A kiss in itself meant nothing at all. Richard had kissed me because I was there. It might be much the same for John Quinn. He was here in Gallagher, and I was convenient.

Or not so convenient. But maybe he liked a challenge.

And, aside from everything else, there was the matter of my own bloodline. Mother absent. Father unknown.

"Damn you, Quinn," I said. "Why didn't you stay in Philadelphia?"

I got dressed. Then I remembered Clovis. I still wanted to talk to her. Preferably before Quinn told De Angelo about her, and De Angelo and Williams turned up at her door. Although, I was surprised Diane hadn't already told the police about Clovis.

Of course, until Clovis came to see her, Diane had believed Richard was having an affair with his high school sweetheart. It would probably have been humiliating to tell the police that. And after Clovis's visit, Diane might have been concerned about what Clovis would say to the police about her own relationship with Scott.

I found Miss Alice's home telephone number and dialed it.

"Hello?" I said, when someone picked up the receiver on the other end. "Hello, is someone there?" I could hear music, a woman singing. Something bluesy. Billie Holiday?

"Hello?" I said again. "Clovis? It's Lizzie Stuart. I need to talk to you—"

The person on the other end replaced the receiver. A gentle, but definite "no."

So either De Angelo and Williams had already been there, or Clovis just plain didn't want to talk to me. Well, I couldn't say I really blamed her.

But while I was at the library looking for the article about Quinn's commendation, I could also check for articles about Richard's son, Kevin, and his suicide. Delores had mentioned an accident on graduation night in the car that Richard had given him. There was the off chance that one or both events had made the newspaper.

I would have to go to the university library. The public library might not have the newspapers I wanted.

A disguise would be nice, but I didn't own a wig. Dark glasses inside would only attract attention. I would just have to hold my head up high and brave the whispers.

I'd gotten enough practice doing that when I was growing up in Drucilla. My teenage mother's reputation for wildness had preceded me. Everyone had watched to see if I would follow in her footsteps.

Chapter 28

NO ONE STOPPED in his or her tracks to watch my progress through the front entrance of the university library and down the stairs to the microfilm room in the basement. I saw a few glances in my direction, but that was about it.

Relieved, I turned my attention to the reason I had come there. It took me about ten minutes to find the article about John Quinn's commendation. It had been for the "suicide by cop" incident. A reporter had used that phrase in his story about the fourteen-year-old science and math honor student, from a middle-class home, who had walked into a downtown Philadelphia deli and drawn a gun. John Quinn, an off-duty police detective, had been among the customers. He had identified himself and tried to talk the boy into putting down his gun. But the teenager, "visibly nervous and agitated," had grabbed a young woman and threatened to kill her. When the young woman struggled, he pushed her to the floor and shot her. It was at this point that Quinn—who was wounded in the process—had shot the "teenage gunman." The young woman, a mother of two, had been seriously injured but had survived. The other customers in the deli had credited Detective Quinn with saving their lives. The honor student with the gun had left behind a note in his jacket pocket apologizing to the police officer he had forced to kill him.

And the city of Philadelphia had given Quinn a commendation.

I thought about that for several minutes—until I started to get a headache from thinking about it. Then I rewound the microfilm. Two suicides. Kids—two of them, this boy and Richard's son—who couldn't think of a good reason to live. Not slum kids. Kids with bright futures. One dead at a cop's hand, the other from a drug overdose. What was wrong with that picture?

I went back to the cabinets to get the Baltimore newspaper microfilm. Delores had said Kevin had crashed his car on graduation night and then been packed off to a drug treatment center. So start with May of that year, just to be sure. I found the microfilm I wanted and brought it back to the machine.

May had been a busy month for crime in Baltimore. But no more than one would expect in any metropolitan area. By the time I reached early June, I had read several stories and a couple of editorials about drugs, drug dealers, and youth gangs.

My hand froze on the knob of the microfilm machine. I stared down at the words on the page:

Medical Student Left to Die

> Last night he was struck by a car and left to die. Today his family—his parents, two brothers, and his fiancée—keep vigil at his bedside, praying he will regain consciousness.
>
> Over and over his mother asks, "How could someone do this? How could someone leave my son there in the street, in the rain, to die?"
>
> Gary Braun is an intern at the hospital where he now fights for his life. . . .

I scanned the rest of the story. Gary Braun, a marathon runner, had gotten off duty at the hospital and, in spite of the weather, had gone out for his nightly run. He had been struck by a car. He had been found by a man who had come out to walk his dog.

"I saw him lying there," the man was quoted as saying. "As if someone had tossed him down. Blood all over his face and head. How could someone have hit him and left him like that. If I hadn't been out walking Rex. . . ."

I twisted the knob so that I could see the date of the issue of the newspaper I was reading. June 7. Fishing a VendaCard from my shoulder bag, I pushed it into the slot and pressed "print."

The machine swished. A moment later, a grainy copy of the story slid out.

I scanned two more weeks of the newspaper before I found another story about the intern. The same reporter had covered his funeral on June 23. The article began, "Gary Braun was buried today. The hit-and-run driver who left him to die has not been found. . . ."

It was crazy. I probably wouldn't even have thought of it if I hadn't been reading *The Great Gatsby*. A hit-and-run accident in a novel was no reason at all to imagine one in real life. But now that I had, I needed to prove myself wrong.

I had Delores Colby's telephone number with me in my address book. I found the calling card the telephone company had sent me and went out into the basement lobby to use one of the booths.

In Baltimore, Delores Colby answered her telephone on the fourth ring. She sounded rushed.

"Mrs. Colby, it's Lizzie Stuart. I'm the colleague of Richard's who called you a couple of days ago."

"I don't have time to talk to you anymore, Miss Stuart. I have a party I'm catering tonight. I have to meet my staff there in less than an hour."

"Please, this will only take a minute. Could you tell me the date of Kevin's graduation from high school?"

"The date? Why do you want to know that?"

"I was reading something and I . . . I wondered if Richard was here or in Baltimore on that particular date."

"June 6. Kevin graduated on June 6."

"Four years ago?" I said. I repeated the month, day, and year.

"That's right. What is it that you were reading?"

"Nothing important. I'm sorry to bother you again. I know you're in a rush."

"Wait—if this is something involving Richard—about his death—his murder—"

"It's nothing, really. Thank you, Mrs. Colby. Good-bye." I hung up quickly.

She would probably call De Angelo and ask what was going on. Quinn had said she had spoken to De Angelo when the detective called her. But Kevin's accident in his car on graduation night had probably not been the main topic of their conversation.

Diane had quoted Kevin's suicide note to me during lunch. What was it she said Kevin had written? "Sorry, Pops. I tried. I really did. But I couldn't do it."

Couldn't forget an accident? Couldn't forget Gary Braun, whom he had left to die?

I took a deep breath. As usual, I was taking a flying leap into my imagination. There was no reason to think Kevin Colby had hit anyone with his car. His mother had said he had run into a streetlight and come home bloody and frightened. If Kevin had hit someone, how could Richard have possibly covered up a hit-and-run accident? The police would have been searching for the car.

But he had shipped Kevin off to a drug treatment center the next day.

And that was exactly what any father would do—or want to do if he could afford it. Richard had discovered that the son he loved was on drugs, and he had sent him away for treatment.

What Kevin had not been able to do was stay off drugs or live up to his father's expectations. That was why he had killed himself. That was what had been haunting Richard on Halloween night—that he might have pushed his son too hard and driven him to drugs and suicide.

It was hardly necessary to conjure up a scenario involving hit-and-run to explain Kevin's despair and Richard's remorse.

I pushed open the telephone booth. I had left my briefcase by the microfilm machine. I'd better get it before it developed legs and walked away on some student's shoulder.

All right. Suppose Kevin had hit Gary Braun, and Richard had managed to cover it up. If that was what had happened, then discovering that his son had committed suicide because he had made him conceal his crime would certainly have been enough to send Richard into a second depression. Enough to explain his mood swings of the past few months. But it still didn't explain what had happened on Tuesday night.

I kept telling myself that my hit-and-run theory was pure conjecture as I sat in a back booth at Shoney's, eating comfort food in the form of liver and onions and mashed potatoes. I told myself that until I thought I believed it.

And then I found myself thinking "what if" again.

But even if it had happened—even if Kevin had been driving that car—even if someone who cared about Gary Braun had found out—would that person then come after Kevin's father? Come after him four years later? Revenge was a dish best served cold. But that was a little too cold. Why wait all that time?

So it was unlikely that a bereaved Braun family member had come from Baltimore to kill Richard. Especially since it was even more unlikely that Kevin Colby had hit anything other than a streetlight.

I signaled to my waitress and ordered the hot fudge cake. I had been good and eaten my salad and veggies. My overactive imagination deserved a treat for its creativity.

The problem was that ever since I was a child, I had found it hard to let go of an idea once it occurred to me. As my grandfather had sometimes informed me with a certain amount of frustration, *It takes a crowbar to pry you loose from something once you get hold of it.*

Borderline obsessive, that was me. That was why I ended up on Diane Colby's doorstep at around four o'clock. I had tried to distract myself. I had even gone back to the mall that I was beginning to hate the sight of and spent another hour wandering around in the stores. But I ended up at Diane's anyway.

And I really should have called first. Polite people called first.

Diane seemed to be of the same opinion when she opened the door. A flash of annoyance passed across her pale, elegant face. I'm sure only good breeding kept her from saying "What do you want?"

Instead, she gestured me in with a wave of her glass that almost sent red wine splashing onto the tiled floor of her foyer.

"A drink?" Diane offered after she had invited me to sit down.

"No, thank you," I said. I sat down on the sofa. It was butter colored and butter-soft leather. Quite comfortable.

Diane sat down, legs akimbo, on the Oriental carpet. She was wearing blue jeans and a white T-shirt. She would have looked youthful if she hadn't looked so worn out.

I glanced toward the window. It was getting late. I had wanted to be tucked in behind my locked door before nightfall.

"What I wanted to ask, Diane," I said, when she said nothing, "I was wondering about Kevin. About his suicide."

"What about it?" she said.

"I have an idea. A wild idea about what might have happened that night when Kevin crashed the car that Richard had given him."

"He ran into a streetlight," Diane said.

"Are you sure?" I said. "I mean, did Richard ever say anything that made you think that there might be more to the story?"

"What else could there be?"

"I think— You said Kevin's suicide note—"

"I burned it," Diane said. "Richard carried it around in his wallet for months. He would take it out and read it. He would sit there." She nodded toward an easy chair beside a reading lamp. "Sit there with it in his hand, staring into space."

"And you burned it?"

Diane leaned back, both hands behind her. "One night when he was sleeping. I took it from his wallet and burned it. He never forgave me for that. He said it was the last message he would ever have from his son and I had destroyed it."

Her head was up. Tears were rolling down her face.

I found my packet of tissues and handed them to her. We were both silent as she blew her nose and reached for her wine glass on the coffee table.

Then I said, "When you burned the note, you must have intended to help."

"Yes," she said. "Makes me a pretty rotten psychologist, doesn't it?"

"I have this wild idea, Diane. There was a hit-and-run accident on the night of Kevin's graduation."

"A hit-and-run accident?" She pushed back her blonde hair from her face.

"On the night that Kevin crashed the car his father gave him," I said.

I had her full attention now. "What are you suggesting?" she said.

"I know it's a crazy idea. But there was something about the way Delores described Kevin running into the house bloody and scared— I just need you to tell me that Kevin hit a streetlight. That you're sure that's what happened."

Diane's blue gaze held mine for a moment. I couldn't read her expression.

Then she stood up with a minimum of wasted motion. Graceful in spite of the alcohol she had been consuming. Either she hadn't been drinking as much as she had on Thursday, or she was learning to hold her liquor.

"How did you learn about this accident?" she asked. She was beside the bookcase, kneeling down.

"A Baltimore newspaper from four years ago," I said.

She stood up, rising with fluid grace again. She had a book in her hands, a paperback. She walked over and held it out to me. "Kevin's," she said.

It was Du Bois's *The Souls of Black Folk*. "Is this the book that he left the suicide note in?" I asked.

Diane nodded. She dropped down on the sofa beside me. The leather gave a soft whoosh. "It was on Richard's night table. I didn't want to look at it anymore. But I couldn't bring myself to throw it away, so yesterday I stuck it in the bookcase."

"What am I looking for?" I asked her. "You said you burned the suicide note."

She gestured. "Open it to the flyleaf. Richard wrote a note to Kevin. And Kevin wrote something beneath it."

I opened the book and read what Richard had written. "To my beloved son, Kevin. May you scale mountains and build empires. Your proud father, Richard."

Beneath that message, in a slanting childish hand, Kevin had written, "Me hit, me run. You proud of that, Pops?"

It was not proof of anything. I sat there looking from the book to Diane and back again. She smiled and picked up her wine glass. "The plot thickens," she said.

"But even if this is so," I said, "it can't have anything to do with Richard's murder."

"Can't it?" Diane asked with a shrug. "There must have been some reason someone wanted him dead."

"We should call De Angelo," I said.

She gestured toward the telephone on the table beside me. "Be my guest."

"I don't know the number," I said.

Diane got up and walked over to the counter in the kitchen. She came back with a business card that she held out to me. She sat down and picked up her drink again.

I dialed De Angelo's number at the campus police station but got his voice mail. I followed the instructions to speak to a real person. The officer who came on the line said Detective De Angelo was not there. I told him who I was and asked if he could reach De Angelo. There was an odd little pause. "Did you say Professor Stuart? I believe Detective De Angelo was looking for you earlier."

"Why?" I said.

"I think he had some concerns about your safety, ma'am."

Because Quinn had given him the letter from my windshield? But I rather doubted De Angelo was busting a gut over his concerns about my safety.

"I'm fine. But I—we—do need to speak to him."

"We, ma'am?"

"I'm at Professor Diane Colby's house. Could you have Detective De Angelo call us here as soon as possible?" I gave him the number.

There was another odd little pause. Then he said that he would have De Angelo get right back to us.

"What was that about?" Diane asked.

"De Angelo's been looking for me. Seems he's suddenly concerned about my safety."

I didn't go into the matter of the letters. There wasn't any need. Diane pulled her legs up on the sofa and leaned back with her eyes closed. She didn't look as if she was in the mood for conversation. Neither was I.

We sat there in silence for several minutes until the doorbell rang. "That's service," Diane said.

She went to open the door. I got to my feet.

"I want to see Lizzie Stuart," Clovis said. She charged by Diane, shoving her aside. She was wearing a black and white checked raincoat over a white flannel night gown. She had sneakers on her feet.

I started toward her. "Clovis, what's wrong?"

She came at me. I tried to dodge her fist, but her glancing blow to my jaw sent me sprawling. "You have the nerve to sit there in my grandma's café smiling at me?" she said. "That cop told me. He told me about you and Richard kissing in your car."

I tried to raise my head, and the pain shot all the way to my toes.

Someone was pounding on the door. "That will be the police," Diane said to Clovis, enunciating each word as if Clovis were hard of hearing. "They're here to take you away."

Clovis stood there with her hands on her hips.

The person who came through the door when Diane opened it was Scott Novak. He pointed at Clovis. "I saw that woman come in. I thought you needed help."

Diane said, her voice weary, "Scott, I've told you to stop this. Why do you keep coming here?"

He held out his hand to her. "I couldn't stay away, Di. You need me now."

Diane said, "Need you? Need you for what?"

Scott flushed. He gestured toward Clovis. "I saw her drive up in that truck. She's the woman Richard was sleeping with, isn't she? I thought I should come in and help you."

Clovis looked him over, with her hands still on her hips. "Help her do what, little man? Do you think you're man enough to move me?"

His eyes widened. "What do you mean by that?"

Clovis laughed. "Richard told me all about you." She nodded her head at Diane. "You could do better than this little boy, honey. You better leave him in the sandbox over at his little school, playing with the rest of the children."

Scott flung himself at Clovis. She grabbed his upraised arm and twisted it behind him. He cried out in pain as she drove him down to his knees.

That was when the doorbell rang again. Perfect timing in the farce we were enacting.

This time it was De Angelo. Williams was behind him. He glanced around. His gaze settled on me, still on the floor. "Now, why is it, Professor Stuart, that everywhere you go, there's a ruckus." He turned to Clovis. "I've been looking for you, Ms. Durham. We heard from Professor Stuart's neighbor that you made a few threats when you were over there today."

Clovis, with Scott still curled up at her feet, smiled at De Angelo and said, "But when you told me about Richard kissing this one here"—pointing at me—"you were hoping you'd get a little trouble going, weren't you?"

De Angelo forgot to smile. "You'd better come with us," he told her.

"Are you charging her with something?" I said. The words came out muffled by the hand I had pressed to my face.

De Angelo turned and looked down at me. "Pardon me, Professor?"

I pushed myself up and started the slow climb to my feet. Detective Williams came over and held out her hand to help.

"Thank you," I said. "I asked if you were charging Ms. Durham with something, Detective."

De Angelo found his smile. "Since you were sitting down there on the floor—"

"I tripped and fell," I said.

De Angelo gestured at Scott. "And what happened to him?"

"He attacked Ms. Durham," Diane said.

Scott looked at her as if she had kicked him.

Diane said, "I would appreciate it, Detective, if you would escort all of my visitors out. I believe I've had enough excitement."

De Angelo glanced from one of us to the other.

Williams said, "Ron, let it go."

She won that round.

De Angelo said, "Allow Detective Williams and me to escort you people out to your respective vehicles."

I walked with great care back over to the sofa to get my shoulder bag. That was when I saw Kevin's book. "Diane?"

She turned from watching Scott pick himself up from the floor, and I pointed at the book.

"Detective De Angelo," she said. "Before you go, there is something else I need to discuss with you. Something Professor Stuart brought to my attention."

"Now, what would that be?" De Angelo asked, looking at me.

"You'll tell him?" I asked Diane.

"Yes."

"Then I'm going to go home now," I said. "Please excuse me."

Williams walked behind me to the door. I turned as I remembered Diane didn't have the name. "Gary Braun," I told her. "His name was Gary Braun. A medical student."

Diane nodded. "I'll explain."

I said good-bye to Williams and walked out to my car. Clovis's truck and Scott's white sedan had me blocked in. They came out of the house a few minutes later. Scott looked angry. Clovis was half-smiling. She raised her hand in a salute to me as she passed.

Scott was barely out of the driveway before Clovis shot out behind him in her enameled blue pickup, her tires squealing. I left at a more sedate pace. I drove home sedately too.

Mrs. Cavendish came to her door when I pulled into my driveway. "Are you all right?" she said, starting across the street. "A crazy woman in a truck was here looking for you."

"She found me," I said as I locked my car.

The porch light came on as I started up the walk. Mrs. Cavendish yelped. "Sweetie, what happened to your face? Did she do that?"

"Could we talk tomorrow, Mrs. Cavendish?"

She surprised me by nodding. "You go inside and put an ice pack on that. You can tell me all about it in the morning."

I was in bed with the ice pack on my jaw when I thought of Delores Colby and what it would do to her if her son had been the hit-and-run driver.

I got up and took three more aspirin. I slept fitfully, waking at every sound.

Chapter 29

SUNDAY, NOVEMBER 5

If I had known how it felt, I might have been more sympathetic. I might have cringed every time I saw a garish supermarket tabloid with a photograph of some poor celebrity who had been caught unaware, image snapped in a situation that was open to—and invariably given—the worst possible interpretation. If I had known how it felt, I might have been outraged for him or her.

Well, now I knew exactly how it felt. I was staring down at my own noncelebrity face on page three of the Sunday edition of *The Gallagher Gazette*. There we were, John Quinn and I, on my front doorstep. Quinn standing behind—close behind—me as I unlocked the door. The caption beneath the photograph read, "University Police Chief Responds To Professor's Late Night Call For Help."

My hands shook as I tried to read the accompanying article in which Quinn apparently had answered questions about my late-night call and his response.

But nothing he could have said would be enough to explain away that photograph. The caption might as well have screamed, "CAUGHT IN ILLICIT TRYST! SCARLET WOMAN IN MURDER CASE AND COP IN CHARGE." And, yes, folks, as you can see in this zoom lens, close-up photograph, she's black and he's white.

I thrust the newspaper away from me and stretched out on the sofa, with the ice pack I had made for my jaw pressed to my forehead. It didn't help.

After I had spent a half hour or so feeling completely miserable and sorry for myself, it occurred to me to wonder about that photograph. It was more of a tabloid shot than the kind one would expect to appear in a respectable hometown daily. I sat up and reached for the newspaper. There was no photographer's credit.

I let my eyes scan down the article. The reporter stated in the first paragraph that the *Gazette* had received the photograph from an anonymous source. Sent special delivery to the newspaper office.

I carried my dripping ice pack and page three out to the kitchen.

Fortified by the mug of tea on the table in front of me, I settled down to read the article. When university police chief Quinn had been contacted about the photograph, he had verified its authenticity. Most of the rest of the article was a statement from Quinn about how we had come to be together on my doorstep on Friday evening.

He stuck more or less to the truth. I had called him after finding an anonymous and threatening letter on my windshield. Because I was nearby, he had advised me to come to his house while he contacted Detective De Angelo. However, Detective De Angelo was off-duty, and when he failed to return his call, Quinn explained, he had questioned me himself. Then he had thought it advisable to provide me with escort home and to contact the Gallagher Police Department to request additional drive-by patrol of my street. He and his dog had stayed only long enough to search and secure my residence.

I liked that phrase—"to search and secure." Very military, Quinn.

In the next paragraph, the Gallagher PD police chief confirmed that Chief Quinn had made a request for additional patrol and that the request had been granted.

In the final paragraph, President Sorenson expressed his continued confidence in Quinn's stewardship of the university police department. The article ended with a quote from Sorenson: "One wonders who would have a motive to engage in this kind of covert and offensive surveillance of Professor Stuart's home."

Yes, one certainly did wonder. If this was the work of Richard's killer, I was getting the deluxe treatment.

But, at least—unless Sorenson had been talking out of both sides of his mouth—Quinn still had his job.

But it was a mess, as Mrs. Cavendish would say.

I groaned as I realized how much more of a mess it might have been if Quinn hadn't thought to close my front door before he kissed me.

Mrs. Cavendish did not come trotting across the street, waving the Sunday newspaper. She called instead. I stood there listening to the message she was leaving on my answering machine:

"Lizzie? It's Adele Cavendish. Blast it all! I didn't see a thing. My daughter-in-law had me over for dinner Friday evening. By the time I'd spent three hours listening to her witless chatter, all I wanted was my bed when I finally made it home. Worst luck. If I'd been here, I might have seen whoever it was prowling around with a camera. I've got to go to Mass, sweetie. I'll be over when I get back. Keep your chin up."

I kept my chin up by dressing for church in my best Sunday-go-to-meeting black suit and high heels. I made one stop on the way—the drugstore to buy concealer for my jaw that was displaying an interesting array of colors. The young woman behind the checkout counter looked at me and then cast an uneasy glance toward the entrance.

Either she expected my battering husband to appear with gun in hand or she had recognized me from my photograph in the *Gazette*.

I didn't know if Miss Alice and Clovis attended Mt. Zion Baptist. But Mt. Zion had been my grandmother's family church. And as my grandfather had once observed about a county supervisor who had made it a point to attend Sunday services on the day before he went on trial for embezzlement, *Ain't nothing like showing your face among church folk when everybody thinks you been up to mischief.*

So I was coming out to show my face—including my battered jaw. That was preferable to hiding inside my house as if I had done something wrong.

And if my luck was in, I might find Miss Alice occupying one of Mt. Zion's pews. And Miss Alice might be able to persuade Clovis to talk to me.

Chapter 30

I GOT TO THE CHURCH just as the minister was giving the opening prayer. The white-uniformed usher, a tidy woman with beauty-parlor-fresh silver curls, smiled at me and indicated with a gesture that I would have to wait there in the foyer until he was done. When his "amen" had been echoed by "amen" from the congregation, she opened the double doors and turned me over to another uniformed usher.

Fiftyish and stern-faced, usher number two started to lead me up the aisle toward the front, but I gestured toward the half-empty second pew from the door. With reluctance, she allowed me to slide in beside three teenagers, two boys and a girl. Undoubtedly, she expected them to carry on teenage nonsense during the sermon and me to try to sneak out before the offering was collected. I gave her my best reassuring smile and she retreated. The teenage girl grinned at me, greeting me as a fellow heretic. I had the feeling the usher was going to be speaking to that girl's mama.

Except I did have a certain feeling of rebellion. My grandmother, Hester Rose, had never allowed me to sit in the back of the church. Even as an adult, I usually moved obediently toward the front. But not today. I was there on other business.

I hadn't spotted Miss Alice or Clovis. Instead I stared with honest admiration at the marvelous hats the women around me were wearing. These were women who knew how to carry off a feather, a flower, or a daring tilt. I loved hats, but I always felt a little silly wearing one.

However, hats were not the point. As the usher passed, I almost stopped her and asked if this was Miss Alice's church and if she was here. But the twitching of the usher's nose as she looked in my direction made me think better of inquiring.

The Reverend Jebidiah Jones was a preacher of the fire-and-brimstone, call-and-response school. He set the church rocking. People were ready to stand up and shout even before the gospel choir swung into action.

Hester Rose had never cared for—or approved of—ministers who ranted and raved in the pulpit. But unlike my grandmother, I had no objection to being kept awake in church. My only quibble was when the choir started singing and people started shouting and they didn't know when to stop. I was giving serious thought to facing down the usher and slipping out the door to wait in my car, when things finally settled down.

The offering was collected, and announcements went on for a while. Then came the call for visitors to stand and identify themselves. I looked over my shoulder at the usher. Her steely gaze was trained on me. I got to my feet. And that was when I had an idea.

"Good morning. I'm Lizzie Stuart from Drucilla, Kentucky. I'm a visiting professor at Piedmont State University. But. . . ." I glanced around the room and tried to smile at all the faces turned in my direction. "But I feel as if I have a connection to Gallagher. My grandmother, Hester Rose—she was Hester Rose Robinson when she lived here—my grandmother was born here in Gallagher. And I would especially enjoy talking to anyone who remembers her family." I looked around. "Miss Alice, if you're here. . . ."

"I'm here, child." She was in one of the front pews. I hadn't spotted her because of her wide pink hat with two pink roses. The hat had concealed her face.

"Thank you," I said. "It's a pleasure to be here in my grandmother's church this morning."

I sat down to a murmur of approval and a wave of whispers. They had seen my photograph in the *Gazette* too.

Hester Rose would not have approved of my making a spectacle of myself. But if one was shoved into the limelight, one might as well make use of it.

Then what Reverend Jones was saying penetrated. I had heard the word *university*.

"A painful thing," he said. "A young man who grew up in our midst. Whose mama and her sisters attended this church. Whose father worked in this church until his untimely death. A young man graced by God, who went out in the world and obtained success. Who came back to his hometown and was generous in giving to his mama's church. It's a painful thing, Church. I tell you that it's a painful thing to think of Richard Colby, an intelligent young man, a gifted and generous young man, struck down by some godless person. Let us pray for Richard Colby's soul, Church. And let us pray that the spirit of God will enter the soul of his killer and bring that sinful person to confess and repent. Let us bow our heads and pray, Church."

Reverend Jones began to pray. I had not cried for Richard until now. But Reverend Jones's voice was the voice of pain and sorrow.

So was the song that followed his prayer. "Sometimes I Feel Like A Motherless Child" soared out above the pews. The soloist sang it as a wail from the heart. When I wiped my eyes and looked up at her, I realized it was Clovis. She was singing with her head thrown back and tears streaming. By the time she was done, sobs were coming from most of the pews. Even some of the men had pulled out their white handkerchiefs.

The reverend had us all stand as Clovis ended her solo. I slid out of the back pew and out of the door as people began to shake hands and hug each other.

The air felt like rain. I looked up at the sky. Cloudy, chance of showers, the weatherman had said.

Miss Alice finally appeared, leaning on her cane, shifting down the steps, one hip at a time. She was talking with the two women who were following behind her. Clovis trailed behind the trio. When Miss Alice saw me waiting, she called out in her gruff voice, "You'd best come on home to dinner, child."

I said, "Yes, ma'am."

"You got your car here? Just follow on behind us." She pointed. "That's my nephew's car over there. I don't ride in Clovis's truck."

"Yes, ma'am," I said again.

"Come on in, child. Come along," Miss Alice called to me when we all reached her house.

My eyes met Clovis's. Her eyes were red. She nodded her head in acknowledgment of my presence and turned to follow her grandmother up the walk. We both paced our steps to Miss Alice's slow progress.

The swing in the corner of the porch reminded me of the one my grandfather had put up long ago on our front porch back in Kentucky. Of all the summer nights we had spent swaying gently back and forth in that swing as he told me stories. The swing was still there, but at the moment, someone else was living in my grandparents' house. I had rented it out during my year here in Gallagher.

Clovis unlocked the front door and we stepped inside. Miss Alice's house smelled of collard greens, lemon furniture polish, and BenGay. Miss Alice pointed me toward the flowered blue and white sofa in the living room. "You have a seat there, child. I'm going to go get my feet out of these-here shoes. Then I'll come back and we'll talk some."

"Thank you, ma'am," I said.

"Clovis," Miss Alice called to her granddaughter, who had disappeared into one of the other rooms. "You start getting dinner on the table."

"May I help?" I asked, starting to rise.

Miss Alice waved me back. "No, you just sit yourself down, child. Clovis can do it." Her voice dropped to a huskier whisper. "I'm trying to keep her busy, you see. That's the best thing for her."

I nodded and sat back down.

* * *

When Miss Alice shuffled back into the living room—still wearing her dusky pink suit, but now with her feet in men's leather bedroom slippers—I was flipping through a photograph album that had been out on the coffee table.

"See all my fine-looking boys and girls?" she asked me. "Children and grandchildren and nieces and nephews and great-nieces and nephews. I got me a family a woman can be right proud of."

"Yes, you do," I agreed.

I had come to see Clovis, but I might do better to wait until after we had sat down at the dinner table together before I tried to talk to her. In the meantime, I could ask Miss Alice about something that had been nagging at the back of my mind.

Miss Alice had lowered herself into the recliner across from the sofa. She lifted her legs one at a time onto the footrest. I waited for her to get settled, and then I said, "Miss Alice, could we talk some more about my grandmother?"

"What about her, child?"

"The first time we talked, you said that you were glad that she had found a good man. You said that she'd had a hard life here." I hesitated, not really sure I wanted to go on. "I had the feeling there was more you could have said, ma'am."

"There's always more a body could say," Miss Alice said. "Don't mean you should always say it."

"Yes, ma'am. But sometimes—" I shook my head. "I never really understood my grandmother, Miss Alice. That's a part of why I came here. Because I want to understand who she was."

Miss Alice massaged her knee with a gnarled hand. "Got rheumatism in my knee. It bothers me when it's gonna rain."

"Yes, ma'am," I said.

"You might not want to know, child. Sometimes it's better to leave things alone."

"I said that to someone not too long ago," I said. "But you see, I don't really believe that."

Miss Alice sighed. A long, weary, old woman's sigh. "Hester Rose didn't tell you no more about what happened that day when Mose Davenport was killed?" she asked.

"What else would she have told me, ma'am?"

"I don't remember nothing much about that day except the grown folks huddled together whispering and talking and us children being told we couldn't go outside. And my daddy getting out his shotgun, and my mama telling him to put it away. And I remember my daddy saying if any white man—but *man* weren't the word he used—if any white man tried to come in his house. . . . 'Cause sometimes back then, when white folks got started on something, sometimes they would come into the colored part of town—and didn't make no difference about innocent or guilty. All of it was the same. But they didn't come that afternoon. And we stayed inside that night. And the next day, the grown folks decided it was going to be all right. They had heard that from some white people—the mayor, I think. He was a real good mayor for a white man. He told the white folks they shouldn't do no more. And some of them didn't want to anyway. So in a week or so, things just went on back to like it was."

"But what about my grandmother, Miss Alice? She left town that day when Mose Davenport was lynched."

Miss Alice came back from the scenes she was seeing in her head and looked at me hard. "Your grandmother didn't talk about that day?" she asked me again.

"She said that the shooting of the police officer was an accident. She said Mose Davenport didn't kill the doctor. She told me about how Mose Davenport was killed as he ran out of the house. And then later Ophelia Hewitt hanged herself in jail with a sheet from her cot."

Miss Alice nodded her head. "Least, that was what they claimed happened to Ophelia. We heard it later that day, just as my mama was putting supper on the table. One of the men who worked for Mr. Clark, the man who owned the big general store—"

"Yes, I know about the store," I said.

"Well, this colored man who worked for Mr. Clark was over there when all the trouble started. And Mr. Clark told him to stay right there and keep on working while he went to see what was going on. Then later Mr. Clark come on back with these two other white men, and they was talking about Mose being killed. And this colored man kept on working like Mr. Clark had told him to—trying to keep himself out of their sight so they wouldn't think about him. Anyway, he was still out there in back unloading when a man come running in and said that nigger girl had hanged herself in her jail cell. And Mr. Clark snorted and said, 'Good riddance. That'll save us from having to pay to feed and board her in jail.' When my daddy heard what Mr. Clark had said, he never did have no more good to say about him after that. Had always bought his supplies from Mr. Clark too. Went on buying them there 'cause he didn't have no choice, but he didn't have no more good to say about him. Least not in front of colored people he could trust. There was some colored folk you couldn't trust, you know. Still some like that. Talk too much to the wrong people. Get you in all kind of trouble."

Why did I feel a flicker of guilt about telling Quinn about Clovis when she said that?

"Yes, ma'am," I said. "About my grandmother. . . ."

Miss Alice held my gaze with her sharp old eyes. "Sometimes, child, there are some things . . . if your grandma didn't tell you all about what happened that day—" She shook her head. "Maybe she thought it was better you didn't know. And like I said, I was just a little bit of a thing then. I don't know none of this for myself."

"But you know what the old folks said. Please tell me. What did they say about my grandmother? About her leaving town?"

"She left town 'cause if she hadn't, she would have ended up in that jail like Ophelia did. They would have made no mind that she weren't nothing but a girl. She was there when Mose Davenport killed that policeman."

"Yes, ma'am," I said.

I waited. We looked at each other across the several feet between my seat on the sofa and her recliner. Miss Alice stopped massaging her knee and let her gnarled hands rest in her lap. "There was a boy named Henry. His folks was dead too, and he and Hester Rose was real good friends. Henry came that evening. I remember that much. I remember him sneaking in the back door and how funny he looked—his eyes all scared and wide. And my daddy drew him to the side to talk to him. Then he called my mama over there. And she talked to him too. Then my mama went and got some food from the kitchen. Some of the supper she had been cooking. She wrapped it up in a bundle. Then she went in her room and came back with an old shirt-waist and a skirt of my sister's she had been mending. And she gave Henry that, and she took out some of the ointment she used on our scrapes and cuts, and she give him that too. And Henry went slipping out the back door again."

"My grandmother," I said. "Was Henry— Did he tell your parents anything about my grandmother?"

"They didn't tell us young'uns nothing about it then. Never did tell us. We just heard that Hester Rose was gone. That she'd gone away on the freight train that night." Miss Alice paused, her gaze on my face. "Later, when I was a grown girl," she said, "I asked my sister about it. She was older than me, and she had slipped and listened to what the grown folks was saying. My sister, she told me what Henry had said."

"What was that?" I asked.

Miss Alice shook her head. "Your grandma was hiding there in the woods behind Ophelia's house while everything was going on. One of them white men caught her back there, and he—" Miss Alice fixed her gaze on me and lowered her husky, gruff voice. "That white man used her. Used her bad."

"He . . . you're saying that he raped her?" I said. "She was twelve years old."

Miss Alice nodded. "Too young for that. He hurt her bad. When he was done with her, she made her way to this old lean-to her and Henry had built themselves in the woods. Henry found her there, and he stayed with her till it was almost dark. Then he came to tell my folks and get some food and clothes for her."

"Why didn't they— Why didn't your parents go to her?"

"'Cause someone might have seen them. Caught them all. Better to let Henry take her what she needed."

I stood up. "Thank you for telling me about—" I swallowed and tried again. "I don't think I can stay for dinner. But thank you very much for inviting me."

"Now, child, don't you take on about this," Miss Alice said. "It happened a long time ago, and your grandma came through it all right. You said your grandpa was a good man."

I nodded. "Yes, he was a very good man."

"Then, Hester Rose came through it all right. Colored women back then, they knew that if a white man wanted her, it didn't make no difference if she weren't nothing but a girl. White men. . . . They still think like that. But now they ain't so bold with it. Know colored men ain't scared of them like they used to be. Shoot 'em soon as they look at 'em now." She tapped her cane. "Your grandma went on and married and had children. It was her burden, not yours. Don't you go taking it on."

"Yes, ma'am." I glanced toward the kitchen, where I could hear Clovis moving about. "I'll just speak to Clovis before I go."

Miss Alice looked at me and sighed. "All right, child. But there ain't no reason for you to leave."

"I don't think I could eat right now," I said. "Excuse me, please."

When I paused in the kitchen doorway, Clovis glanced over her shoulder. "The food's almost ready," she said.

"I'm not staying," I said. "Clovis, I just wanted to tell you how sorry I am about Richard. I know the two of you were close once."

She turned around with the metal spatula in her hand. Meat juice dripped from it onto the white and blue tile floor. "That was a long time ago." She smiled, but it was more like a grimace. "He came back. And he told me he was having trouble with his fancy blonde wife. And maybe I let myself think that he might leave her and we might get back together after all these years."

"It might have happened," I said.

"No. It wasn't going to happen. At least, not the way I wanted." She realized the spatula was dripping and turned and dropped it onto the counter. "Richard was never going to feel about me like that. That was what Filmore tried to tell me."

"Filmore?"

"My husband. The man I married after Richard went away. He was a good man, as men go. And he loved me. He had joined the Navy, and I thought I would get away from here and travel."

"Did you?"

Clovis smiled. "From one Navy base to another. One sad little apartment after another. I spent a whole lot of time waiting for Filmore while he was out there on those ships. And when he came home, he said I wanted him to be Richard. And he said he was never going to be. And even if Richard had come back for me, it wouldn't have been the way I told myself it would have been. Filmore called me a fool." Clovis picked up the spatula and turned back toward the stove. "I guess he was right. I was a fool then, and I'm still one."

"What happened to your husband?" I asked.

"He filed for divorce and told me to take myself on back home. Said he could do better than a woman who wanted another man."

"I'm sorry," I said. "Clovis—about Richard—I know you talked to De Angelo. But is there anything that you can think of that Richard said to you. Did he ever talk about Kevin?"

"He loved that boy," Clovis said. "It almost killed him when he died."

"Did he talk about him? About how he died?"

She shook her head, making her beaded braids sway. "No more than to say he died of a drug overdose." She frowned. "Why are you asking about Kevin?"

"I had a wild idea that somehow his death might be related to Richard's," I said. "I'm going to go now."

"All right," Clovis said. She turned back to the stove.

"You come see me again, child," Miss Alice said as I passed the living room on my way to the front door.

"Yes, ma'am," I said. "Thank you for talking to me."

My grandmother had been raped. My twelve-year-old grandmother had witnessed a lynching and then had been raped in the woods by a member of that white mob.

I turned the car onto upper Main Street and drove slowly past the Victorian houses. Had the owners of those houses been in that mob which had gathered across the street from Ophelia Hewitt's house? Had they known that the child who had been in Ophelia's house had been discovered and raped? Had they considered that punishment enough for her crime of being there in that house when a white man was shot?

I turned down the hill past the building which had housed the local Sears store before it moved to the mall. The building was empty now. A boarded-up hulk.

I made a right turn at the traffic light. I knew where I was going now.

I parked my car on the residential street across from the city cemetery. At the end of the street, two boys were riding their bikes. A man was sitting on the porch of the house across from the cemetery. He watched me walk toward the ornate black wrought-iron gates. Then he went back to the book he was reading.

It took me a while to find Officer Thomas Kincaid's grave. There were two other gravestones. Thomas Kincaid's father and his mother. But no gravestone for his wife. Had she stayed in Gallagher? Had she married again? On that day in 1921, both she and Hester Rose had their lives shattered.

I sunk down on the grass. I sat there in my black suit and my high heels, with my face turned up to the overcast sky. A cool breeze was blowing, and two crows had settled on a branch of the oak tree above me. They watched me there on the grass until they became bored, and then they flew away. I sat there thinking about that August day in 1921.

"Excuse me. But haven't we met before?"

I turned my head and looked up into Officer Thomas Kincaid's pale eyes.

He thought it was funny. By the time I had finished my tea and the bowl of soup he had persuaded me to have, I was able to see the humorous side of it too. I suppose the expression on my face must have been—as he put it—"something to behold." After all, it wasn't every day that one saw a ghost. Except this ghost was flesh and blood. His name was Ethan, and he was Thomas Kincaid's great-grandson. A "throwback" to the old man, he told me.

We were sitting in a diner not far from the cemetery. It had started to rain while we were talking, and he had suggested we get in out of the wet.

"I read about the movie about Amanda Norris that they shot here last spring," I said. "But I don't remember seeing your name mentioned as one of the backers. The name Kincaid would have registered."

Ethan laughed, his ice-blue eyes warm. "I'm a silent partner," he said. "I threw the idea out there, and my buddy picked it up and ran with it." He leaned back, resting his head against the booth as he looked across the table at me. "As you can imagine, my family's memories of this place aren't that happy. But my great-grandmother did tell stories about the town. And they were passed down, including the one about how she and Amanda Norris were both married in the summer of 1919. Of course, there was a lot more excitement in Gallagher about the Norris nuptials."

"And so you thought the story of Amanda Norris, the adventurous heiress bride, would make a great movie," I said.

"No, it was my buddy who thought that when I told him the story. He'd been wanting to do an historical romance, preferably one that involved a little globe-trotting. Amanda Norris's story was perfect for that."

"Did you come to Gallagher last spring when he was filming?"

Ethan shook his head against the booth. "No, at the time, I was lucky enough to have a couple of big assignments."

"Assignments?"

"I'm a photojournalist."

"That sounds like fun."

"It's a living," he said with a smile that said it was more than that. "Anyway, that was why I missed the filming here. But when I saw the rushes—the first print—I knew I had to come and have a look around."

"Was that what you were doing on campus that day I saw you?"

Ethan nodded. "My dad attended Piedmont State for a year as a freshman. I stopped by Alumni House to see if they had anything on him in their files."

"And you've been here in Gallagher for almost three weeks?"

He laughed. "No, I don't think I could entertain myself in Gallagher that long. I was here for a couple of days, and then I flew to New York. But then my buddy called and asked if I would swing back through and take a few photographs. Some still shots. I got back to town last night."

"Did you read about the murder on campus?"

"Read it and saw it on the news." He grinned. "So your name was not completely unfamiliar."

"So you can see why I've been driven to hanging out in graveyards," I said.

"This, too, shall pass," Ethan said.

"So I've been told. It's strange, isn't it. The two of us sitting here like this. The only connection between us a tragedy that happened eighty years ago."

"Nothing like a good tragedy to bring people together," Ethan said. "Another cup of tea?"

"And a hamburger, please. I'm starving."

My ghost raised his hand to attract our waitress's attention.

And I considered the fact that neither ghosts nor lynchings nor rape seemed to affect my appetite for very long. Undoubtedly, tonight when I was tucked in bed, I would have ample time to ponder what I had learned today.

"Sweetie?" Mrs. Cavendish said. "I saw you come in. Do you have your TV on? If you don't, turn on Channel 13 fast. Your young man's giving a press conference, and they're grilling him about you."

I dropped the receiver and grabbed up the remote.

Quinn was back at the podium in that room in the police station.

A reporter was saying, "Is it true that you and Professor Stuart knew each other before you both arrived here in Gallagher?"

Quinn's face revealed nothing at all. "I have an announcement—"

he started to say.

Another reporter said, "How did you and Professor Stuart know each other?"

"How long have you known each other?" someone else called out.

"Is it a coincidence that you're both here in Gallagher now?" came from the other side of the room.

Quinn said, "There would be a highly unlikely coincidence, wouldn't it? Professor Stuart and I met in Cornwall, England. We were both there on vacation."

"Then your meeting had nothing to do with police matters?" the Channel 13 reporter asked.

Quinn paused for several beats. "Actually, it did," he said. "Someone was murdered."

At that, chaos broke out. Hands went up all over the room. All of the reporters were trying to ask questions at once. Finally, one of them yelled louder than the others: "Was Professor Stuart a suspect in that case?"

"No, she was not," Quinn said. "She was instrumental in helping to apprehend the killer." He glanced around the room. "Now, getting back to my announcement. I have decided that it would be best to remove myself from direct supervision of the investigation into Professor Colby's homicide. As the questions I've had from all of you would suggest, speculation about my relationship with Professor Stuart is making me less effective than I would like to be in that role."

"Are you saying you're resigning as police chief?" a reporter called out.

"No, I am not resigning," Quinn said. "I will continue with my other duties. However, Assistant Chief Granger will take over as the supervisor in charge of the Colby case. Investigators on the case will report to him. He will make all administrative decisions concerning the investigation. He will also do future press briefings regarding the case. That's it for now. Thank you, ladies and gentlemen."

He turned and walked away from the podium as they called out more questions to him.

I slid off the sofa and sunk down on the floor.

Chapter 31

MONDAY, NOVEMBER 6

I had a class to teach at 1 P.M. I got up early—much earlier than I normally would have—and drove into campus. I had spent most of the night sitting up in bed thinking. First, I'd thought about Hester Rose leaving town on that freight train. When I couldn't think about that anymore, I thought about Quinn and how he would probably like to hand me the shovel when I dug that hole and pulled the dirt in after me.

And then I thought about my conversation with Ethan Kincaid. He had not been able to tell me anything I didn't already know about what had happened that day. But he had told me about the aftermath of that day for his family. With the widow's fund that had been collected for her, his great-grandmother had left Gallagher, a place she now hated. She had gone to stay with a sister in West Virginia until her child, a son, was born.

It was while she was in West Virginia that the package had come. The package had been delivered by a well-dressed gentleman who said that he had been commissioned to ensure the safe conveyance of said package into Mrs. Kincaid's hands. When it was opened, the package was found to contain $2,500 in cash. A small fortune in those days. The gentleman had already departed. There was no name or address on the wrapping. The young widow never learned the name of her benefactor.

Twenty-five hundred dollars was an extremely generous gesture. Why hadn't the contributor simply donated the money through the widow's fund the city had collected? Unless the person had not wanted other people in the town to wonder about the money and why it was being donated.

The name that kept running through my head was Jonathan Caulder. Jonathan Caulder had been a friend of Dr. Daniel Stevens's. He had gone to the jail to try to help Ophelia, his murdered friend's housekeeper. Maybe he had also wanted to help the slain policeman's widow. But why would he have wanted to help her that much?

I had come to campus early to try to finish those last four months of *The Gallagher Gazette*, September to December 1921. I wanted to see if there was any more mention of Jonathan Caulder and his sister, Laura. Miss Alice had said Laura had gone into a depression following Daniel Stevens's murder and eventually been sent to her relatives in Atlanta. Maybe there would be subtle references to that in the society notes in the *Gazette*, comments on the social butterfly's decline.

As I sat down at a microfilm machine, it occurred to me that I should probably be more concerned with the present situation. De Angelo had not called or stopped by yesterday to ask about my brilliant theory concerning Kevin Colby as a hit-and-run driver. That probably meant he thought it was pure fantasy. But I needed to follow up with him anyway. I needed to make sure Diane had actually told him about it after I left.

But it was still early yet, not even nine o'clock. I could call De Angelo before my afternoon class. I wanted to do this now. I didn't want to talk to De Angelo yet and hear him mock me about Quinn. I needed to do this now.

I went back to the newspaper coverage for spring 1921 to look for a report on the auto accident involving Laura Caulder that Miss Alice had told me about. The accident had happened on April 2. The *Gazette* had reported it the next day in an item at the bottom of page four. That explained why I hadn't noticed it the first time I had gone through the paper. With these microfilm machines, one had to shift up or down to read all of a page. I had been focusing on the society notes at the top.

<u>Lucky Escape</u>

> Yesterday afternoon Mr. Robert Mason and Miss Laura Caulder had a lucky escape when the motorcar Mr. Mason was driving with Miss Caulder as his passenger left the road and went off into a ditch. The mishap occurred on the Westview Avenue Extension as Mr. Mason and Miss Caulder were returning to town after a drive in the country.
>
> Although both suffered bumps and bruises, and Miss Caulder some more serious injury to her back, everyone agrees that the young couple were lucky to escape with their lives, as the automobile flipped over onto its top. Miss Caulder was taken to the hospital emergency department, where she was seen by Dr. Daniel Stevens. She is now recuperating at home and assures her many friends that she will soon be recovered.

I sat back in my chair. Not much there other than the name of the young man Laura had been out with. Had Daniel Stevens considered Robert Mason a rival? Or since Dr. Stevens was the one who had been murdered, should I think of it the other way around?

The accident had happened in April. Laura had been in a back brace. Then in June, she had gone to Charleston to visit friends. So she must have been recovered by then.

As I was going over the timeline in my head, I idly turned the knob on the microfilm machine, moving through the months from April to June. Corsets, 89¢. Maxwell House coffee. A balloonist expected to land in a field near Annapolis. Red Devil lye. U.S. to retain fingerprints from the draft. Greensboro policeman killed by whiskey runners. May 31, the devastating race riot in Tulsa. And then life going on, with summer furs and the Studebaker Series 21. Mutt and Jeff. Politics. Softball.

"The bloom of womanhood restored." The ad was in the form of a letter. A testimonial from a woman who had been rescued from the ravages of female problems by the pictured patent medicine. Mrs. G. Salinger was now the mother of a healthy, plump baby boy.

Yes, and if she had breast-fed her baby boy, she'd given him mother's milk laced with alcohol. The alcohol content in the patent medicines from that period. . . .

"'High strung and nervy,'" I said.

"Pardon me?" A woman, probably faculty, was sitting at the next table.

"I'm sorry." I hit the button to rewind the microfilm. "I was talking to myself. I just remembered something someone said to me."

The woman smiled. "I get those too. Delayed brain connections."

Most definitely that. Of course, I could be off on the wrong track again. Another flight of the imagination. I deposited the box containing the microfilm on one of the library carts on my way out.

Humidity hung in the air again. Other than that rain shower in the cemetery yesterday, the promised storm over the weekend had not materialized. I had a feeling it was coming today. Miss Alice had her rheumatism. I had my jittery nerve endings.

Parnell, in his bright red aviator's scarf, was back at his place on the portico of Andrew Clark's boarded-up store. This morning his bottle was not raised to his lips. He seemed to be sleeping. Too early for drinking. Or for causing a ruckus.

But not too early for Miss Alice to be seated at her table in her café. "Good morning, child. I'm sure seeing a lot of you these days."

"Yes, ma'am," I said. "I hope you don't mind."

"Don't mind at all. You want some breakfast?"

"No, ma'am, I've already eaten."

Her old eyes studied my face. "You all right this morning?"

I wasn't sure whether she was referring to Quinn's news conference or to what she had told me about Hester Rose.

"Yes, ma'am, I'm all right. " I said. "But there's something else I wanted to ask you about."

"Ask away."

"Remember when we were talking earlier about Laura Caulder and her accident and how your sister used to keep house for the Caulders. I was reading something at the library this morning about the medicines that women used to take—the tonics and so on. And I wondered if your sister might have mentioned Laura taking any kind of medicine."

Miss Alice looked at me. I waited for her to ask why I wanted to know something like that.

But she said, "Miss Laura had asthma. Now and then, she'd get an attack and wouldn't be able to catch her breath. My sister used to say it happened when she weren't getting her way."

"You mean your sister thought Laura's condition was psychosomatic? All in her head?"

"She thought that sometimes it was plain, spoiled rotten and nothing but."

"But the attacks—they looked real?"

"They was real. She'd be huffing and puffing and wheezing. I saw her one time. That one was so bad, they had to call the doctor."

"Dr. Stevens?"

"No, not him. Miss Laura had another doctor. An older man—what was his name. . . ." She tapped her cane on the floor. "It'll come to me."

"Yes, ma'am."

"Cahill, that was it. Dr. Cahill."

"Do you know if he gave Laura any kind of medicine for her asthma?"

"He gave her medicine for her asthma," Miss Alice said. "And medicine for to help her sleep and for those bad headaches she used to get now and then. Medicine for her nerves too."

"She was taking all those different kinds of medicines?"

"I guess she was mixing and matching them," Miss Alice said. "For whatever ailed her at the time."

"Do you know what Dr. Stevens thought about it? About Laura taking all those medicines?"

"He didn't approve. My sister said he and Miss Laura's brother had words one time 'cause he didn't want to give her no more medicine when she started complaining about how her back was still acting up."

I could feel the blood pounding through my head. It might have been lack of sleep. "When was that?" I asked.

"'Bout a month or so after her accident happened."

"So that would have been before Laura went to Charleston to visit her friends. She went there in June."

"Then it would have been before."

I nodded, going through the timetable in my head again. I needed to go back to the library and do those last four months of 1921.

Miss Alice said, "You sure you had your breakfast this morning? You looked peaked."

"Yes, ma'am, I've eaten. I just have this idea."

She cackled. "You don't want to be thinking too much. You'll wear out your brains that way. Least that's what an old auntie of mine used to say. I never did hold to that notion."

"No, ma'am." I stood up and reached out my hand to her, and she took it in her gnarled one. "Thank you, Miss Alice, for all your help."

She held onto my hand. "You watch out for yourself. You hear me, child?"

"Yes, ma'am." I leaned down and kissed her cheek. "I will. Thank you again."

She patted my hand and released it. "Little help that I been."

Chapter 32

ON CAMPUS, the day appeared to be proceeding without incident. No riots, no demonstrators. I entered the lobby of Brewster Hall in a pre-class surge of students. It was almost 12:50. But no one would have thought it odd that I hadn't turned up. By now, they had learned I was not a morning person. On the days when I didn't teach, I usually was not there until after noon. Given my brand-new notoriety, they were probably taking odds in the faculty lounge about whether I would show up at all.

As I waited for the elevator, I went over everything one more time in my mind. Since I had been downtown anyway, I stopped at the public library to ask Miriam Lockwood, the archivist, for another look at great-aunt Sophie's scrapbook. She had kindly obliged, with no more than a glance at my jaw.

I had thought I might find another clue about Laura Caulder in the scrapbook. Something I had missed before. But there was nothing else. There seemed to be nothing else in the newspaper microfilm for the rest of that year either. A microfilm machine had been free, and I had gotten the reel for September to December and gone through it quickly while I was there.

There had been only one passing mention in the society notes: "Laura Caulder left today to visit with relatives in Atlanta." That note was in the September 9 issue of the *Gazette*. As for Jonathan Caulder, he had continued to appear in court. He had been back in Corporation Court for the September session representing that tobacco warehouse owner who had shot his partner. The court had found the man guilty of manslaughter.

After class, I would do the first few months of 1922 and see what I could find. I had forgotten to ask Miss Alice if she remembered exactly when Jonathan Caulder had left Gallagher for good. When he had come on back to the city to settle his affairs on that last trip she had mentioned.

But I could call her after class.

Laura Caulder had been nervy and high-strung. Restless and constantly on the go. She had been taking a variety of medications for an assortment of real or imagined illnesses. Daniel Stevens—who was not her doctor but who was her brother's friend and who was probably in love with Laura—had not approved.

Daniel Stevens had been murdered one August day in the office that adjoined his house. He had died from a blow to the head. The police had supposed that Mose Davenport, who was a drifter and gambler and suspected of selling cocaine to the local colored people, had killed him. Dr. Stevens had drugs and perhaps money and other valuables in his office. They had assumed he had caught Mose Davenport in his office and Davenport had killed him.

That theory was supported by the fact that Davenport and Ophelia Hewitt, Dr. Stevens's deaf-mute housekeeper, had been seen leaving the house shortly before the body was discovered. If they hadn't committed the crime, then why hadn't they reported it?

That was what the police had thought.

I frowned as I stepped out of the elevator. But did my own half-formed theory make any more sense? Laura might have had a drug dependency of some sort. But why would she have to kill Daniel Stevens to get those drugs when her own doctor—this Dr. Cahill—was providing her with prescriptions?

Dammit, I was missing something.

Which was to be expected when you were trying to solve an eighty-year-old mystery and probably jumping to all kinds of far-fetched conclusions in the process.

"Lizzie!" Greta had come out of her office. "Lizzie!"

Wonderful. I was hoping not to have to talk to anyone before class.

"Hello," I said. "Did you need me?"

"Lizzie, Amos has been trying to reach you. He wants to speak—"

Amos appeared in his office doorway. "Lizzie, could I speak to you for a moment?"

I followed him into his office.

Gesturing me toward a chair, he closed the door. He sat down. "Lizzie, concerning this situation with . . . the publicity that you've been receiving. I've received several calls."

"From whom?" I said.

"Various administrators offering their thoughts."

"I take it you want to share their thoughts with me," I said.

Amos frowned and glanced at his watch. "I don't think we have time for that now. I tried to reach you earlier. I wanted to talk to you about your class today—"

"Which starts in about seven minutes," I said, glancing at my own watch.

"Yes, well, that's what I wanted to speak to you about." Amos tried to smile. "Perhaps you should cancel it today."

"Are you telling me to cancel it?" I asked.

"No—no, my dear—I'm only suggesting you consider— I thought

you might be uncomfortable—"

I stood up. "I've been uncomfortable lots of times in my life, Amos. Sometimes it feels like I've spent my whole life being uncomfortable. So unless you have instructions from above that I am not to show my face in a classroom, I'm going to go teach now."

He stood up. "Of course, my dear, of course—if you think you're up to it." He tried again to smile. Then he shook his head and waved his hand at me. "Go teach."

"Thank you."

Joyce Fielding was standing in the mail room doorway. I almost walked into her. "What's in the bag?" she asked.

"Excuse me, please," I said. I gestured her aside and stuck my head in the door to look in my mailbox. Nothing there.

"What did you say was in the bag?" Joyce asked again.

I looked down at the big plastic bag I was carrying. I had stopped at the bookstore. "Poster paper," I said. "Sometimes when I'm trying to think something through, I like to do a timeline and put it up on the wall so that I can see what I'm thinking about."

"Very efficient," Joyce said. "And that was a really nice picture of you and Chief Quinn in the *Gazette* yesterday." She was grinning.

I said, "I always try to be photogenic when photographers are hiding in the bushes."

"Our very own Jessica Fletcher," Joyce said. "How exactly were you instrumental in bringing—"

"Joyce, if you are wise, you'll leave it alone," I said.

She laughed. "Want to have dinner tonight? I want to hear all the dirt."

"There is none. And, yes, dinner sounds good. If we can make it early."

"When are you out of class?"

"Four," I said.

"I'll meet you at your office at five."

I nodded. "I've got to run. I've got class in five minutes, and I need to find my lecture notes."

"When all else fails, show a video," Joyce called after me, as I scurried down the hall.

I really didn't have time for dinner tonight. Dinner tonight with anyone was the last thing I wanted. But I wasn't about to turn down a friendly overture. Besides, Joyce and I had never really had a chance to talk about Richard's murder.

Of course, dinner might turn out to be rather unpleasant if Joyce was the murderer. But somehow I couldn't quite see Joyce with a knife in her hand. And we would be in a public place.

* * *

The class was an undergrad seminar, "Violence in American History." We were taking the topics in chronological order. Today the subject was the American West. Or, more accurately, the mythology of the western frontier.

Forty pairs of undergraduate eyes watched my every move from the moment I walked into the classroom. The smile I'd pasted on my face before I walked through the door felt as if it were glued to my lips.

"Today's topic is the mythology of the American West," I said. "The men of the West. The Indian fighters protecting the settlers. The cowboys on the dusty trails protecting their herds from rustlers. The town tamers who rode in and cleaned up Dodge City and Tombstone. The strong, silent heroes with gun belts strapped to their waists. Do we still respond on some level to those images?"

Hands shot up, and I sighed in relief.

"Yes?" I chose a hand to acknowledge. "Is it David?"

The lanky kid nodded.

"All right, David? What do you think?"

"I was wondering, Professor, do you have a theory about who killed Professor Colby?"

So much for my lyrical introduction. I looked around the room at the gazes focused on my face, waiting for my response.

"No, I don't, David. And I've been asked not to discuss the case."

Another hand went up. "But, Professor, couldn't you just give us a hint?"

The eager expressions that had started to fade perked up again.

"That, Lisa, is based on the assumption that I know something to hint about," I said.

Malcolm (one of the senders of the "problem with your assignment" E-mail) said from his seat in the front row, "Does that mean you don't know anything, Professor?"

I grinned right back at him. "It means if I knew anything about the case, Malcolm, I wouldn't be standing here chitchatting with you." I picked up my cup and took a sip of water. "I'd be somewhere telling everyone how smart I am. And how really unimaginably privileged you are to be in my class."

He didn't look particularly pleased to be the butt of the laughter that rippled through the room. He'd probably call President Sorenson and tell him I'd taken to publicly harassing students. And then poor Amos would have his worst fears confirmed about letting me in front of a class. Oh, well.

I turned back to David, who was grinning. Probably because he didn't like Malcolm either. "David, getting back to my original question," I said, "do you have any thoughts about the 'man with a gun' popularized in Western mythology?"

He looked uncomfortable. He hadn't anticipated having to answer the question. He squirmed in his seat. "Well, uh. . . ."

"Yes, David?"

"Well, don't we still see some of that today?"

"Do we? In what form?"

"How about vigilantes?"

"What about them?" I asked.

"Modern ones. The guys who take the law into their own hands. You know, the ones who think they're Charles Bronson and start patrolling their neighborhoods—"

"But some neighborhood watches are legitimate," the student behind him (Russell?) objected.

"And vigilantes were around long before the American West," a young woman added.

"You're Susan, right?" I said. "Examples of what you mean?"

"Groups like we talked about. The South Carolina Regulators. Or even before that, the Puritans who punished people they thought were witches—"

"But that's not the same thing," David said. "The Puritans weren't vigilantes. They had courts. . . ."

The class went well after that. Voices from the left, right, and middle chimed in. And I took a deep breath and decided that with the videos in my briefcase, I might actually make it through the next three hours.

I did. Just barely. As I took the elevator back up to fifth floor, I was leaning against the wall for support. Tonight, I had to get some sleep, even if I had to knock myself over the head to do it.

I glanced at my watch. 4:10. I was supposed to have office hours from four to six, but the students who wanted to talk to me always talked to me during break or right after class anyway. And these days, most students preferred E-mail messages to face-to-face meetings whenever possible. So no one was likely to miss me if I skipped out early. Just in case, I would leave a note on the door saying that I would be in tomorrow afternoon.

So another fifty minutes here. Then dinner with Joyce. Then home and bed. And then I might actually be able to get my brain to function again. I was suffering from overload.

I needed to call De Angelo too. I could do that now.

But when I unlocked my office door, the first thing I saw was the red message light on my telephone. Someone had called me. Maybe De Angelo was going to save me the trouble.

Or maybe it was Quinn. But he should know that it was the better part of common sense not to be in communication with me today. President Sorenson's good will might not survive another media fiasco.

I had three messages. Two from students. The third was from Ted James.

I scribbled down his office number at Emory University as he recited it. I had it somewhere, but I wanted to get back to him before he left for the day. He had been away all last week, he said. In Seattle, attending a conference. He had heard about Richard this morning, and he had just spoken to Diane. Please give him a call.

Absolutely. I dialed the number and waited, hoping he was still there.

"Diane says there won't be any kind of funeral service," Ted said on the other end of the line.

"Is that what Richard wanted?" I asked.

"Hell, no. You know Richard. The guy would have liked to go out New Orleans style—a Dixie jazz band and six white horses drawing his coffin. He wouldn't have minded a few weeping, wailing women either."

Well, he did have the weeping women. But the jazz band and six white horses weren't quite my image of Richard.

"No," I said. "I didn't really know Richard that well. That day at lunch was the first time we had actually sat down and talked."

"He mentioned you a couple of times when he was here," Ted said. He chuckled. "My man Rich didn't know quite what to make of you."

"He— What exactly was he finding puzzling about me?"

Ted laughed again. "Well, never mind that."

"No, tell me about that," I said.

"Another time," he said. "Let's just say Richard had been observing you and found you hard to categorize."

I decided to leave what Richard had said about me alone for now. "Ted, did Richard say anything else about the people here? About anyone in particular?"

When he spoke again, his voice was no longer amused. "I've been thinking about that all afternoon. I keep thinking that there must be something he said. If someone hated him enough to murder him, you would think he would have picked up on the vibes—"

"But he didn't say anything to you to suggest he was worrying about something?"

"The only thing he was worried about was his marriage. And he didn't want to talk about that." Ted paused. "Diane's one chilly lady, isn't she?"

"Did Richard say—"

"No, he didn't talk about her much at all. I picked that up when I spoke to her today."

"You've never met her?" I said.

"And, given her complete lack of interest in who I might be and what I wanted, I don't think I'm likely to."

"Did you ever meet Clovis?" I asked.

Ted laughed. "Our girl, Clo. Never met her, but I'd like to. From what Richard said about her over the years, she sounds like one hell of a woman." Another pause. "But if Richard had married her, she probably would have killed him." Ted groaned. "I didn't mean that the way it came out. It's just that Richard always joked about Clovis's temper. He said you didn't want to get her riled."

I fingered my tender jaw. "No, you don't," I said. "Ted, one more thing, and I'll let you go. You've lived in Atlanta for a long time, right?"

"Right. First as a student. Then back here as faculty, going on nine years now. Why?"

"Have you ever heard of—and this would be more in the way of local history than present day—but have you ever heard of a man named Jonathan Caulder?"

"Judge Caulder? Sure I've heard of him. His granddaughter donated a hospital wing in his name the weekend Richard was here. A big bash was going on when Rich took me to the emergency room."

"Your ankle," I said, willing my pounding heart to slow down. "Richard said you sprained your ankle in a pickup basketball game."

"Still think I'm eighteen sometimes," Ted said. "But why did you ask about Judge Caulder?"

"Because when he lived here in Gallagher, he was a lawyer," I said. "I had read that he moved to Atlanta with his sister, Laura, and I wondered what became of them."

"I don't know about the sister. But he became a judge and one of the richest men in the state. Political connections too. One of his grandsons—also a lawyer—is supposed to have his eye on the U.S. Senate. He's a state representative, right now."

I let go of my hold on the edge of the desk and willed myself to relax. "Do you know anything else about the family?"

Ted said, "There was a story about Judge Caulder in the newspaper when his granddaughter dedicated that hospital wing. I think he was married two or three times. His first wife died. He had a couple of sons, but they were both killed in World War II. He married again when he was in his fifties. His granddaughter's husband was killed in Vietnam. Second time around, she married Texas oil and cattle money. They're real jet-setters, homes all over the place. But heavy into philanthropy. Noblesse oblige."

"And do they have children?" I asked.

"I think she has a couple from the first marriage. But why don't you check the *Atlanta Sentinel* for that weekend? There's where I saw the article, and I may be getting it wrong."

"Yes. Thank you," I said, trying not to spring up from my chair. "I'll go look for it now."

"Hey, Richard brought a copy of that newspaper back with him to Gallagher."

"What?" I said. "What did you say?"

"Richard had a copy of that newspaper. Or, at least, that section of it. We were sitting in the airport waiting for his flight. Someone had left a copy of the *Sentinel* on the seat beside us, and Richard picked it up to read this article about a business merger of some sort."

"A business merger? That was why he brought the newspaper back? Because of a business merger?"

"No, that's why he picked it up in the first place," Ted said. "But he was flipping through it as we were talking, and he saw the photograph."

"What photograph?"

"The photograph of Judge Caulder's granddaughter—Georgina, I think her name is. It was a shot of her at the dedication the night before, holding a glass of champagne and wearing this gown that must have broken somebody's piggy bank."

"And what did Richard say? What did he say about the picture?"

"He was staring at it, and I asked him what was going on."

"And?" I said. "What did he say?"

"You're getting really excited about this, aren't you? What—"

"Ted, please, just tell me what he said."

"He didn't say anything much. Only that the photograph reminded him of something or someone. But he didn't know what."

"And he brought the newspaper back with him? You saw him do it? You're sure?"

"Sure, I'm sure. His flight was called. He started to toss the newspaper back on the seat. Then he picked up that section and put it in the side pocket of his carry-on bag."

"Oh, my—the newspapers," I said.

"What is it?" Ted said. "What's going on?"

"I don't know," I said. "I've got to go find that newspaper."

"Wait! Why—"

"I've got to go to the library, Ted. Thank you. Good-bye."

I hung up the receiver and grabbed my shoulder bag.

No, look for it on-line first. It was only eight days ago. The article might still be there.

My hand was hovering over the mouse on my desk when I remembered Richard's molasses skimmer. He had used the molasses skimmer as a paperweight. When I first saw it on Tuesday afternoon, it was on top of a pile of newspapers in his bookcase. That night, when I stood in the door looking down at Richard's body, the molasses skimmer was on the floor. So were the newspapers that had been beneath it.

What if someone had been looking for the newspaper that Richard had brought back from Atlanta. But why steal it if he had already seen it? If he already knew what was in it?

But if Richard had been killed before he could tell anyone else. . . . If the newspaper had been taken because it might reveal something about the killer. . . .

That Tuesday noon over lunch in the Orleans Café, Richard and I had talked about his visit to Atlanta. We had talked about Daniel Stevens's murder. And then that night Richard was murdered.

I reached for my glasses and tried to focus on what I was doing.

I found the article on-line in the *Sentinel*'s society page. It was a fluffy piece about the dedication of a new hospital wing for children with life-threatening illnesses. The Caulder wing, in honor of Judge Jonathan Caulder, who had died in 1993. The article described the dedication ceremony and gala at the hospital that had been taking place that Saturday evening when Ted and Richard were in the emergency room getting Ted's sprained ankle treated. The guests had been a who's who of Atlanta and Georgia society. But according to the gushing reporter, all eyes had been on Georgina Newsome, the judge's beautiful and elegant granddaughter. Her husband, Aaron, and her brother, Drake, the state representative, also had been present.

But the photograph was not included with the on-line story. And my search for the article about Judge Caulder's life came up empty. But it must be there. Ted James had said he'd read it. Could he have meant an obituary? But that would have been in 1993, and he said he had seen the story when the hospital wing was dedicated.

I needed to go to the library and get the newspaper on microfilm. Then I would have everything in front of me, including the photograph.

I was stepping into the elevator when I remembered. Joyce. I had to tell her I needed to cancel dinner. I half-ran down the corridor toward her office. The only person in sight was Joe Larsen, who was on the telephone. He waved as I dashed past his office door.

I rapped on Joyce's door and turned the knob at the same time. "Joyce? I'm sorry, but I have to—" I was still talking when what I was seeing registered. "Oh . . . oh, I— Excuse me."

Joyce's face was flaming. So was Pete Murphy's.

He stepped away from her and started pulling at his beard. "We . . . uh. . . ," he said.

Joyce recovered her voice first. "I was about to come around to see if you were ready for dinner when I got sidetracked," she said, nodding toward Pete.

"I see," I said. "Well, I need to cancel anyway. . . ."

Pete pulled at his beard again. "Anyway, this is what I was doing on Tuesday night," he said. "Not killing Richard."

Joyce looked at him. "She didn't think—"

"That damn anonymous letter I told you about," Pete said.

Joyce pushed back a strand of her flyaway hair. "He was with me, Lizzie," she said. "We told the police. But we didn't want to have everyone in the school talking."

I couldn't help staring at them. "But the two of you are always arguing. Is that an act?"

Pete looked at Joyce and grinned. "No," he said.

"No," she said.

"Oh," I said. "Well, anyway, about dinner, Joyce. Could I get a rain check?"

"You bet," Pete said and winked at Joyce.

She blushed like a schoolgirl.

"See you later," I said. I backed out and closed the door behind me.

Chapter 33

IN NOVEMBER, the days are shorter. In November, lightning storms are supposed to be over until spring. But as I stepped outside, I saw lightning flickering off to the east. I pulled the collar of my jacket higher against the brisk wind that was picking up. The library was five or six minutes away. There were lots of people on the sidewalks between buildings. If I walked fast, I could beat the storm and be safe inside the library in nothing flat.

I burst through the library doors, panting like a distance runner, a few seconds ahead of the rain and the first clash of thunder. I tried to relax my tense muscles as I went down the basement steps. There were no windows in the basement, so I wouldn't see the storm. Only hear it.

In the periodicals room, I shrugged out of my jacket and threw it over the back of a chair to claim the vacant microfilm machine. Then I went to find the *Atlanta Sentinel.* The last labeled box of microfilm for the newspaper went from April to June.

Had someone been using the microfilm for October?

I searched the library carts provided for used items that needed to be put back in the cabinets. There were microfilm boxes for other newspapers, but nothing for the *Sentinel.*

I was on the verge of screaming out loud, when my brain started to function again. The microfilm for October hadn't come in yet. There would have to be a time lag between print copy and the microfilm that was made available to libraries.

I almost ran across the lobby to the reading room on the other side of the basement.

"The *Atlanta Sentinel,*" I said to the librarian behind the desk. "The microfilm stopped at June 30 of this year. Does the library receive the hard copy—the paper copy—of that newspaper?"

"Just a moment," he said. "Let me check that." He went to another computer screen. "No, I'm afraid we don't have a daily subscription. Only Sundays."

"Sundays," I said. "Yes! Yes! Thank you. That's exactly what I need."

"Then you're in luck," he said, amusement in his voice. Obviously he had put me down as another of the crazed researchers that he had learned to take in stride.

He pushed a card toward me. "Fill this out, and I'll have someone pull what you need from the storage room."

I filled in my name and ID number and the issue of the newspaper I needed, then gave it back to him.

"About ten minutes," he said.

I went over and dropped down into a chair at the table across from his desk.

When the work-study student returned almost fifteen minutes later with newspaper in hand, I could have hugged him. Instead, I opened the newspaper and started to search for the article I had read on-line.

It was on the front page of the society section. Above it was the large color photograph that must have caught Richard's eye. "Judge's Granddaughter Dedicates Children's Wing" the caption said.

I leaned closer, studying the photograph of an elegant woman with smooth shoulders bared above a shimmering silver gown. Diamond drop earrings dangled from her ears. Her reddish-blonde hair was upswept, held back by a silver clasp. Her slender hand, also displaying a large diamond, held a glass of champagne upraised in a toast.

I sat back and then leaned forward again, trying to see what Richard had seen.

After a few minutes of staring at the photograph, I gave up and moved on to the next page. Ted James had said there was an article about Jonathan Caulder's life in this issue of the newspaper. Where was it?

No, not an article. An editorial.

Judge Caulder's Wisdom

> Judge Jonathan Caulder once recalled to a friend that during all his years on the bench, he was guided by but one principle: "Justice should be tempered with mercy." Judge Caulder often said that when a man or woman stood before him, he always paused to remind himself that "There, but for the grace of God, go I or a loved one."
>
> This doesn't mean that Judge Caulder was a weak judge. He was known for handing down some of the toughest sentences in the state. But he was also known for showing mercy to those who deserved it. . . .

I scanned the next three paragraphs that went on in similar fashion, offering examples of Judge Caulder's wisdom. And then I came to the final paragraph. The paragraph Ted James must have remembered:

> Judge Caulder's long life was not always an easy once. He married in his early thirties, after the death of his beloved sister, Laura. His marriage was a true love match, but his young wife died four years later.
>
> The two sons from that marriage would both die in World War II. The judge would marry two more times, each time losing his wife after a few brief years of marriage. But the judge often said he drew strength from these tragedies. He said that his family was the most important thing in his life, the source of any compassion, wisdom, or honor that he possessed.
>
> We beg to differ. We think those qualities came from within the man himself. In the years since his retirement from the bench, we have sorely missed this man who tendered justice with mercy. We can only take comfort from the fact that those who bear the Caulder name have continued in the footsteps of their forebear, bringing decency and wisdom to public service.

As far as this particular editorial writer was concerned, Jonathan Caulder had been a paragon among men. He might have been that in his old age. But what had he been when he lived in Gallagher? If his "beloved sister," Laura, had killed Dr. Daniel Stevens in a moment of drug-induced rage or fear, would Jonathan Caulder have helped her to cover it up? And when Thomas Kincaid was killed when he went to arrest Mose Davenport, would Jonathan Caulder have been remorseful enough about the police officer's death to send his widow $2,500?

If Laura Caulder had killed Daniel Stevens, that would explain why her brother had first kept her isolated in their house and then shipped her out of town to Atlanta. It would also explain Laura's nervous breakdown later.

And it would explain why Jonathan Caulder had gone to see Ophelia Hewitt as she sat in her jail cell and promised to try to help her. He had known that she and Mose Davenport had not killed his best friend, Daniel Stevens.

It all fit. So why didn't it feel right?

And there was still the matter of Richard and the photograph. Richard's bringing back the society page from the *Atlanta Sentinel* and then being murdered in his office. How did that fit?

I went back to Georgina Newsome's photograph and stared at it some more. But I still didn't see what Richard had seen. There was nothing familiar about it to me. Or maybe my sleep-deprived eyes had stopped working.

Giving up, I returned the newspaper to the librarian at the desk. Then I went back to the microfilm room to look for the *Sentinel* for 1993. I needed to find Judge Caulder's obituary. There might be something there.

At least the microfilm for that year was where it should be. But a dull ache had settled in my neck and back by the time I finally found the obituary. Judge Caulder had died in November 1993. There was a photograph, obviously taken years earlier, of a handsome man with strong, aquiline features. His full head of wavy hair was snow-white, but there was the suggestion of youthful vigor and energy about him.

He looked like a person I would have liked.

I reached out to adjust the microfilm focus and realized my hand was shaking again. I arched my back to stretch my cramping muscles and then leaned forward to read Jonathan Caulder's obituary.

The name leapt out at me. It hit me right between the eyes. I stood up, feeling slightly dizzy. "Also survived by a great-grandson, Jonathan Bishop Reed, and a great-granddaughter, Laura Megan Reed."

Megan Reed.

I was in the telephone booth in the basement lobby when the fire alarm went off. Still holding the receiver, I pushed the door half open, listening. Around me, students sitting at the tables or walking through the lobby gave a collective groan.

"What idiot does a fire drill in the middle of a storm?" someone said.

But the students began to gather up their books and belongings. I started to step back into the booth and close it.

"Everybody out! There's a bomb in the building. Everybody get out!" The kid running down the stairs was waving his arms. "Get out! Everybody out!"

A moment later, the PA system crackled on. A woman's voice said, "Please remain calm. We have an emergency. This is not a drill. Please evacuate the library immediately, using all available exits. Please go to the nearest exit in an orderly. . . ."

Whatever she said next about being orderly was lost in the ensuing chaos. On the floor above, there was the sound of pounding feet. Down in the basement, students poured out of the audiovisual room and the periodicals room on the other side. I stood pressed against the telephone booth, trying to decide which way to go.

My gaze locked with Megan's. She was standing beside the stairs, still and focused as people shoved and pushed and stampeded around her. Her eyes were fixed on me. I wouldn't have recognized her if she hadn't been staring at me. She was wearing a black pageboy wig straight out of *Pulp Fiction*. She had a red leather jacket over her arm and something in her hand beneath the jacket.

I started to back away toward the corridor off the lobby. The archives/special collection room was at the end of the corridor, and there was a fire exit in the back of that room. Other people were running in that direction. I stumbled against someone and grabbed a table to keep from falling. Megan was behind me, still focused, still calm. The people in front of me moved as if they were swimming through molasses.

Someone pushed me forward. I fell against the open doorway of an office. I glanced to the side and saw Megan's face.

"Please, I have to get out," I said, trying to shove my way forward in the stream of bodies.

The person I was shoving against shoved back. And something hit me hard on the elbow. I cried out, and a hand shoved me sideways. I landed on the floor inside the office. I heard the door close.

When I had gotten past the pain radiating from my elbow, I looked up. Megan was standing in front of the closed door. The jacket was still over her hand, but now the barrel of the gun she had pointed at me was visible. "Could I speak with you, Professor Stuart?" she said. "It is rather important."

I rubbed at my elbow and levered myself to my feet. "We should get out of here," I said. "There's a bomb threat."

"No one will notice if we talk for a moment," she said.

I glanced out through the half-closed blinds which the occupant of this glassed office had put up to provide some privacy. If I screamed, would someone hear me?

"You wouldn't use that gun here," I said.

"Try me," she said. "With all that noise out there and the sirens coming, do you think anyone would notice?"

I looked into her blue eyes. They were quite calm. Quite determined.

"Why?" I said. "Why did you kill Richard?"

"When I was in his office that afternoon, he offered to loan me a book. He moved the newspapers on the bookcase to get to it, and I saw the Atlanta newspaper. And my mother's face looking up at me." She shook her head. "And the two of you had been to lunch together. Had talked about Mose Davenport. I didn't have any choice."

There were only a few stragglers left now. In another few moments, everyone in the basement would be outside. Everyone except Megan and me. Would someone check to make sure everyone was out? Surely someone would do that.

"Richard didn't tell me anything," I said. "Maybe he never even remembered who the photograph reminded him of. Maybe he forgot about it completely."

She shook her head. "At the murder mystery party, he told me I looked pretty. And then he looked at me again, and he asked if I happened to have any rich, society relatives in Atlanta."

"He probably meant it as a joke," I said.

"If he did, it was his mistake," Megan said, sending a glance toward the half-closed blinds. "Later, in his office," she said, "I asked him if he had mentioned it to anyone else. He looked surprised. And then he made another joke about the big change from my ingenue party clothes to the fright mask and cape I was wearing at the time. He asked if I was on my way trick-or-treating."

"And then you killed him," I said.

"I had to," Megan said. "Sooner or later, you would have mentioned Jonathan Caulder, and he would have remembered what he'd read and mentioned the resemblance he thought he'd seen between me and the woman in the photograph. And you would have started wondering and asking questions."

"And that was why you killed Richard?" I said. "Because of what he might remember?"

"Do you think I could stand by and let the two of you destroy my family? My grandfather was a wonderful man."

"A wonderful man who covered up his sister's crime and allowed Mose Davenport to take the blame?"

Megan was staring at me, frowning slightly. And that was when I knew what I had gotten wrong. Not Laura, Jonathan.

Megan said, "Whatever my great-grandfather did, his life and what he accomplished was more important than Mose Davenport."

"Or Richard Colby?" I asked. "Or Lizzie Stuart?"

"I am not going to let you destroy my family," Megan said. "That is not an option, Professor Stuart." She looked me in the eye as she said that. "First that damn movie company and then you. Why couldn't you leave it alone?"

"My grandmother was raped that day," I said. "By someone in that mob."

"That wasn't my family's fault," Megan said. "You want to destroy us because some redneck in a mob—"

"Your great-grandfather set everything in motion when he killed Daniel Stevens," I said.

"That was an accident. Daniel Stevens said something that horrified him. He lost control for a moment." Her voice wavered, but the gun in her hand was steady. "You don't know what kind of man he was. He would never have deliberately harmed another person."

I nodded. "I'm sure he wouldn't have. It was just an unfortunate accident. His little accident, and now your little murder."

Megan flushed. Then her eyes narrowed. "What are you doing, Professor Stuart? Get away from that desk. In fact, why don't we get out of here now. It looks like everyone is gone."

"Where are we going?" I asked, as she waved me forward.

"Upstairs," she said.

As I walked past her, I turned and swung out my shoulder bag. She ducked. I ran. At any moment, I expected to hear gunfire, to feel a bullet penetrate my skin.

When I got to the fire door, I looked back. She was running toward me, the gun raised. I darted out into the rain. Lightning flashed and thunder crashed around me. I ran up the hill toward the street and the sirens and voices. When I glanced back, Megan was nowhere in sight.

"Well, Professor Stuart. I've been looking for you." I whirled around to find De Angelo grinning at me. "No need to panic now. Probably just a hoax."

"Megan," I said, panting. "Megan Reed killed Richard."

De Angelo's smile disappeared. "What did you say? Megan Reed?"

I grabbed his arm. "I don't have time to explain. She's down there somewhere. She has a gun."

De Angelo's hand moved to the gun holster under his jacket. He took a step in the direction from which I had come. Then he glanced back at me and cursed. "Come on," he said, turning toward the street above.

"Wait! Where are you going? She's down there. She was in the library."

"I heard you," De Angelo said. "But I've got to call for backup. Come the hell on, Professor."

I ran behind him, catching my breath at a display of lightning.

The gray sedan was pulled up to the curb. He opened the driver's-side door and reached inside for a cell phone. "Damn radio's on the blink," he said.

He waved me toward the passenger side. I ran around and yanked open the door and tumbled inside, out of the rain and the storm.

Another fire engine roared up the street and around the corner toward the front of the library. De Angelo was talking into the phone as he got in on the driver's side and slammed the door.

"I've got her right here, Chief," he said. "She's fine."

He listened for a moment. He was frowning. "Don't you think it would make more sense for me to—"

He listened again. Then he said, "Yes, sir, Chief. Absolutely, sir. See you shortly."

He ended the call and put the cell phone inside his raincoat. Then he turned to me. "Chief Quinn is concerned about your safety, Professor Stuart," he said. "My orders are to bring you back to the station."

His tone of voice and the look he gave me said exactly what he thought about those orders. But I didn't particularly care at the moment. I wanted to be inside someplace where it was light and warm and there was no Megan.

"Buckle up," De Angelo told me.

I strapped myself in and grabbed for the dashboard as he made a tire-screeching U-turn. "With all this mess, we're going to have to go the long way around," he said.

"Do you think Megan called in the bomb threat?" I said. "She must have been watching me and realized that I had found it. That I'd found her great-grandfather's obituary with her name in it."

De Angelo swerved onto College Avenue. "She was afraid you'd find that," he said. When I turned my head and looked at him, he was smiling. He said, "You're just like that little pink bunny rabbit with the battery in its chest, aren't you, Professor? We kept trying to get your mind on something else—phone calls, anonymous letters, a tip to SAR about police harassment, that photograph of you and Big Chief Quinn." De Angelo shook his head. "But nothing could keep you away from that microfilm machine for long."

"Are you a member of the Caulder family?" I said, trying to speak above my booming heartbeat.

"Me? Now, do I looked like I'm to the manor born?" He shook his head. "I hate highfalutin rich people. As my daddy used to say, 'They look at you and expect to see *peckerwood* wrote across your forehead.'"

We were stopped at the traffic light leading off-campus onto Riverside Drive. There was a car in the lane beside us. Cars coming in the other direction.

Could I signal? Could I jump out?

I slid one hand toward the buckle of my seat belt and the other toward the door.

"Bad girl, Professor," De Angelo said. He had his gun pointed at me. "Why don't you just put your purse down on the floor there. Then put your hands in your lap and link your fingers together."

I looked from his smiling face to the gun. I put my shoulder bag on the floor and my hands in my lap.

The light changed. De Angelo turned onto Riverside Drive. "Now, I got me a problem with high-and-mighty Quinn too," he said. "How do you think he got the chief's job?"

"Qualifications?" I said.

"Yeah, the fix was in on that one as soon as he said, 'I was Airborne, and my daddy was a major general,'" De Angelo said.

"Did you want the chief's job?" I asked.

"Me?" De Angelo smiled. "Not me, Professor. I'm just a cop trying to get by."

"By taking a bribe to look the other way in a murder investigation?" I said. "She is paying you, isn't she?"

"Now, why else would I be doing this," De Angelo said. "I'm not getting any younger, Professor. I've got to think about my future."

"Did you help her kill him?" I asked as we passed the Vibrations dance club. Even on a Monday night, in the middle of a storm, the parking lot was jammed with cars.

"Nope," De Angelo said. "But I figured out she had. I'm a pretty good detective."

"So Chief Quinn told me," I said.

"He said that? I'm truly touched."

The gun was in his lap now. Could I reach over and grab it? And then what? Force him to stop the car?

"How did you figure out she had done it?" I asked. "What tipped you off?"

"Eric. The boy's a pretty good liar. He played those pranks on Halloween, by the way. But his tongue stumbled over that alibi she gave him."

"What alibi?"

"Miss Megan told him that he needed an alibi for when Colby was killed. She told him to say he'd been with her at her apartment."

"Where had he been?"

"Driving around. After he left the infirmary, he just drove around. By the time he did show up at Miss Megan's, she was at home."

"So when Eric said he had been with her, he also provided Megan with an alibi," I said, remembering Eric's visit to my office before the faculty meeting. If I had really been listening, would I have picked up on something? "Is Eric in on this too?"

"Nope. The boy actually thought I believed him. It was while I was having a closer look at him that I began to have my suspicions about Miss Megan."

I measured the distance between my lap and his. Could I get the gun?

"Bad girl, Professor," he said, taking his eyes from the road to glance at me. "Keep those fingers linked."

"You're going to kill me anyway," I said.

"But if you're good, I'll make it fast."

I closed my eyes and tried to shut out the rain and the lightning and De Angelo's smile.

"Where are we going?" I asked when I could speak again. We were crossing the downtown bridge. The Dan River rushed over its dam, churning black in the rain and lightning.

"Someplace where we can get this done," De Angelo said, in answer to my question. "I really do need to get myself on back to campus so I can help search for you when they realize you're missing."

"Where is Detective Williams tonight? Won't she realize you've been missing."

"Nope. Our Marcia's a single mommy. Today, she called and said she couldn't come in because her son gone and got himself in trouble at school. Mommy had to go see about putting it all right again. So she couldn't make it in to work. I told her I'd do my best to survive without her."

"You probably wouldn't have wanted her around for this anyway," I said above the fear rising in my throat.

We had turned onto Union Street. There were no other cars. The municipal parking lot was empty. The liquor store and bank were closed. So was the Orleans Café.

"The Orleans is closed on Sunday and Monday," De Angelo said, as if he had read my mind. "Which works out real well for us."

He pulled the car into the alley between the café and the barber shop next door and stopped. He took the key from the ignition and picked up the gun in his lap. "Now, what I want you to do is get out, Professor, and move around in front of the car with your hands up where I can see them."

I looked down at the glittering barrel of his automatic. "Maybe I would have been better off if Megan had shot me back there in the library," I said.

"She couldn't," he said. "It was a toy gun."

He gestured with the real gun in his hand. "Out."

I opened my car door and slid out into the cramped space he had left on my side between the car and the wall of the café. De Angelo had gotten out on the driver's side. He gestured with his gun for me to move in front of the car. Then he put his gun into his belt and reached into his raincoat pocket. I watched as he put on the leather gloves he had taken out. He walked toward me. I backed away until I bumped against the metal garbage cans lined up along the wall.

"Now, let's make this easy, Professor."

"Why should I help you do that?" I said as he reached out toward me.

I opened my mouth and screamed. He grabbed me by the throat with both hands. I fumbled behind me, trying to grasp the garbage can lid.

"Hit the deck!" Glass exploded around us, and the smell of whiskey saturated the air.

De Angelo whirled around. He yanked off his gloves and pulled his gun from his belt. As he fired at Parnell, I pulled the slippery, wet, garbage can lid free. I brought it down on his arm with all the force I could muster.

The gun spun away. De Angelo cursed. As he turned toward me, I slammed the lid into his face. He staggered and grabbed for me.

I ran, scrambling back up the alley toward the car.

I yanked open the driver's-side door and beat down on the horn, hitting it with the palm of my hand.

He was coming after me. I reached across the car seat and

snatched up my shoulder bag from the floor.

I ran into the empty street, yelling at the top of my lungs. "Help! Someone help me!"

There was a telephone booth across the street in the municipal parking lot. I ran toward it. Behind me I could hear De Angelo reversing his car out of the alley.

I didn't look back. I ran. Slipping on the wet pavement in my black pumps. Catching my breath at the zigzag of the lightning. I fell against the telephone booth and shoved the door open. As I reached for the receiver, the lights of De Angelo's car swept over me. He was driving straight at the booth. I screamed and scrambled out of the door.

The car swerved in front of me. De Angelo slammed on the brakes. I fell against the car and down on my knees.

He jumped out of the car and ran around it. He grabbed me up. I raised my knee and aimed it at his groin. It was a glancing blow, and he cursed and reached for me again. I sprayed the contents of the bottle in my hand in his face. He cried out and staggered back with his hands to his eyes.

I tumbled over the trunk of the car as I tried to get to the driver's side of the car. De Angelo came from the other direction, still rubbing at his eyes. "You want to play games, Professor?" he said. "Is that what you want to do?"

I was breathing in pants that shook my body. I watched him and measured the distance we each were from the open car door. Was the warning buzzer screeching because the key was in the ignition or because the headlights were on?

"Come on," De Angelo said. "Go for it."

And then he froze, with his head up. I froze too. Sirens. Sirens coming toward us.

De Angelo cursed and ran around the car.

Police cruisers screeched into the parking lot, coming from both directions.

De Angelo stood there beside his car with his gun in his hand.

Uniformed officers came out of the two cruisers, guns drawn over their cars. Quinn and Williams came out of a blue sedan. Their guns were drawn too.

"Put the gun down, De Angelo," Williams said.

De Angelo smiled. "Now, would you really shoot me, Marcia, honey?"

Quinn said, "I would. Just give me a reason."

De Angelo laughed at that. "That's the trouble with you soldier boys. You can't take a joke." He bent down and placed his gun on the ground in front of him. He stood up with his fingers linked behind his head.

I sunk down on the wet asphalt. The wind lashed the rain, blowing it around us. But the lightning was moving away, the thunder only a dull rumble now.

Quinn came over and squatted down beside me.

Williams was giving De Angelo his rights. Two uniformed officers were handcuffing him. One of them said, "Geez, what's this guy been doing? Bathing in perfume?"

The other laughed. "He smells like my wife's flower garden."

Williams stepped closer and sniffed. "Yeah, you do smell kind of sweet, Ron, honey."

Quinn said in my ear as he drew me to my feet, "Lizabeth? Not the healing therapy body mist?"

I pulled away from him. "I do not run around with mace in my purse, Quinn. I had to use what I had."

"Gotta use what you got," a voice trilled out behind us.

I whirled around. "Parnell?"

He was being held up by a patrolman. There was blood on his leg. But he was alive.

"Parnell, oh, thank God, you're all right." I threw my arms around him. "Parnell, thank you. Thank you so much." I kissed his cheek.

He batted me away. "Don't be kissing me, woman. Man's got a gun."

I kissed his bristly, smelly cheek again. "You saved me," I said.

"And wasted my good liquor." But he smiled, a twitch of his chapped lips. "Used to have a pretty good arm. Ain't used it in a while."

"It's still good," I said. "Best arm I've seen in years."

Parnell raised his face to the rain and sung out, "Hit the deck. Hit the damn deck."

The patrolman winced. "Come on, buddy. Let's see about getting you to the hospital."

Chapter 34

ANY PASSING EXUBERANCE I might have felt at besting De Angelo was gone. I was sitting in Marcia Williams's office in the same visitor's chair I had occupied the last time I was there. Someone had found me a dry Gallagher PD sweatshirt. The Gallagher PD did not run to tea bags. I had declined offers of coffee.

I got up and went over to the window and stared out into the darkness. I sat back down.

Almost an hour later, Williams and Quinn strolled in. Williams went over and poured a mug of coffee. She handed it to Quinn and poured another for herself.

She went around her desk and sat down. He sat down in the other visitor's chair.

"Well, did you get her?" I asked when they both seemed content to sit there sipping their coffee. "Did you get Megan?"

"We got her," Quinn said.

I left that for the moment and turned to Williams. "Did Diane Colby tell you my theory about Kevin Colby being involved in a hit-and-run?"

Williams nodded. "And De Angelo and I contacted the Baltimore PD."

"And?" I said.

"They went to see Mrs. Delores Colby. She said you were a crazy woman and suggested you had been romantically involved with her ex-husband and that accusing Richard's son of a crime was some kind of warped revenge."

"Revenge?" I said.

"For something Richard had done to you."

"So she didn't believe it might be true," I said.

Williams said, "Whether it's true or not, Professor Stuart, it's going to be tough for the Baltimore PD to prove unless they can find the car. Mrs. Colby told them Richard Colby disposed of it after the accident. She thought he sold it. She denies knowing to whom."

"So what you're saying is that the police probably won't be able to link Kevin to the hit-and-run?"

"There were no witnesses. There's no car. The suspect is dead." Williams took another sip of her coffee. "No one's likely to put in overtime on this one."

"Good," I said. "I didn't want to hurt Delores Colby. I hope she really does believe that I'm a vengeful woman. And I was probably wrong anyway."

Quinn sighed. "Lizzie," he said. "Care to see what we found when we picked up Megan Reed?"

"What?" I asked, looking from him to Williams.

Williams opened the manila envelope she had brought in with her. She took out a plastic bag. Yellowed pages of stationery were inside.

She opened the bag and took them out. "Megan tried to burn this when we arrived. I don't know why she kept it in the first place."

"What is it?" I asked again.

"A letter her great-grandfather wrote," Quinn said. "She said it was in a secret compartment of the desk he left to her when he died. The desk stayed in his house until she moved into her own apartment and sent for it. That was when she found the letter."

I held out my hand. "May I see it, please?"

Williams said, "You're not going to enjoy reading it. Parts of it are offensive."

"Forgive me, Detective Williams, but I can't imagine how a letter could be more offensive than what Jonathan Caulder actually did. Back in 1921, he was responsible for one murder, one lynching, one jailhouse suicide by a pregnant woman, another pregnant woman left widowed. And, of course, we mustn't forget one twelve-year-old girl raped. And then Megan picked up "

"A twelve-year-old girl raped?" Quinn said.

I turned to look at him. "Hester Rose. She was raped by one of the men in the mob. Miss Alice told me."

He reached out for the letter. "Maybe you shouldn't read this right now."

"When would you suggest I read it?" I said. "Actually, I would like to know what Judge Caulder had to say for himself."

But I didn't have my reading glasses. And there were tears in my eyes and I couldn't see. I shoved the pages toward Quinn. "Please, read it to me."

"Lizzie—"

"Just read it, Quinn."

He said, "It's dated August 11, 1944.

"My Dear Detective Kingston:

"I don't know if this letter will reach you after all these many years. In fact, it is unlikely that I will even post it. No, this letter is more in the form of an exercise in remorse, an examination of a crime and the punishment that seems to be visited upon those that I love—a sister and two wives dead, a son lost. Perhaps another son dying even now.

"You once asked a favor of me. You asked me to satisfy your need to know the truth. I couldn't oblige at the time. Even now, there is reason to keep my silence. I have one son left, you see. If he should return to me, then I will go on preserving the silence I kept first to protect my sister. But Laura is long dead, and there can be no further consequences to her.

"All those years ago, you told me that you could prove nothing. There was no evidence, you said. Nothing you or anyone else could prove. Mose Davenport was dead.

"The girl Ophelia had hanged herself in her despair. And, Detective, to satisfy your mind, I did sincerely want to help her when I entered her cell. But she looked at me as if I were the devil incarnate. Undoubtedly, before he was killed, Mose Davenport had shared with her some suspicion he harbored.

"But to return to the conversation we had that day before I left Gallagher for good. No proof, you said. Of what, I asked you. What reason could I have had to do what you suspected? You suspected it only because you had seen my sister, Laura, look at me with loathing and draw away from the touch of my hand. She was ill, I said.

"And she was. That was the crux of it. Daniel had told me of her illness. He had told me that she had become addicted to the drugs that old Cahill had prescribed for her.

"But I refused to believe him. I loved my sister dearly, Detective Kingston. She was my life's breath. And because of that, I refused to believe something so ugly could touch her. But on that day, Daniel called me to his office. He, this man, who called himself my friend and who claimed to love my sister, looked me in the eye and slandered her. He said her addiction had become so desperate that she had approached Mose Davenport and asked him to get her some of his foul stuff—the stuff he supplied to the niggers. He said Davenport had come to him because he had been frightened by my sister's request. Daniel, my friend, stood there and looked me in the eye as he besmeared my sister's name.

"He said to me in all earnestness that we would have to do something to save Laura from herself. And in a moment of blind fury, I picked up the statue from his desk and struck him with it. As to whether I might have come forward if Mose Davenport had not killed Officer Kincaid, I doubt it. I am a man of honor. But Davenport was a colored no-account, and if he had not died for that crime, he would have for some other. And, as you know, my sister's condition at the time was fragile. Hate me, she might have. But she still needed me.

"Now you have the whole of it, Detective Kingston. The truth you wanted. And perhaps one day this letter will indeed reach your hands. I remain,

"Yours,

"Jonathan Caulder"

Quinn's voice that had hardened with anger and irony as he read, faded to silence.

"The bastard leaves that for his great-granddaughter to find," Williams said. "And she gets it into her head that she should kill to protect the family secret."

"To protect a dead man's honor," I said. "Judge Caulder was an honorable man. He passed his legacy down to his descendants. It was up to them to preserve it."

Quinn expressed what he thought of that with one of his more incisive turns of phrase. Then he stood up. "Come on, Lizabeth. Time to go home."

I looked up at him and remembered what I had been about to ask back in the parking lot before he shoved me into a patrol car and went off with Williams to find Megan. "Did you know De Angelo was up to something?"

"We knew," he said, his mouth grim. "We just didn't know what."

"So we had to give him enough rope to hang himself," Williams said from her desk.

And Hester Rose said in my head, *Shoulda give him a ladder while you was at it, and pointed him at a tree.*

I burst out laughing.

Quinn drew me up out of my chair. "Lizzie—"

"It's all right," I said. "A bad joke. A really bad joke. But it is more than a philosophical question, isn't it, Quinn?"

"What is?"

"How to get past all the pain and the rage. How to deny yourself the satisfaction of avenging an insult or a wrong, of meeting violence with violence."

"Lizzie, I know this—"

"No, you don't know," I said.

"All right," he said. "I don't know."

"But I could try to explain. When I wake up, Quinn—which will probably be sometime next week—if you still want to talk, then we will. And I'll try to explain. In fact, I will tell you all about Lizabeth Theodora Stuart and her world."

"I think I'd better brace myself for that one," he said. But his scowl was dissolving into a smile. The one that started in his eyes and worked its way down to his mouth.

That much felt right. I would think about all the rest of it after I'd had some sleep.